The Man in the High Castle and Philosophy

Popular Culture and Philosophy® Series Editor: George A. Reisch

Volume 1 *Seinfeld and Philosophy: A Book about Everything and Nothing* (2000)

Volume 2 *The Simpsons and Philosophy: The D'oh! of Homer* (2001)

Volume 3 *The Matrix and Philosophy: Welcome to the Desert of the Real* (2002)

Volume 4 *Buffy the Vampire Slayer and Philosophy: Fear and Trembling in Sunnydale* (2003)

Volume 9 *Harry Potter and Philosophy: If Aristotle Ran Hogwarts* (2004)

Volume 12 *Star Wars and Philosophy: More Powerful than You Can Possibly Imagine* (2005)

Volume 13 *Superheroes and Philosophy: Truth, Justice, and the Socratic Way* (2005)

Volume 17 *Bob Dylan and Philosophy: It's Alright Ma (I'm Only Thinking)* (2006)

Volume 19 *Monty Python and Philosophy: Nudge Nudge, Think Think!* (2006)

Volume 30 *Pink Floyd and Philosophy: Careful with that Axiom, Eugene!* (2007)

Volume 35 *Star Trek and Philosophy: The Wrath of Kant* (2008)

Volume 36 *The Legend of Zelda and Philosophy: I Link Therefore I Am* (2008)

Volume 42 *Supervillains and Philosophy: Sometimes Evil Is Its Own Reward* (2009)

Volume 49 *Zombies, Vampires, and Philosophy: New Life for the Undead* (2010)

ume 53 *Martial Arts and Philosophy: Beating and Nothingness* (2010)

Volume 54 *The Onion and Philosophy: Fake News Story True, Alleges Indignant Area Professor* (2010)

Volume 55 *Doctor Who and Philosophy: Bigger on the Inside* (2010)

Volume 57 *Rush and Philosophy: Heart and Mind United* (2011) Edited by Jim Berti and Durrell Bowman

Volume 58 *Dexter and Philosophy: Mind over Spatter* (2011) Edited by Richard Greene, George A. Reisch, and Rachel Robison-Greene

Volume 60 *SpongeBob SquarePants and Philosophy: Soaking Up Secrets Under the Sea!* (2011) Edited by Joseph J. Foy

Volume 61 *Sherlock Holmes and Philosophy: The Footprints of a Gigantic Mind* (2011) Edited by Josef Steiff

Volume 63 *Philip K. Dick and Philosophy: Do Androids Have Kindred Spirits?* (2011) Edited by D.E. Whittkower

Volume 64 *The Rolling Stones and Philosophy: It's Just a Thought Away* (2012) Edited by Luke Dick and George A. Reisch

Volume 67 *Breaking Bad and Philosophy: Badder Living through Chemistry* (2012) Edited by David R. Koepsell and Robert Arp

Volume 68 *The Walking Dead and Philosophy: Zombie Apocalypse Now* (2012) Edited by Wayne Yuen

Volume 69 *Curb Your Enthusiasm and Philosophy: Awaken the Social Assassin Within* (2012) Edited by Mark Ralkowski

Volume 71 *The Catcher in the Rye and Philosophy: A Book for Bastards, Morons, and Madmen* (2012) Edited by Keith Dromm and Heather Salter

Volume 73 *The Wire and Philosophy: This America, Man* (2013) Edited by David Bzdak, Joanna Crosby, and Seth Vannatta

Volume 74 *Planet of the Apes and Philosophy: Great Apes Think Alike* (2013) Edited by John Huss

Volume 75 *Psych and Philosophy: Some Dark Juju-Magumbo* (2013) Edited by Robert Arp

Volume 79 *Frankenstein and Philosophy: The Shocking Truth* (2013) Edited by Nicolas Michaud

Volume 80 *Ender's Game and Philosophy: Genocide Is Child's Play* (2013) Edited by D.E. Wittkower and Lucinda Rush

Volume 82 *Jurassic Park and Philosophy: The Truth Is Terrifying* (2014) Edited by Nicolas Michaud

Volume 83 *The Devil and Philosophy: The Nature of His Game* (2014) Edited by Robert Arp

Volume 84 *Leonard Cohen and Philosophy: Various Positions* (2014) by Jason Holt

Volume 85 *Homeland and Philosophy: For Your Minds Only* (2014) Edited by Robert Arp

Volume 86 *Girls and Philosophy: This Book Isn't a Metaphor for Anything* (2015) Edited by Richard Greene and Rachel Robison-Greene

Volume 87 *Adventure Time and Philosophy: The Handbook for Heroes* (2015) Edited by Nicolas Michaud

Volume 88 *Justified and Philosophy: Shoot First, Think Later* (2015) Edited by Rod Carveth and Robert Arp

Volume 89 *Steve Jobs and Philosophy: For Those Who Think Different* (2015) Edited by Shawn E. Klein

Volume 90 *Dracula and Philosophy: Dying to Know* (2015) Edited by Nicolas Michaud and Janelle Pötzsch

Volume 91 *It's Always Sunny and Philosophy: The Gang Gets Analyzed* (2015) Edited by Roger Hunt and Robert Arp

Volume 92 *Orange Is the New Black and Philosophy: Last Exit from Litchfield* (2015) Edited by Richard Greene and Rachel Robison-Greene

Volume 93 *More Doctor Who and Philosophy: Regeneration Time* (2015) Edited by Courtland Lewis and Paula Smithka

Volume 94 *Divergent and Philosophy: The Factions of Life* (2016) Edited by Courtland Lewis

Volume 95 *Downton Abbey and Philosophy: Thinking in That Manor* (2016) Edited by Adam Barkman and Robert Arp

Volume 96 *Hannibal Lecter and Philosophy: The Heart of the Matter* (2016) Edited by Joseph Westfall

Volume 99 *Louis C.K. and Philosophy: You Don't Get to Be Bored* (2016) Edited by Mark Ralkowski

Volume 100 *Batman, Superman, and Philosophy: Badass or Boyscout?* (2016) Edited by Nicolas Michaud

Volume 101 *Discworld and Philosophy: Reality Is Not What It Seems* (2016) Edited by Nicolas Michaud

Volume 102 *Orphan Black and Philosophy: Grand Theft DNA* (2016) Edited by Richard Greene and Rachel Robison-Greene

Volume 103 *David Bowie and Philosophy: Rebel Rebel* (2016) Edited by Theodore G. Ammon

Volume 104 *Red Rising and Philosophy: Break the Chains!* (2016) Edited by Courtland Lewis and Kevin McCain

Volume 105 *The Ultimate Game of Thrones and Philosophy: You Think or Die* (2017) Edited by Eric J. Silverman and Robert Arp

Volume 106 *Peanuts and Philosophy: You're a Wise Man, Charlie Brown!* (2017) Edited by Richard Greene and Rachel Robison-Greene

Volume 107 *Deadpool and Philosophy: My Common Sense Is Tingling* (2017) Edited by Nicolas Michaud

Volume 108 *The X-Files and Philosophy: The Truth Is In Here* (2017) Edited by Robert Arp

Volume 109 *Mr. Robot and Philosophy: Beyond Good and Evil Corp* (2017) Edited by Richard Greene and Rachel Robison-Greene

Volume 110 *Hamilton and Philosophy: Revolutionary Thinking* (2017) Edited by Aaron Rabinowitz and Robert Arp

Volume 111 *The Man in the High Castle and Philosophy: Subversive Reports from Another Reality* (2017) Edited by Bruce Krajewski and Joshua Heter

In Preparation:

The Americans and Philosophy (2017) Edited by Robert Arp and Kevin Guilfoy

Jimi Hendrix and Philosophy (2017) Edited by Theodore G. Ammon

American Horror Story and Philosophy (2017) Edited by Richard Greene and Rachel Robison-Greene

Iron Man versus Captain America and Philosophy (2018) Edited by Nicolas Michaud and JessicaWatkins

Stephen King's Dark Tower and Philosophy (2018) Edited by Nicolas Michaud and Jacob Thomas May

Amy Schumer and Philosophy (2018) Edited by Charlene Elsby and Rob Luzecky

1984 and Philosophy (2018) Edited by Ezio di Nucci and Stefan Storrie

Scott Adams and Philosophy (2018) Edited by Dan Yim, Galen Foresman, and Robert Arp

Twin Peaks and Philosophy (2018) Edited by Richard Greene and Rachel Robison-Greene

For full details of all Popular Culture and Philosophy® books, visit www.opencourtbooks.com.

Popular Culture and Philosophy®

The Man in the High Castle and Philosophy

Subversive Reports from Another Reality

EDITED BY

BRUCE KRAJEWSKI AND
JOSHUA HETER

OPEN COURT
Chicago

Volume 111 in the series, Popular Culture and Philosophy®, edited by George A. Reisch

To find out more about Open Court books, visit our website at www.opencourtbooks.com.

Open Court Publishing Company is a division of Carus Publishing Company, dba Cricket Media.

First printing 2017

Printed and bound in the United States of America.

The Man in the High Castle and Philosophy: Subversive Reports from Another Reality

ISBN: 978-0-8126-9963-0

Library of Congress Control Number: 2017942595

This book is also available as an e-book.

Contents

Thanks

We're deeply grateful and very much indebted to a number of people who helped make this project a success. Thank you to everyone at Open Court, including (but not limited to) David Ramsay Steele and George Reisch, and also to Richard Greene, for their guidance on a number of matters. Thank you to our institutions—the University of Texas Arlington and Iowa Western Community College—without which we might not be in a position to work on projects such as this. The people who work in the Interlibrary Loan Department at UT-Arlington deserve special mention for their efforts to hunt down items for research. Thank you to all of the fine and thoughtful contributors to this volume. And finally, we must thank you, the reader, for your interest in and commitment to thinking carefully and critically about the events in history, including fictional history, alternative history, and history in many kinds of possible worlds.

I

Now Wait for Last Season

1
Juliana in Plato's Cave

DENNIS M. WEISS

Amazon's most successful television show begins with an evocative reminder that we're living in a media culture in which life is screened. As the opening credits begin to roll, the first thing we viewers hear is a film projector.

What we see are images projected against a patriotic screen. We hear the Austrian folk tune "Edelweiss"—more about that later. We're reminded that we're watching television. We're at home with our televisions—or maybe, given current technology and the challenges of managing "peak" TV—we're watching *The Man in the High Castle* on our smart phone or tablet while commuting (both hands on the wheel please).

As if to drive this message home, the first scene of the pilot episode features the sound of a projector and light spilling from a projection booth. This time it's a commercial playing in a movie house. "It's a new day"—an almost Reaganesque evocation of "Prouder, Stronger, Better." "It's morning again in America." Except these Americans happen to be Nazis. This is a television show about living in a media age of screens, images, and televisions—with Nazis!

Further underscoring its self-referential nature as a television show about watching television, in an early pivotal scene setting up the backstory, we watch as Frank Frink and Ed McCarthy, sitting at a bar, watch Hitler on television as they spin conspiracy stories about Hitler's Parkinson's and the jockeying of his underlings to succeed him. We're watching the watchers.

Immediately after this scene, Trudy Walker, just prior to being shot by the Japanese Kempeitai, hands off a film canister to her half-sister Juliana, telling her that it is "a way out." Juliana returns to her basement apartment and, pulling out a film projector, immediately screens the newsreel, *The Grasshopper Lies Heavy*. Once again, we hear the sound of a movie projector and see light projected on a basement curtain. Juliana is transfixed. She's pulled into this screened world—to the point where she watches the film over and over again, her eyes welling up with tears. She smiles. Frank comes home and recognizes the anti-fascist newsreels made by the "Man in the High Castle" and he and Juliana debate whether the films are "real."

This early scene with Juliana is an interesting screening of Plato's Cave, where Plato imagines prisoners, chained deep in a cave, watching shadowy images cast on a wall, mistakenly assuming them to be the sole reality, oblivious to the world that lies outside the cave. Juliana is in her basement apartment, underground, watching images flicker on an old curtain. But rather than assuming that the images are illusory, underground second-rate deceptions of a more real world lying outside the basement door, Juliana takes these images for reality and it changes the direction of her life. It's the screened image that sets Juliana free and not the "real" world in which she lives. Juliana, turning Plato on his head, prefers image to reality and it's these illusory screened images that provide her with a way out.

But things aren't so clear, at least for us viewers, for we've already seen that the status of screened images is ambiguous. We've seen Nazi ideology masquerading as commercial shorts in movie theaters. And over the course of the first several episodes of *The Man in the High Castle* we see several scenes of television shows playing in the background: a Nazi version of the gameshow "What's My Line?"; Japanese wrestling entertaining a bored housewife doing the laundry;

a Reich version of *Dragnet*. Later, John Smith gathers his family and Nazi buddies around the television on VA Day to watch a patriotic speech from the Führer. And then there's that opening song—"Edelweiss." Meant to be an evocation of the folk spirit of the Nazi homeland, and thought by many to be an authentic Austrian folk song, if not its official national anthem, it's actually a song penned in 1959 by Rogers and Hammerstein for the Broadway musical *The Sound of Music*. Scratching a bit beneath the celluloid surface then, we're led to believe that what appears to be authentic is in fact suspect. And yet, Juliana comes to believe in these newsreels, to the point that she assumes her sister Trudy's identity and travels to Canon City to discover more about these mysterious films.

Two Julianas

It might seem perverse to watch *The Man in the High Castle* with a view toward its commentary on television and the screened image. After all, here's a television show dealing with the aftermath of the atomic bombing of Washington, DC, a television show in which Nazis and Japanese Kempeitai brutally oppress Americans while wiping out East Coast Jews and the disabled. Much of the discussion revolving around *The Man in the High Castle* has to do with the "what if" of World War II ending in a different way. But in fact, there is another intriguing what-if this series implicitly explores: What if the Nazis had invented television?

In Philip K. Dick's counterfactual science fiction novel, originally published in 1962 and re-issued as a Vintage paperback in 1992, it's the victory of the Axis powers in World War II that gets the lion's share of attention. But the counterfactual world Dick built is interesting on many levels, not least for what it has to say about technology. As in the television show, the Nazis are clearly more technologically advanced than the Japanese and those vanquished Americans. In both novel and television show, Japanese trade minister Mr. Tagomi admits that Japan has fallen behind Nazi technological progress, underscored by Nazi rockets that transport individuals across the country in two hours and, in the novel, allow the Germans to populate Mars. In the world of the novel, those technological advances extend even to television. In the novel Juliana is divorced from Frank Frink and living in Canon City. While shopping in a drugstore she glimpses an article in *Life* magazine: "Television in Europe: Glimpse of Tomorrow."

Turning to it, interested, she sees a picture of a German family watching television in their living room. Already, the article said, there are four hours of image broadcast during the day from Berlin. Someday there would be television stations in all the major European cities. And, by 1970, one would be built in New York.

Once again, Juliana is transfixed by the thought of staring at a screened image. She wonders, "what it's like to sit home in your living room and see the whole world on a little gray glass tube." If the Nazis can fly back and forth between Earth and Mars, why, Juliana wonders, can't they get television going? Recall that Dick is writing this in the early 1960s. *The Man in the High Castle* was published in 1962. The first golden age of television ran from 1949 until approximately 1960 and by 1960 television had reached a saturation point. In 1950 only nine percent of American households had a television set. By 1960 that figure had reached ninety percent. Dick was living in a world newly dominated by television but was imagining a world in which it was largely absent. Although, that's not altogether true.

As in the television show, Dick's counterfactual world includes a counterfactual narrative, *The Grasshopper Lies Heavy*, only in this case the narrative is not a series of newsreels but a novel written by the "Man in the High Castle," a novel-within-a-novel rather than a newsreel-within-a-television show. Later in the novel, as Juliana is reading *The Grasshopper Lies Heavy*, we learn about "the fabulous television." In the novel's alternate history novel, Juliana is enthralled to read about how through Yankee know-how and mass-production, inexpensive little television sets were shipped off to backward people in Africa and Asia where, through educational TV shows, they learned how to read and dig wells and heal their sick (p. 157). Meanwhile, in the "real" present of Dick's alternative history novel, television is mostly absent. Characters largely depend on radio and the printed page, whether *The Grasshopper Lies Heavy* or the *I Ching*, plays a dominant role.

Amazon Adapting Dick Adapting History

Two vignettes involving two Julianas living in two very different worlds. One Juliana revolves around the printed word and the search for the truth behind a novel. The other Juliana revolves around screening images and searching for a way out. Reading and watching our two Julianas together ought to inspire us to think about the place in our lives of images and screens, the printed word and the electronic media.

Amazon's television adaptation of Dick's novel offers something of an alternative take on the printed page, this from a company that started out as a bookseller. Where television is largely absent from the book, books are largely absent from the television show. In episode 3, Joe and Juliana separately visit a used-book store, where the books, according to The Marshall, have "got the stink of their owner. Cigarettes and coffee, cat piss, smell of decay." Joe had never heard of *The Adventures of Huckleberry Finn,* and selling Bibles gets the bookstore owner killed. This world is not a print-based world but a world of the visual image. As Frank Spotnitz, the show's creator, observed to ScreenerTV.com in November of 2015, he was much more interested in creating a visual culture that works better on television.

> In the novel, Hawthorne Abendsen has written a novel where the Allies won the war. In the TV series, it's a film showing we've won the war. I did that because this is a visual medium and a film is going to be so much more powerful to watch than hearing about a book that people have read. . . . That one change obviously

> changes an awful lot, because a film is a physical object and there's a reality to that that we have to account for in the series that wasn't dealt with in the novel.

There's more going on here, though, than Spotnitz lets on, for that "one change" indicates a far greater shift in the worlds of our two Julianas. It's not just that we have newsreels rather than novels. It's that the televisual world of *The Man in the High Castle* is fascinated with images and our visual culture. Consider that the series is bookended by two movie references. In the opening scene we see an extended shot of a movie marquee advertising *The Punch Party*, starring Rock Hudson and June Allyson, a totally fictional film. The season closes with Tagomi in a counterfactual San Francisco staring up at a billboard for Stanley Kubrick's *Lolita*.

Consider, too, that the television show is fascinated with the visual iconography of the Nazi regime, going so far as to unfavorably compare the films of Leni Riefenstahl to the newsreels. As Erich comments to John Smith in episode 2, "Reich Minister Goebbels says that not even Fräulein Riefenstahl could make films of such sophistication." In Dick's novel, no scenes are set in the Nazi-occupied states and we only hear about Berlin second-hand. In the television show, though, numerous scenes take place in New York and it relishes presenting us with images of Americana into which it can insert the swastika. In a November 19th 2015 interview with *Village Voice*, Spotnitz recognizes the links between Hollywood and the Nazis:

> Hitler, tragically, was an incredibly evil and dangerous villain who managed to kill people with a hateful ideology and on an unprecedented scale. He also happened to have costumes and production design that were tailor-made for Hollywood. They really were amazing, their aesthetics for their cause: their buildings, their military uniforms, their parades, their marches, their Leni Riefenstahl films.

While recognizing the evil of the Nazis in one breath, Spotnitz is attracted to their made-for-Hollywood glamour in the next. The buildings! The uniforms! Leni!

Then there's the role of photographs in the television show. Frank's sister and her two children are photographed just prior to their being gassed and it's all that Frank has left of her. John Smith learns that his son has a rare genetic disease and we later see him going through a family photo album, which includes pictures of his dead brother in a wheelchair. Juliana's search for her sister leads her to an abandoned house where she finds a photo of Trudy. Tagomi often stares wistfully at photos of family members arrayed on his desk. We're very much in a visual-based culture of the image.

And we shouldn't forget that *The Man in the High Castle* is a television show debuting during television's second golden age and facing what John Landgraf (proclaimed "the philosopher king of FX" by Slate's television critic Willa Paskin) has called "peak TV," the problem of keeping up with the overwhelming number of scripted shows being produced for television—more than four hundred in 2015. And it's a television show adapted from a novel in which television shows were absent, an adaptation that comes from a mammoth former bookseller adapting to our new digital environment and battling for dominance of our media ecosystem. What are we to make of all this?

Newsreels for Novels

We might find a clue in the year 1962—the year that Dick published *The Man in the High Castle*, the year in which both novel and television show are set, and a pivotal time period in our social and cultural history. We're moving from the age of print to the age of television and the full-blown emergence of media culture. Our two Julianas are facing a world about to change, and not because of some crack in the Axis powers, but because of the changing media environment.

Dick's novel is still a literary world. It's a world where people read—whether the *I Ching* or *The Grasshopper Lies Heavy*. It's a world that still doesn't have television. It's a world where people can still look forward to television's being fabulous. But the world of the TV show is a world that already revolves around the visual image: television, movies, newsreels, photographs. And it's debuting in a world already remade by the media. Where Dick's own world was just entering the media-dominated 1960s and he could still look forward to the possibility that television was fabulous or educational, Amazon's TV show is looking at a world already remade by television and now being remade yet again by social media, smart phones, and peak TV. For good or ill, we're all now living in a visual, image-dominated culture.

This suggests that as we watch *The Man in the High Castle*, a television show coming from a bookseller trying to make it as a media giant, what we're really watching is a show about the cultural shift we have lived through and continue to live through. It is indeed a new day, as Joe is reminded sitting in a movie theater and watching the latest Nazi propaganda commercial. Spotnitz implicitly recognizes what's happening here when he suggests that with that "one small change" of novel for newsreel, "an awful lot" changes.

Writing is linear and focused on the diachronic while the world of electronic media is more fragmentary and synchronic. Neil Postman famously characterized the world of television as the world of "and now . . . this," suggestive of the manner in which the televisual world lacks order and meaning. The world is made different by the introduction of TV. As we skip from one channel to another we inhabit first one world then another. In *The Medium Is the Massage* that sage of media philosophy Marshall McLuhan sums up the implications of this change from print to pixels:

> Electric circuitry has overthrown the regime of "time" and "space" and pours upon us instantly and continuously the concerns of all other men. . . . Its message is Total Change, ending psychic, social, economic, and political parochialism. . . . Nothing can be further from the spirit of the new technology than "a place for everything and everything in its place." You can't *go* home again. (p. 16)

In *No Sense of Place* media scholar Joshua Meyrowitz explores the shift from a print-based culture to an electronic-based culture and argues that the emergence of electronic media in the 1960s, especially television, caused fundamental shifts in the structure of society and social behavior, which led to the transformative social developments of the 1960s and 1970s. By merging formerly distinct public spheres, blurring the dividing line between private and public behaviors, and severing the traditional link between physical space and social place, electronic media are deeply implicated in the restructuring of our sense of space, time, and place. As places lose their distinctive characteristics we feel increasingly rootless because our roots can no longer be defined in terms of some distinctive location.

> Our world may suddenly seem senseless to many people because, for the first time in modern history, it is relatively placeless. The intensity of the changes in the last thirty years . . . may be related to the unique power of TV to break down the distinctions between here and there, live and mediated, and personal and public. (p. 308)

Television, Meyrowitz argues, reprocesses our physical and social environment in a revolutionary way and thereby creates a new metaphysical arena (p. 146).

Seeing with Many Eyes

This new world created by electronic media was a constant source of inspiration for Dick and probably accounts for his continuing popularity as a source of movie and television adaptations. In "The Second Coming of Philip K. Dick," *Wired* magazine suggested that Dick's vision "all but defines contemporary Hollywood science fiction and spills over into other kinds of movies as well." Dick's novels and short stories explore themes of illusion, authenticity, simulation, multiple realities and their impact on the human condition, themes that emerge out of the media revolution taking place at the time he is writing.

Returning to Amazon's television show, this new metaphysical arena created by the media helps illuminate some of the more interesting features of the television show, especially the connection between Juliana and Tagomi. Consider that our two Julianas, for all their differences, initially share a pursuit of the truth. Both are impelled by their different encounters with *The Grasshopper Lies Heavy* to search for the truth behind the novel or newsreels. Dick's Juliana confronts the author of the novel and ultimately turns to the *I Ching* to vouchsafe the truth of the novel's alternative narrative.

Our television Juliana, though, follows a different path. Initially the newsreel suggests a way out, another reality, perhaps *the* reality. Initially she hasn't broken through to the recognition that she's living in a different world, a world constituted by the media in which our screens don't promise us Reality with a capital R—whatever that might be. Indeed, our own experience of reality TV ought to inform our appreciation of this series. We no longer look to Reality TV as a window on to reality. We know that it is edited, constructed, spliced. Juliana too is learning how to look at her screens. Over the course of the series she goes from being transfixed by the images on the screen to doubting their veracity.

In the first episode she is transformed by the newsreels, leading her on her path to Canon City. The season's final episode, "A Way Out," opens on the lens of a film projector as it screens another newsreel, suggesting that the reels are indeed a way out. But even as we witness the film's images reflected on the eyes of Frank and Juliana, Frank asks, "What was that?" and Juliana responds, a tear running down her cheek, "A nightmare." Juliana is now less sure about the status of the newsreels and less sure that they provide a way out. When confronted with the possibility that Joe Blake is a Nazi who murders Frank Frink, Juliana makes a choice to trust Joe and not the film. As she says to Joe in episode 10: "I don't believe the film. I don't believe it. I believe you." As Juliana learns more about the newsreels, including their possibly competing and contradictory visions of the future, she ultimately disavows them as a possible way out. Having repeatedly violated the Resistance's core principle—"You don't ever watch the films. No exceptions. It doesn't matter to us what you saw."—Juliana gains a newfound skepticism regarding the media's power to provide a way out.

Juliana has learned to see with new eyes. In *Postphenomenology*, the American philosopher of technology Don Ihde has suggested that as image technologies reshape culture they induce a kind of bug-eyed compound vision which has an acidic effect on more foundational and romantic visions of culture.

> Compound vision is multiple vision. One scans the multiple screens, focusing here, then there and, out of the mélange, forming new directions and possibilities. (p. 29)

Ihde compares this compound vision to the multiple displays found in newsrooms and suggests that the compound eye gives a panorama beyond the boundaries of binocular vision. Juliana's experiences over the course of the first season of *The Man in the High Castle* perhaps endow her with something like Ihde's compound vision and suggests to her new possibilities for "a way out" other than looking to another reality. Juliana is learning to navigate this new, image-dominated, electronic media world.

Something similar is perhaps suggested for the most puzzling scene of the series—Tagomi's seeming immersion in another reality, a scene that occurs as well in the novel. While in the novel, Tagomi and Juliana have nothing to do with one another, the television show clearly suggests a bond between the two. Living in their mediated world, they long to see differently. Tagomi and Juliana both learn to see with many eyes. Treating Dick's source material less as metaphysical fiction and more as media fiction might suggest that rather than breaking through to some alternative timeline or parallel universe, Tagomi's intense meditation leads to the recognition that reality may be a lot like television.

As Meyrowitz says, television breaks down the barriers between time and space, here and there, live and mediated. Tagomi comes to embrace compound vision and the recognition that new directions and possibilities can be found in new ways of seeing. If you don't like what you see, find a way to change the channel and see things differently. Our novel's Juliana wonders what it would be like to see the whole world on a little grey glass. Wouldn't it be fabulous?

It may not help feed starving Africans but perhaps in inducing a new media metaphysic and instilling compound vision television shows us, if not a way out, at least a way forward.

2
Say Heil! to Architecture

FERNANDO GABRIEL PAGNONI BERNS AND
EMILIANO AGUILAR

The last scene of Season One of *The Man in the High Castle* ("A Way Out") rests heavily on the viewers' ability to understand how monuments, architecture, and spectacle work in social settings.

Trade Minister of the Pacific States of America, Nobusuke Tagomi, meditates in the middle of a public square. He is circled by Nazi iconography ornamenting the buildings. He closes his eyes and when he opens them up, all his surroundings are now completely different in aspect, but the same in some ways. There is no Nazi imagery anymore, but there are, indeed, monuments and visual spectacle. He's in the same location in a timeline in which America won World War II.

He gazes upon the billboards and colorful scenery decorated with red, white, blue, *Lolita* posters, and Ronald Reagan ads for cigarettes. This change is enough for viewers to understand that an uncanny journey has taken place. Audiences recognize the other reality by seeing the buildings.

This ending connects full circle with the sequence of credits opening each episode. The title credits roll, backed by the tunes of a seriously creepy version of "Edelweiss." Almost every image accompanying the titles refers to American monuments, thus underlying the importance of this theme within the series. First, Nazi and Japanese flags are projected on the outline of a United States map, pointing to an alternative historical stream in which the Axis powers have won World War II. Next are briefs shots of well-known American monuments, all of them familiar and yet eerily changed: Mount Rushmore and the Statue of Liberty, both of them cohabiting with Nazi effigies such as the Imperial Eagle. Viewers know that one of the official posters of the series has the Statue of Liberty wearing a Nazi flag, another sign indicating that monuments are significant. Audiences see American emblems transformed into National Socialist monuments since they now stand for Nazi America. *The Man in the High Castle* reminds viewers of the culpability of architects and architecture in furthering a totalitarian political agenda.

The series pilot begins, after the initial credits, with Joe Blake watching a newsreel in a theater. Monuments and movies are both tools which tell us about history. In a show about *alternate* history, monuments are critically important. Monuments and architecture can be "read" in a similarly way to literary texts. Monuments provide indexes for remembering and forgetting that accompany any political or cultural change. Their durability through history exposes them to multiple readings that make monuments fascinating material for philosophical thinking about the unstable nature of the past, wrongly believed as fixed.

What's So Bad about Monuments?

Monuments are very visible in many parts of the world and tend to highlight significant historical events or individuals. Monuments are interesting artifacts, since they tell about a past event that has been so important that it deserves a monument. And why we know that that past event has been important to history? Because it has been memorialized through the creation of a monument. What comes first? The importance of the event, which warrants a monument? Or, we understand the episode as important precisely because it has a monument erected in its honor?

Still, how many times we, common citizens, stop our walking to carefully observe a monument representing some person when we have no idea who he or she is? But we think that he or she has been important for history. Because a monument has been erected about him or her. The chicken or the egg? A monuments refers not only to an event, but also to itself, who constructed it, and why. Monuments point to something more than the past: they become monuments of power.

The bigger the monument, the bigger the statement. A colossal monument is someone screaming at us how important the event was (all the same, viewers may have no idea who she or he was).

Monuments run the risk of turning historical events into myths through a recounting of history that is far from the truth. Monuments have the virtue (or, sometimes, defect) of fixing a story. They are not malleable, versatile. They scream history, and the big ones are really hard to ignore. When a regime falls, monuments and statues are torn down, so the community can begin to write a new history. This is easy to see in some of the newsreel films that the fabled "Man in the High Castle" distributes. The anti-fascist images depict Americans tearing down Nazi imagery. In one of the scenes, an Imperial Eagle is knocked down from a cupola. Juliana Crane, watching the scene in "The New World," immediately infers what the scene represents: an alternate history. A statue is knocked down so that another (alternative) stream line can be written. Monuments record memories or, better say, *selected* memories. They are selections about what is to be told and what is to be *forgotten*. That's why monuments are potentially dangerous.

Nazism and fascism in general loved with passion the fixity and immutability of big buildings and monuments. Fascist parties felt that monuments and displays of giant architecture represent them: big, strong, spectacular and, more important, everlasting. No one can ignore them. The huge monuments bespeak power, even when they can be ugly. Architecture and monuments were considered indelible "words in stone." The Nazi intention was that the built heritage would endure and continue to "speak" about the

National Socialist glory over time. Fascist parties were inclined to monuments on a massive scale, so the reconversion of America into Nazi architecture observed in *The Man in the High Castle* rests on real assumptions.

Huge monuments and architecture are forms of spectacle that allow wider dissemination. Big works of architecture are there to *impress* people. In "The New World" episode, the swastika can be observed prominently adorning buildings and bright advertisements decorating facades. There's a direct link between spectacle and monuments: the latter are mostly architectural arrangements meant to impress an audience. Just like any spectacle. As the German philosopher Walter Benjamin argued in his classic essay "The Work of Art in the Age of Mechanical Reproduction," fascism turned political life into spectacle as a way to narcotize people, and this idea is central in the construction of *The Man in the High Castle*.

What You See Is What You Get

In the first episode, Nobusuke Tagomi prepares the visit to America of the Japanese prince and his wife. The scene takes place inside a huge Nazi embassy within the Japanese Pacific States. The camera offers a wide shot of the embassy's monumentality, the embassy dwarfing the buildings circling it. The next shot depicts the Nazis preparing ceremonies using a scale model of the same building. Tagomi, however, feels uncomfortable. He considers that the furniture and all its pieces within the room are "wrong" because it lacks "chi," the spirit of good or bad faith living within material things.

The German Nazi surreptitiously mocks the idea, but Tagomi, in turn, mocks Nazi philosophy: they believe only in things they can see. Big things. Tagomi points to the preference of German Nazis for visual spectacle, as the building where the scene takes place testifies. In the episode "The Illustrated Woman," the SS headquarters in New York City is highlighted. The building is clearly taller than all the skyscrapers circling it. The building includes the Imperial Eagle at the top, thus literately taking Nazism to new "peaks." In contrast, the Kempeitai headquarters also consist of tall buildings, but not especially striking in altitude or architectural form, with only a tiny Japanese flag on the top. They mostly blend in with the other buildings ("Kindness").

All the Japanese festivities and receptions (as seen in "The Illustrated Woman") are elegant but not exactly "spectacular." They tend to be rather simple and performed in natural spaces: they are spiritual rites of respect for the ancestors rather than demonstrations of power. When the Japanese prince is presented to the people, however, the parade is organized by Germany, so it has to be a huge spectacle. The audience is shown an aerial shot from high altitude, with the Imperial Eagle at the center of the image.

The use of monuments and architecture as fascist tools is emphasized briefly in two episodes: in "Kindness," John Smith takes Captain Connolly to the highest balcony of the Nazi headquarters. His purpose is interrogation, and the altitude is both oppressive and foreboding. Any viewer familiar with Western film and TV fiction knows that Smith will push the man into the abyss to kill him. And he does so. In that scene, the incredible altitude links three items: Nazism, death, and noteworthy architecture.

In "A Way Out," Heydrich states his motto: the strong must overcome the weak. Cut to the next scene in the Austrian Alps, where we see Hitler's headquarters, a monumental castle dominating the surrounding mountains. The castle is positioned at a peak. The Führer resides in a monumental structure at the top of the world. Nazi ideology is speaking through this architecture.

In this sense, one of the most important holidays within *The Man in the High Castle* is Victory Day, another form of spectacle. VA Day comes to replace July 4th as the national holy day par excellence. Every building is adorned with Nazi flags. Fireworks dominate the night sky, and all give a cheerful "Sieg heil!" The Pacific States, however, choose not to observe these festivities, another example of the differences between Imperial Japan and Nazi Germany ("Three

Monkeys"). Japan chooses instead to celebrate Marine Day, more related to military efforts, imperialism, and honor, all issues important to Imperial Japan before the American occupation (in the real world).

Walter Benjamin warned of the dangers of allowing spectacle to infiltrate politics to disguise the workings of totalitarian regimes. The recurrent use of huge architecture and monumental spectacle "traps" people within a visual regime that downplays a critical attitude, stultifies the masses, and turns them into passive spectators whose only action is to cheer. Sieg heil!

Countermonuments or Flow My Tears, the Americans Said

Why do Mr. Kasoura and his lovely wife decide to begin a lifestyle that pays homage to American culture (notably in "Truth"), considering that the American occupation and Americanization of Japan has never taken place in this alternative history?

Beyond the obvious symbols—Kasoura saying "Call me Paul"—the interest in American culture by the Japanese conquerors has subtle causes. This concern for forgotten cultures (and in this alternative history, American culture has been colonized by Nazis) is connected with memory and the forgotten. For example, when dinning with "Paul and Betty", Robert Childan calls jazz "nigger music." American culture has lost its values at the hands of other cultures and ideologies, Nazi Germany and Imperial Japan, the ones in charge of composing history through social discourse and architecture. But alongside official memory, fixed in monuments and Victory Days, there are other objects that we could call "countermonuments", indexes of the past which, unlike common monuments, highlight the fleeting and the overlooked.

A memory contrary to the official one evokes alternative memories of the past. Many times, this "counter-memory" is materialized in the form of counter-monuments. When Mr. Tagomi gives Juliana one of his chrysanthemums ("Truth"), he is not only giving her a present in honor of her sister, but through a subtle movement, he seeks to reaffirm the memory of Trudy, killed by the terrorism of the State. There is hardly anything more counter-hegemonic than Tagomi's gesture. That same flower, which represents Juliana's search for truth, also refers to the memory of Tagomi's family, whom he lost in a war that Japan won but that brought him only loneliness. Later, Juliana begins to bring him flowers ("End of the World"), thus strengthening her connection with the past and reaffirming the need for that memory.

Alongside monuments there are counter-monuments, which challenge monumentality as an index of the past. The counter-monuments serve to destabilize the idea that the past is fixed and help us to reconsider the ways in which history is narrated and magnified by the symbology materialized in the big monuments. Juliana and Tagomi's exchange of flowers is the perfect countermonument. Flowers work here as links to the past but, unlike Nazi architecture, they are small and fragile, ephemeral objects doomed to quickly disappear.

There are other counter-monuments within the series. Amid the displays of fascist political theatricality, film as a medium emerges as the means for the very reproduction of the masses, in contrast to more traditional aesthetic categories, such as "creativity" or "genius." Film is a more "democratic" medium. Unlike monuments, which represents only someone important enough to be recreated in stone or marble, home movies or photography can recreate anyone, a member of royalty or someone from the working class. In this sense, the medium of film is an enemy of fascism within the series, a form of counter-monument.

The films show the possible existence of an alternative world in which the political and social reality would be completely different. The notion of the isolated image blasted out of the continuum of history is important within Benjamin's philosophy of history, reflecting one of his most interesting preoccupations and claims: that *the past is constructed by the present*, and must therefore be read in and through that present. The short films circulating illegally, in turn, constitute different interpretations of history. Film is here an art made for the masses, bringing new points of view, since more people can access the means for recording. Monuments can be erected only by the State (with large sums to spend, of course). Filmmaking, even in 1962, was more accessible than the construction of monuments.

In turn, the films must circulate in an underground way, rather than being a proud display of history as Nazi monuments are. The problem is that *all* counter-monuments tend to disappear underground in the course of time. The nature of counter-monuments is frailty, minimalism, all things that tend to disappear or to go unnoticed. Memory is best represented by the big monuments, which serve to fix memory and historical references. Counter-monuments survive only through circulation: the clandestine circuit of exchange must not die. Regardless of whether the Man in the High Castle really exists, the films must be produced and continue to circulate as a counter-narrative to the monuments.

A counter-monument is counter-cultural, a piece looking to break with the "aura" of empowerment of monuments. That is why the newsreels in *The Man in the High Castle* work against the grain without denying the existence of history, because, "the counter-monument does not intend to negate memory but to call attention to the impossibility of permanence" (Kattago). History is not fixed but malleable according to your point of view. Ultimately, this is a brave statement within the show. A kind of anti-hegemony prowls around the newsreels, and the fact that these movies show possible futures opens up paths to hope and routes of rebellion.

Little Actions, Big Meanings

A counter-monument is not necessarily an object; it also could be an action. In "Three Monkeys," after arguing violently with Juliana, Frank Frink roams the streets, ending up at Mark Sampson's house. In the privacy of his home, they both dedicate a prayer in Hebrew to the dead. The ceremony and all the manifestations of pain must be attended underground.

Something similar happens in "Truth": Frank tells Juliana about his foiled assassination attempt during the reception for the Japanese prince, and how he feels himself reflected in the eyes of a Japanese boy. For Frank, the reception was a farce, a fake. The chosen word is interesting if we keep in mind that both Frank and the antiquarian work together to create fake historical pieces to sell. This action confirms that history is a performance, a practice that can be literally fabricated by means of fake documents, or through the exhibition of monuments that point to a seemingly univocal past.

At the beginning of "Three Monkeys," in a context that might have come from a mid-twentieth-century American story, or from a family home video, Joe plays baseball with Thomas Smith as they talk about their experiences within the spectacular frame of Victory Day. As in real life, baseball, a typical American practice, has survived the Nazi occupation. Its presence points to something absent: American freedom. The game is a memory. Even more, during their conversation, Thomas realizes that Joe does not possess a stellar record with the Nazi espionage service. In other words, a critical recuperation of the past is done in a double way: through the practice of baseball and through dialogue. Both practices question the idea of a perfect, pure regime. In the same episode, the denial of Obergruppenführer John Smith regarding memories of fishing shared with the traitor Rudolf Wegener presents a dilemma, because, despite the former following strictly the law when he punishes his old friend, a hint of nostalgia overwhelms Smith: the longing for the little things of the past, the counter-memory of what might have been.

Hitler, ill and frail, is kept out of sight of the citizens until the last episode. Recurrently through the series, the Führer's health is brought up, confirming his delicate state. Hitler exists through his monuments, all of them indexes of his presence. Frailty is not a characteristic of a monument. Hitler's body makes him subject to ephemerality, and that is exactly what monuments hide from citizens. Hitler-as-body is, at the end, a counter-monument. He will, eventually, *pass* and become invisible.

Monumental Invisibility

In "Three Monkeys," Wegener and Smith discuss spectacle. Smith talks about Berlin and its grandiosity, while Wegener interrupts him, pointing to the fact that nobody seems to care about the decorations any more. This exchange foregrounds some problem with monuments. After a while, they work only with tourists, who mostly take pictures, sometimes without noticing to whom or to what the constructions refer. Monuments run the risk, big as they are, of being naturalized as part of the landscape. Their effect upon history fades away. Nobody in *The Man in the High Castle* seems to notice these colossal structures anymore, since they undermine, as most monuments do, the complexities of history.

As Robert Musil put it, "There is nothing so invisible as a monument."

3
Saving Hitler's Life

DONALD MCCARTHY

In 1943, painter Norman Rockwell debuted *Freedom from Want*, a painting that portrayed a family setting down for Thanksgiving dinner, with the matriarch of the family placing the Thanksgiving turkey in front of the patriarch, who sits at the head of the table.

In *The Man in the High Castle*'s sixth episode, "Three Monkeys," a warped version of this image plays out: Obergruppenführer John Smith cuts a turkey in front of his wife as they await dinner. The scene has a more suburban element than Rockwell's painting as it is set outside on a sunny day, in the backyard of Smith's house. In the background is a flag: at first glance it looks American, but where one would normally find the stars on the flag is the swastika. It's a perverse joke, taking one of the most iconic images of Americana and twisting it into the darkest vision possible.

While "Three Monkeys" is not the most pivotal episode in terms of plot, the above scene is imperative to understanding *The Man in the High Castle*'s relationship with duality, a relationship that extends outside of the show, wrapping in the viewer. Duality is usually associated with the idea of two opposites existing together, such as yin and yang, but it comes from a much wider background. The philosophy of dualism, which is where duality comes from, explores how the mind and the body exist as separate entities.

The human body and the conscious mind are not opposites, this line of thinking states, but they are distinct from one another and should therefore be treated as separate entities. This can easily be taken in a religious direction, but *The Man in the High Castle* instead looks at dualism via speculative fiction, specifically alternate universes. By presenting multiple alternate universes, *The Man in the High Castle* shows the audience various forms of history playing out on the same physical sphere. The place is the same, but reality is different. In this sense, the world is the body and history is the mind. However, where dualism tends to present two entities, *The Man in the High Castle* eventually presents many entities existing at once, taking dualism and dividing it again and again

Previous television shows, such as David Lynch and Mark Frost's masterpiece, *Twin Peaks*, used dualism to explore the darker side of the American Dream. David Chase's *The Sopranos* also used dualism, specifically at the start of its sixth season, exploring how Tony Soprano would be if he was not a mobster. Because of the long form nature of television, character development can take interesting routes that a film, which is limited to so short a period of time, cannot go down.

The Man in the High Castle goes a step further than most other television shows, breaking the characters not into two, but into many. It is aware of television's prior history with dualism, showrunner Frank Spotnitz worked on *The X-Files*, which had a number of episodes revolve around this very concept, but it is moving the conversation forward. It also uses dualism in its original meaning to establish a relationship with the audience that is unique in television history.

The Fracturing of the Single Person

In the first episode, appropriately titled "The New World," Juliana Crain discovers the newsreel movie *The Grasshopper Lies Heavy*, which displays footage from a timeline where the Allied powers won the war against the Axis powers. While watching the movie, Juliana seems to have a personal philosophical awakening. She begins to cry, both from the shock of the video and the possibilities it offers. She is becoming aware that the nature of the world is broader than she had previously thought. Her fiancé, Frank Frink, on the other hand, wants to get rid of the movie, seeing it as a threat.

The scene encompasses the two main reactions people have to a revelation: awe and fear. Director David Semel shoots the scene so that the viewer feels both reactions. By cutting back and forth between a close-up of Juliana's face as she reacts to the footage and to the footage itself, film that the audience is already very familiar with because it is from the actual Allied victory, he preps the audience to feel the fascination she does. When Frank enters the room, he is first framed in a dark doorway and then through a window pane, signifying how his reaction will be different from Juliana's, and the audience becomes suspicious, not necessarily of Frank, but of the situation in general. Should Juliana have access to what she is seeing? She sees it as a blessing, but Frank sees it as a curse, that seeing this other world will only make theirs worse; is he correct? Whether ignorance of the wider world is, in the end, better is left for the audience to decide as the series unfolds.

However, the specifics of this scene come back in the ninth episode, "Kindness," when Juliana and Frank see yet another film. By this point, the two have evolved, especially Frank who has gone from a laid-back blue-collar worker to a man with a deep sense of anger and betrayal. Frank is as suspicious of the film as he was in "The New World," but he is ready to see it, to accept what it will reveal in a way that he had not been nine episodes earlier. Juliana, on the other hand, is not quite as capable of accepting this film as she was at first. Because her first experience was one of awe, the opposite nature of the second film comes as a blow, which results in her character coming across as unmoored after the newreel, similar to Frank's in "The New World."

To show the evolution of the characters, this scene, directed by Michael Slovis, is staged opposite from the scene in "The New World." Here, Juliana and Frank stand next to each other in an empty auditorium. They are no longer separated nor are they in a confined space. The reality of the world, of its multifaceted nature, is no longer a secret. It is well that their viewpoints have changed, because the Frank and Juliana at the start of *The Man in the High Castle* could not have stomached what this video presents. Gone are scenes of victory. Instead, they are first presented with footage of a nuclear wasteland in the United States. The footage then cuts to prisoners of war being forced to their knees by their German captives. One of the captives is Frank. He is then shot in the back of the head by Joe Blake, a supposed ally of Frank and Juliana's in the timeline most of the season takes place within.

The moment is chilling, but in a fashion only *The Man in the High Castle* can deliver. Frank and Juliana don't learn anything about Joe's allegiances in the universe of the show; they are both well aware that they are seeing an alternate history. Yet the fact that Joe can become such a cold-blooded killer, even in an alternate timeline, is unnerving and forces them to view him in a different light. It's not that Joe has changed, but rather their perception of what Joe could become has shifted. Now that they know what he can do, they view him differently.

It's tragic, in its way, because just the thought of what a person could be, not what they are, can change perspectives. They embrace a dualistic viewpoint of humanity in this moment, one where a person who is good can just as easily be a person who is evil. Yet, *The Man in the High Castle* does not entirely embrace this concept even as it plays with it. The direction of this scene certainly plays as an opposite of the scene in the first episode, but the writing adds an extra layer, questioning if the idea of a person flipping between good and evil is as simple as it sounds.

Unspoken is also the fact that both Juliana and Frank must have the capability of being different individuals, like Joe. The show has alluded to this on multiple occasions in previous episodes, even if the characters are only just realizing it in the ninth installment. Juliana spends time in

Canon City from the second to fifth episode, and here she's more daring than the Juliana seen in the first episode. While Juliana is away, the mild-mannered version of Frank is replaced with a homicidal one after the death of his sister, leading to a scene where he attempts to assassinate the crown prince of Imperial Japan. These changes are not just to increase the drama; they signify the various possibilities for joy and violence hidden not just within each person, but within the world itself. Juliana and Frank do not go back and forth between good and evil, but they do show how there are many facets of the same person.

The Limits of History

In "A Way Out," the first season's finale, the relationship between the audience and that of *The Man in the High Castle* fully reveals itself, showing that the themes the show has explored with the characters are also being explored on an even broader level. During "A Way Out," the audience meets Hitler in the flesh; it is he who has been collecting at least some of the footage that Frank and Juliana found. However, what makes Hitler's appearance so shocking is not that he has been hoarding the mysterious films, but rather that the audience wants him to survive an assassination attempt.

In a deft bit of writing, showrunner Frank Spotnitz and his writers set up Hitler as an evil man who has even worse men just beneath him (there is at least some historical precedent to the idea that Himmler and Goebbels were worse than Hitler when it came to brutality). Should Hitler be assassinated, a war between imperial Japan and Nazi Germany will break out, likely ending the lives of all the characters the audience has grown to know and, to some extent, love. For the audience to want a world where Adolf Hitler is *not* assassinated sounds disturbing, but *The Man in the High Castle* manages to craft the story in a way that makes Hitler's survival a moral necessity.

Not content to end there, the two characters who are involved in ensuring Hitler's survival, and thus the two characters the audience cheers on, are also Nazis: the previously mentioned John Smith and Rudolf Wegener. Wegener is sent by a faction of Nazis, led by Reinhard Heydrich, who want Hitler dead, to assassinate the Führer during a visit to the Führer's castle (which is quite high, I might add, leading to some convincing speculation that Hitler is the titular character of the show; barring a future reversal, this appears to be a legitimate read). Wegener, though, does not want to be a partner to this; he has, in fact, been one of the key behind-the-scenes players in orchestrating peace between Imperial Japan and Nazi Germany. However, both his life and, implicitly, the lives of his family members are being threatened by Heydrich.

At the same time, Heydrich, who is in America, senses that John Smith's loyalties lie with Hitler and not with the overall values of the Nazi party. Heydrich takes Smith on a hunting trip into the woods, leading him to a cabin where he holds him prisoner, giving him an ultimatum: throw his support behind Heydrich before Heydrich receives the call Hitler has been assassinated.

Episode director Daniel Percival cuts between these two plots, escalating the tension. Before long the audience is worried John Smith will die and that so, too, might Adolf Hitler. During Wegener and Hitler's confrontation, Hitler makes it clear that he is aware of the fractured nature of life. He has been watching footage from alternate universes for some time, he reveals, and from each of them he learns something new. He declines to go into details—understandable since he also has to talk Wegener out of killing him—but, considering the schisms within the Nazi ranks, it seems likely that Hitler has embraced a new perspective on global conquest.

What once seemed paramount to Hitler, now seems a little less important. No matter what occurs, Hitler knows there are other worlds where he lost, some where he won even greater than he did in *The Man in the High Castle*'s main universe, and some where he landed somewhere in the middle. He understands the fickle nature of the universe, how the world's history is not set in stone, how factions and people can morph under the right circumstances. This reflects the journey the audience has made, as well. At the start of the season, *The Man in the High Castle* seemed to reflect the worst possible world; by the end, it shows that, no, it could be even worse.

The unique sympathies *The Man in the High Castle* managed to bring out of viewers did not go unnoticed by critics upon the show's release. Todd VanderWerff, *Vox*'s television critic, had this to say: "By the end of its finale, this is legitimately one of the weirdest things on television, a show that takes questions of just what evils we're willing to be complicit in when living in any society, then gives them a sci-fi coating that makes them go down a little more easily." *Salon*'s Sonia Saraiya also picked up on this: "The most amazing thing Spotnitz's show pulls off (in the finale—spoilers!) is in bringing you to the point where you see someone able to kill Hitler—pointing a gun at his head—and as you are watching, you are hoping that he won't. The unstable alliance between Japan and Germany will crumble if the old man is assassinated; nuclear war will surely follow. The man holding the gun is a good man—a Nazi who loves his family, who cannot sleep at night because of the atrocities committed by his party. But he can't do it."

The power of forcing the audience to align, even briefly, with Hitler, is one of the show's lasting accomplishments, because it forces the audience to question just how easily its allegiances can be swayed under the right circumstances. By using an actual historical figure, *The Man in the High Castle* starts to become metatextual, which brings it to a new, darker level, one that challenges the audience's own humanity and sense of self.

The Dualism of the Viewing Experience

The Man in the High Castle TV show is adapted from the novel of the same name by science-fiction author Philip K. Dick. The differences are many, but one of the most telling is that in the novel, *The Grasshopper Lies Heavy* is not newsreel footage; it's a book. That Frank Spotnitz changed it to video shows that the medium the story is being told within, originally a novel and now a streaming television show, is part of the story itself. Most television dramas do not call attention to the fact that they are television dramas, but *The Man in the High Castle* does this several times, most noticeably in the opening credits which features images of video footage played across a map of the conquered United States. This forces the audience to be aware that they are watching images within an image. That Juliana and Frank also watch video footage is key, because they are, in fact, doing what the audience currently is doing: watching an alternate narrative of life.

The message Juliana and Frank received from the first video is the opposite of the message received by the audience, which is, in the simplest of terms: this world could be yours. You could live in a world where a Nazi regime is in power. You could be the police office Joe meets on the highway who casually comments that those who are mentally ill or physically handicapped are burned alive. You could be Smith's neighbors who jovially say "Heil Hitler!" Or you could be John Smith, an American hero and an American Nazi.

This does not need to be taken literally, just as the alternate universes do not need to be taken literally. *The Man in the High Castle* is not stepping into the scientific debate on whether alternate realities exist or if there is an America that lost to Germany and happily became National Socialist. Instead, it is questioning the historical narrative that America is necessarily a place that fights off oppressors. The show is telling the audience that simply because a country is democratic does not mean it will always remain so. There are many possibilities within every country, and the possibility for fascism is one of them.

Just as Juliana and Frank are forced to witness other versions of themselves, either directly through their experiences or through what they see on the footage, viewers of *The Man in the High Castle* must confront that they are watching a possible version of themselves whenever they stream another episode. *The Man in the High Castle* is a television show; it's also a presentation of our own alternate reality, meaning the show is, by its very nature, dualistic, existing at once as fiction and a very skewed version of history.

In its relationship with the audience, *The Man in the High Castle* uses dualism in its original sense: providing a fictional world and contrasting it with the real world, subtly asking the audience how different the two are.

II

The World Dick Made

4
Cruel Optimism and the Good Nazi Life

LUKASZ MUNIOWSKI

Lauren Berlant's term "cruel optimism" describes what happens when the object of your desire, the goal of all your strivings, keeps you from enjoying a full life.

The term "cruel optimism" is used especially in reference to something that can be summed up as "the good life," which may be understood as a typical suburban life, dominated by notions of family, community and work. The attachments and expectations that are supposed to make Frank Frink and Obergruppenführer John Smith happy are actually the cause of their misery. Their vision of "the good life" and everything that it promises is more important than what actually makes them feel good. In order to fulfill society's expectations they forfeit their own happiness, which leads to a dismal existence.

The first episode of *The Man in the High Castle* opens up with a propaganda movie about what can be summed up as the Greater Reich's version of the American dream: people are happy no matter whether they spend time with their families or at work, as they are contributing to the greatness of their country. The shots used in this film-within-a-film look as if they might have been taken directly from the propaganda of 1950–1960s America, while the voiceover informs the viewers that in order to achieve happiness they should produce and consume, fueling the economy with their labor and earnings.

Joe Blake leaves the theater as the message is being delivered, moments after we learn that he's there only to get directions for his assignment. His early exit suggests that Joe is either resistant to the propaganda or has internalized it to the point that he does not need to hear the message—he knows it by heart. Whether he believes it or not is a different story, as proved by his actions throughout the first season of the series. Not so in the case of John Smith and Frank Frink, who are completely caught up by the American dream.

The vision of suburban happiness is powerful and suggestive. It should be, as it is key in sustaining the current order. The citizens of the Greater Nazi Reich are supposed to contribute to making their country stronger, as it will benefit them in the long run. The same is the case with the citizens of the Japanese Pacific States, although here the propaganda is more about respect and control. Calm and collected, no matter the current events, Japanese characters want to instill the same mentality within American citizens.

Two characters who are almost obsessed by the idea of the good life are John Smith and Frank Frink. Frink wants to fit in, start a family and have children. He stopped being an artist in order to provide for himself and his girlfriend, Juliana Crain. Smith already has a wife, three kids, and a house in the suburbs. His American Dream is fulfilled, so it is in his best interest to sustain the current order. Both characters fall victim to what can be characterized as "cruel optimism."

In her book *Cruel Optimism* Lauren Berlant writes that "a relation of cruel optimism exists when something you desire is actually an obstacle to your flourishing" (p. 1). The term is used to describe your relation to a goal—usually an object of your desire—that's supposed to make everything better, yet the end result is usually the opposite. The relationship with the object is problematic, because obtaining it usually involves a lot of time and effort.

The supposed happiness is delayed, which makes it more promising and precious. Instead of focusing on the present, your activity is directed towards the future, which means that all action is concentrated on saving for later. This is at the heart of the capitalist model, as the citizen is supposed to blindly follow the ideal of the good life, stuck in a cycle of creation and consumption. The attachment to the postponed happiness gives the worker motivation and creates an appealing storyline for him to follow. If he fails to reach his goal it will be his fault, as this story is supposedly written by the system and the worker's "job" is simply to "connect the dots." The blueprint for happiness is in front of him, he must just follow it.

The idea of the good life varies across times and cultures. Its most basic and concrete definition was presented by Bertrand Russell, one of the most important philosophers of the twentieth century, who argues that "the good life is one inspired by love and guided by knowledge" (*What I Believe*, p. 10). Only a combination of both leads to a certain fulfillment in life, but Russell gives love the upper hand, as without it knowledge is basically useless.

Knowledge is best used to benefit our loved ones. Russell writes that "in a perfect world, every sentient being would be to every other the object of the fullest love," but in reality we are simply unable to do this, as we are repulsed by some people or by creatures like fleas, bugs, or lice (p. 12). Coincidentally, these names are used throughout the series by the Nazis to describe Jews. That sort of hostility proves that Russell's ideal vision, originally conceived in 1925, is out of reach for the citizens of the 1960s Greater Nazi Reich and Japanese Pacific States. If fellow man cannot evoke any positive feelings among them, and his race is the sole reason for the lack of compassion or empathy, than this vision of the good life seems far from ideal. Still, a vision of the good life must exist in order to keep the society under control and give its members something to aspire to.

The opposition between the idea of the good life and the ideal of the good life is based on the relationship between social desire and social need. Henri Lefebvre, another influential twentieth-century philosopher, recognizes the opposition as essential to constructing human reality. He observes that "need is determined biologically and physiologically," hence it is natural and essential to human existence, while "desire is at the same time both individual and social; in other words it is recognized—or excluded—by a society" (*The Critique of Everyday Life*, p. 301).

The conflict stems from the opposition between nature and nurture, and it is the successful combination of both that leads to a successful existence. Since the balance between them is hard to attain, desire is presented by those in the position of power as natural, because without it there is no direction for the economy and its subjects to follow. Lefebvre observes that desire is equipped with "motivations that give meaning to the desired object and to desire itself" (p. 302).

Desire is essential in understanding the good life, as it is desirable, but not necessary. This refers to the idea of the good life, not the ideal good life. It is my desire that fuels the other's desire. By wanting and obtaining, I am instilling the desire to want and obtain in others, who decide to perform these actions if only through mimicry. This creates a social order that is so appealing to individuals like Smith and Frink.

The Case of John Smith

During the VA Day—Victory over America Day—Americans are supposed to celebrate their defeat by the Third Reich on their home soil. The holiday is more important than the Fourth of July. It takes place on the eighteenth of September. Its two main elements are: a traditional dinner of turkey and apple pie, and an address by the Führer, Adolf Hitler himself.

It is also during this holiday that societal aspirations and illusions are most visible. As Joe Blake arrives to the party organized by John Smith's family, he is welcomed by Smith's seemingly perfect son, two daughters and wife, Helen. An exemplary citizen of the Third Reich, Smith of course lives in the suburbs. His neighbors are also exemplary, as they can be seen with their whole families, preparing flags and greeting each other with the traditional "Sieg Heil!", smiling throughout the day. That's also the way the family greets Joe at the door.

Soon, Joe is in the backyard, playing baseball with Smith's son. Known as "American pastime," the activity is referred to as "lazy" by Smith himself, who prefers track or soccer—typically European sports. That could signify that through his rejection of a typically American sport the Obergruppenführer wants to be more German than the Germans themselves, if it were not for the fact that he does not condemn turkey, apple pie, or whiskey, which in fact are quintessentially American. It is therefore impossible to qualify him as anti-American, and he has a typically American vision of the good life.

As Smith already has a perfect house and a perfect family, his main occupation as a family man is sustaining both. In the case of the latter he does so by constantly presenting himself as respectful and righteous to his kids, inspiring in them the desire for similar virtues. In the house there are certain rules that need to be obeyed: children should not run around the house, they must help their mother with the chores, and so on. Since an early age his daughters are preparing for the role of housewives—at one point Smith calls it "the most important job in the Reich"—as they put cutlery at the dinner table. Everything must be in order, even during a simple family breakfast. The family eats all of its meals together and there should be no distractions.

When Thomas wants to prepare for a test at the table, he must get his father's permission to do so. Everything must be organized and done the right way, which in this case means just how Smith wants it. The problem with the rules is that they are not his, nor of his making, but are his way of mimicking how things are done in the Third Reich. Everyone should act without hesitation, following orders from higher authorities—in this case, the kids should listen to their father, who is an authority figure and simply knows best.

When Thomas talks to Smith about a boy at school that is questioning the current order, the Obergruppenführer teaches his son that the best way to approach such individuals is to simply ignore them, as they will eventually fail. The boy's name is Randolph and he does not respect the teachers. Thomas wants to prove him wrong not by beating him up, as most boys his age would do, but by getting the highest score in class. While it is doubtful that Randolph will be impressed by someone doing well at school, as he clearly rejects the validity of education, Thomas thinks that this is the only way to show his superiority. When asked by his father why he wants to do well at school, Thomas answers: "To make my family proud. To bring honor to my school. To serve my country."

Smith is naturally proud of his son and declares that his goals will be fulfilled because he wants to be a "useful member of society," while Randolph is egotistical, focused solely on himself. He is instilling within Thomas the same cruel optimism that drives him. The boy is studying and playing sports not because he enjoys them, but because both will benefit him in the long run. This is the exact same reason behind his father's actions. Instead of taking a day off during the national holiday and being the family man he so eagerly wants to be, Smith uses VA Day to capture a conspirator.

Smith's occupation does not allow him to act otherwise. As the Obergruppenführer, his obligation is to defend and preserve the community in which he lives. This means that he is constantly under pressure to find cracks in the system, and the people responsible for them. Throughout the series he either kills or orders the killing of multiple individuals. His actions are in no way ethical, unlike the image of himself he tries to project on his children. He might soon be oppressed by the same system that he is trying to sustain, as shown by the dilemma regarding his son.

The family doctor reveals to Smith that Thomas has Dejerine-Roussy syndrome and will be paralyzed within a year. It is only thanks to the doctor's good will that the authorities have not yet learned about Thomas's disease. Even though his function is to eliminate such behavior as the doctor's failing to report the case, Smith is glad that the doctor leaves the information to himself. Firm believers in eugenics, Nazis kill all the diseased and crippled. During a conversation with Smith Helen calls it "a blessing," as the sick do not have to suffer anymore. Smith does not reveal to her that her son, just like his brother, is also sick. He was of the same opinion as Helen until the sickness attacked Thomas.

When the workings of the system turn out to no longer be in his favor, and he is directly under threat from the system he has so eagerly protected, Smith unknowingly experiences the cruelty of his optimism. If he wants to keep his son alive, he must act against the system and expose the idea of eugenics as simply unjust. Furthermore, if one element of the system is wrong, he may soon learn that other parts of it are flawed as well.

Helen, his wife, is already aware of that, as she needs to take pills in order to keep up the façade of a perfect housewife. When she tells Joe Blake that one day he could also have "this"—referring to a house in the suburbs and a family—she does so not because she believes in the good life, nor because she's truly happy, but because that behavior, as well as the appreciation of what she has, is expected of her. Berlant's view that "cruel optimism is the condition of maintaining an attachment to a significantly problematic object" (p. 23) applies to the case of John and Helen Smith.

Helen's need for pills implies that she is not happy, even though she has attained the object of her desire. She is expected to feel accomplished and she attributes her inability to feel this way to herself, not to the artificiality of the ideal that she and her husband are chasing. Their attachment to the good life in the Greater Nazi Reich is a perfect example of cruel optimism.

The Case of Frank Frink

Berlant observes that "in a relation of cruel optimism our activity is revealed as a vehicle for attaining a kind of passivity, as evidence of the desire to find forms in relation to which we sustain a coasting sentience, in response to being *too* alive" (p. 43). This quote might as well describe Frank Frink's attitude.

As Juliana exposes Frank to a movie made by the Man in the High Castle, his first reaction is to destroy it. When

Juliana wants to take a stand and act, he also tries to convince her to do otherwise. Frink's vision of the good life is to leave, get married with Juliana and have kids. His actions are actually directed at passivity—his main goal is to settle and stay put. His motivations correspond with the idea of cruel optimism, as he is solely concerned with the future. His idea of the good life is connected to the discovery of television, which allows for such (in)action.

While Frink is rarely seen watching television, he is under the direct influence of its "anti-nomadic" effects. Jonathan Crary claims that it is because of television that "individuals are fixed in place, partitioned from one another, and emptied of political effectiveness" (*24/7*, p. 81). Television promotes idleness, simultaneously creating the impression that something's happening, while the individual does not even leave his house. Even when Frank becomes the direct subject of politics, he still wants to get away instead of defending himself. His sister is killed, his fiancée is on the run from the Kempeitai (Japanese military police), yet the only solution he can come up with is to hide in the Neutral Zone. When Juliana's sister dies, Frank coldly underlines the fact that she was actually her half-sister and that they were supposed to stay together and have a family, not get involved in a fight for freedom. His vision of the good life is threatened, so he does everything possible to convince others—and in consequence himself—that happiness under the Japanese regime is still possible. Frank is convinced of his political insignificance, even after he comes very close to making a difference by shooting the Japanese prince.

When describing after-war reality of the 1950s, Crary writes that it was television that "quickly redefined what constituted membership in society. Even the pretense of valuing education and civic participation dwindled, as citizenship was supplanted by viewership" (p. 79). This passivity is exactly what Frank is aspiring to, as whenever Juliana wants to leave, his first action is to stop her rather than join her in a battle for something she so eagerly believes in. It is only when Frank is personally touched by the system—his sister and her two children are killed by the Japanese—that he wants to act. Still, he is stopped by his immediate environment, personified by his friend Ed McCarthy, who tries to convince Frank that: "you take it or you get yourself killed."

Frank does not listen and goes out, but still finds himself unable to assassinate the Japanese prince. Before, when he is locked in a cell next to a member of the Resistance, at some point during their conversation the man declares: "takes a lot of effort, not being free," perfectly summing up Frank's inaction. Instead of motivating Frank, the words have their effect only to a point—Frank does not act and is fixated on the idea of leaving with Juliana for the Neutral Zone.

Juliana's different: moved by her sister's courage, she also wants to do something brave. Frank is holding her down, and so is her mother, who's even more hypocritical that Frank. Anne Crain Walker constantly criticizes the Japanese and their culture, but cannot stop watching Japanese television, and at one moment is actually caught enjoying a sumo bout. Her husband was killed in the war, so obviously she has more than her fair share of reasons to hate the oppressors, yet she's reluctant to admit that there are certain aspects of Japanese culture that she clearly enjoys. Plus she is still a housewife, stuck in front of the TV, so she is allowed to do the same thing she would do in a country not occupied by the Japanese.

That model of life is something Frank clearly aspires to. He wants to be caught up in the rhythm of work and home, factory and family, not allowing himself the freedom to do something out of the norm. Even when he's able to make a difference, he's quick to run away before having an actual impact on reality. That is because the idea of the good life is too appealing to simply let go of and the cruel optimism instilled by this idea ultimately leads to his unhappiness.

The False Promise

Both characters aspire to what they're supposed to, but while Smith is more like Juliana Crane in his awareness of the significance of the historical moment, Frink constantly looks for a way to avoid it. Even after being exposed to the films made by the Man in the High Castle, regardless of believing them, Frink wants to destroy them and just run away. Juliana wants to act, while her fiancé just wants to hide and lead what he assumes is a normal life, marry her and have children.

This is the life that Smith aspired to and succeeded in reaching, yet he fails to enjoy it, because he constantly needs to defend the current order. While he's right that it is under threat, Smith fails to allow himself just a moment to enjoy the fruits of his labor. His wife is clearly stressed, while the children do their best in keeping up appearances—something they have learned from both of their parents. Is this what Frink would want? Doubtful, just us it is doubtful that Smith envisioned his life to be that way.

Both of them are perfect case studies of Lauren Berlant's "cruel optimism," as their attachments failed to make good on their promise of the good life.

5
In the Neutral Zone, A Libertarian's Home Is Their (High) Castle

M. BLAKE WILSON

> The greatest menace in the twentieth century is the totalitarian state. It can take many forms: left-wing fascism, psychological movements, religious movements, drug rehabilitation places, powerful people, manipulative people; or it can be in a relationship with someone who is more powerful than you psychologically.
>
> —PHILIP K. DICK in Charles Platt, *Dream Makers*, p. 150.

Philip K. Dick exorcised many psychological demons through his work—those involving the appearance-reality distinction, the difference between madness and sanity, and the fractioning of the self—but a coherent and clear political stance does not emerge.

However, by combining Dick's paranoia with the moral positions he takes in *The Man in the High Castle* and other works, it's possible to decipher what kind of political mind is at work behind the idea that the United States lost World War II. Throughout these works, Dick takes a strong stance about self-ownership and privacy rights. These rights destabilize the powerful—Nazis, in particular—and strengthen the powerless and humble characters, like Juliana and Frank, who act as Dick's heroes. Like Juliana, in her staggering journey to the High Castle in order to topple fascism, we are also morally obligated to prevent her fictional world from becoming our reality. Libertarianism—the moral and political philosophy that stands for more rights and less government—is the best way to fulfill that obligation, and the desire for liberty is what motivates these characters as they struggle against totalitarianism.

To the High Castle

Unlike Ayn Rand, whose fiction repeatedly slams readers over the head with its political standpoint (as in *Atlas Shrugged* and its defense of free-market capitalism), Dick's political views in *High Castle* are more subtle. Some of those views, however, are obvious. For starters, it's evident that *High Castle* is anti-fascist. Nazis are bad. Don't be like them. Actually, if you're a Nazi, life in *The High Castle* looks pretty good. But for the rest of us, life looks pretty lousy, and that's because you have few or no rights.

Totalitarianism is bad because it violates rights, and one of the rights it violates more than others is the right to privacy. This right protects many of the other rights that totalitarian governments want to take away: your decisions about self-determination, how you use your property, whether you have children and what kinds of sex you have, and with whom. Dick himself was wary—no, he was downright terrified—of power and authority in general: bosses, teachers, and, most importantly, the police and the governments they defend.

Libertarians share similar fears. Like Dick, they fear the loss of privacy, the punishment of so-called deviant or esoteric lifestyles, and the imposition of state-imposed racism. They also fear the military, particularly when it gains the upper hand over other institutions. These fears, of course, are the realities of those persecuted by the Nazi and Imperial Japanese elites in *The Man in the High Castle*.

From the 1950s through to his death in 1982—*The Man in the High Castle* was published in 1962—Dick believed he was living in an increasingly totalitarian United States, an evil empire marked by political corruption (Watergate, the Pentagon Papers), the decimation of civil rights (privacy in particular), and violence (such as state violence in the form of police brutality and war, and also crime or street violence). So, Dick's alternative to the fascism of *The Man in the High Castle* is not "the real world" where Dick lived: that real world was, for Dick, the inspiration for the novel.

During the Eisenhower era Dick feared that there was a "great movement toward a totalitarian state," where "anybody who is a dissenter is labeled as a traitor" (*Philip K. Dick: In His Own Words*, p. 121). In this sense, *The Man in the High Castle*'s world is just a fictionalized version of the world Dick inhabited, where all it takes is selective amnesia about rights—and privacy rights in particular—to turn the world of *The Man in the High Castle* into political reality.

Give Me Libertarianism or Give Me . . .

As D.E. Wittkower writes in *Philip K. Dick and Philosophy*, "it is not so surprising that Dick will turn out to be a social-political philosopher rather than an epistemologist or metaphysician. His questions are still about value and how we should live" (p. 107). Questions about value and how we live are ethical questions, while epistemologists deal with questions about truth and knowledge (how can I claim to know something?) and metaphysicians field questions about being and reality (what kinds of things exist? What is real?). *The Man in the High Castle* is about *who* has political power, *how* can that power be used (control, benevolence, violence), and *what* can be done when the power is abused. It indeed deals with ethics, but also with politics and law which are subsets of ethics.

Dick's own political thinking—revealed primarily through interviews—tends to be naive and self-contradictory. In an interview shortly before his death, Dick effused that he was "anti-capitalist" yet "not a Marxist," that "Mussolini was a very, very great man," and that the "paradigm of evil" is the "totalitarian state." Although Mao was one of the greatest totalitarian leaders in the modern world, Dick admitted he cried when "that great man" died, while paradoxically considering himself an expert in "opposing authority" (*Philip K. Dick: In His Own Words*, pp. 119–121, 142, and *Philip K. Dick: The Last Testament,* p. 89).

Despite these quotes, the political message of *The Man in the High Castle* and other writings (particularly *A Scanner Darkly*) is clear: the loss of privacy is a major moral and political problem. Privacy protects how people make moral decisions and how they choose to live, and it's one of the primary rights in the libertarian's quiver. The opposite of libertarianism is totalitarianism, and totalitarianism is recognized by the absence of a right to privacy. A person has a right to privacy—in their thoughts, home, or actions—if they have the right to exclude others from those places and if others are under a duty of not to interfere with them. No right to exclude? No duty of noninterference? Then there is no right to privacy, and the results are the terrifying worlds of both *The Man in the High Castle* and another classic literary dystopia about the loss of privacy, George Orwell's *Nineteen Eighty-Four*. So who's a libertarian and why is privacy so important to them?

Libertarianism is based upon the idea that, as John Locke writes, you have a property in your person, which "nobody has any right to but" yourself. This, of course, is the right of self-ownership. Human beings, by virtue of the fact that they are not an android or a rock, possess certain rights just like they possess DNA or possess an arm or leg. From here, libertarianism splits off into right and left branches.

A conservative libertarian (we'll call them "right libertarians," or just the "right") opposes the state because it's coming for their God-given rights to their guns, property and their religion, while a liberal (or "left") libertarian opposes it because they want to use drugs, choose (or not choose) to have an abortion, and not get drafted. They share at least two basic beliefs: first, the basis of liberty is self-ownership, and second, liberty requires privacy. Lockean self-ownership means that everybody owns themselves, and the state acts beyond its authority when it treats people as if *it* owns them. Because you own yourself, you have rights like the right to privacy that the government may never violate—even if violating your rights leads to the greater good. If the state violates these rights, you have no obligation to obey it. In fact, as Locke makes clear, you have an obligation to resist it.

Although they agree about self-ownership, right and left libertarians have very different ideas about property rights. Right libertarians justify world and resource ownership in terms of "finders, keepers" and voluntary transactions, while the left denies that self-ownership can ever translate into world ownership: either everyone owns the world, or no one does. This permits everyone to have a stake in all the world's resources, and that means taking property from its current owners, such as large multinational corporations, through either pitchforks-and-torches-type force or legal force through something like eminent domain. So, unlike many right libertarians who fear governmental power but ignore corporate domination, left libertarians fear the government *and* corporations.

Dick falls into the latter category. In 1982, just two weeks before he died, Dick made this clear when he told biographer Gregg Rickman, "I have no respect for the free enterprise system because it is inequitable. . . . Everything that we left-wingers ever predicted about the free enterprise system has all come true" (*Philip K. Dick: The Last Testament*, p. 148). The system, Dick says, exists "for the welfare of the rich and the powerful at the expense of the poor and the powerless. If you are a human being and you are in danger of freezing to death, you had damned well better throw out this government [the Reagan Administration] one way or another because it will let you die" (pp. 149–150).

Dick's Politics of Paranoia

Both right and left libertarians fear control, spying, manipulation, and limitation on choices, all of which are kept in check by a right to privacy. If you feel secure in your "persons, houses, papers, and effects" (that's the Fourth Amendment speaking), then you probably have strong privacy rights. If you don't feel secure, then you—like the oppressed groups in *The Man in the High Castle*—probably have weak or nonexistent privacy rights. Dick's paranoia about his own privacy seeps into his conceptions of the state and of authority and therefore his characters. Dick was "terrified of Authority Figures like bosses and cops and teachers," and this explains why he became his own boss as a freelance writer (Olander and Greenberg, p. 216).

Dick had an understandable fear of fascism, but also a potentially irrational fear of his own government. His paranoia is often the result of a belief that obvious authorities (the president and the FBI) and not so obvious authorities (corporations, sinister societies) are operating both in front of and behind the scenes. They jointly spy, exploit the weak, dehumanize the disadvantaged, and suppress dissent through charges of treason. Despite his paranoia, it is unlikely that the police in Dick's nonfictional California were defending totalitarianism, but, like the Kempeitai and the SD in *The Man in the High Castle*, when they get too much power they cross the line and violate privacy rights. The Founding Fathers understood that a Constitution ought to prevent the police—and the government that employs and directs them—from crossing that line by establishing the Bill of Rights. From the looks of it, there's no Bill of Rights protecting anyone in the Reich or the Pacific States.

One of the reasons for Dick's insecurity about privacy, and a key event in his biography, was the infamous break-in of 1971. On assignment for *Rolling Stone*, Dick's literary executor and biographer Paul Williams writes that in November of that year, Dick "unlocked the front door of his house in San Rafael, California, and turned on the living-room lights. His stereo was gone. The floor was covered with water and pieces of asbestos. The fireproof, 1,100-pound asbestos-and-steel file cabinet that protected his precious manuscripts had been blown apart by powerful explosives" (*Only Apparently Real*, p. 13). In a 1981 interview, Dick attributed the break-in to a privately organized and government sponsored "nation-wide para-military organization" that harasses self-described left-wingers like him as well as anti-nuclear protestors (*Philip K. Dick: The Last Testament,* p. 86). There's nothing that makes a paranoid feel more secure than proving their fear of the government with facts, and the break-in did just that for Dick. He wrote about the breakdown of privacy in America in *The Man in the High Castle*, and then experienced it himself first-hand.

Dick's paranoia about privacy is a recurring theme in his work. The plot of *A Scanner Darkly* (both the novel and movie) revolves around privacy and its loss in a technologically advanced culture. (As I type this, I pause to check my iPhone. I have a home security camera which gives me a view of the inside of my home and dog through an app. I've often wondered if one day I'll tune in to my own home from my office and see myself sitting there, reading a book or watching TV, oblivious to the fact I am watching a version of myself. If you've read *A Scanner Darkly* or seen the movie, you know exactly what I'm talking about. Paranoia? Sure.)

How Do We Stop It from Happening Here?

Because they support a strong privacy right—again, the right to exclude the state from your body or home—libertarians (both kinds) are committed to limiting the power of police either through legislation or through the courts. One simple set of laws is already contained in the Bill of Rights. When added to other protections in the Bill, such as protections for speech and religious freedoms as well as private property, the courts have located a general privacy right that protects against state interferences with birth control, abortion, wiretapping, and property (unless that property is taken, pursuant to the Fifth Amendment, "for public use," and "just compensation" is provided). This right means that you have the right to exclude the state from those protected areas, and that the state has a duty not to interfere with the exercise of your rights in those areas.

The violation of privacy in the Pacific States was made vividly clear in Season One, episode 6 when Juliana, after getting a job in the Trade Ministry, is horrified to find that her stepfather, Arnold, isn't a bus driver: he heads up the domestic surveillance unit for the Japanese. The usual Phildickian paranoia turns from irrational fear to rational fact: the police and their lackeys are eavesdropping, bugging phones, and keeping tabs on what appears to be hundreds of telephone conversations. The loss of privacy goes hand in hand with the loss of liberty.

Libertarians are committed to a smaller or minimal state that does not engage in this kind of activity. Such a state requires few rules, and it's no coincidence that many contemporary libertarians (mostly on the right) believe that the rules and ideas contained in the Constitution are sufficient to guarantee a secure yet free state. But can the libertarian minimal state prevent a takeover by *internal* fascists? One of the most chilling implications of *The Man in the High Castle* is that the Nazis won by drawing out the domestic bullyboys (John Smith, for example) from the stained fabric of racist America and sucking them into either being traitors during the war, or ambitious pragmatists afterward. As they say, if you can't beat 'em, join 'em. Judging from their rapid and uncompromising rise to power after the war's end, Smith and other American Nazis joined 'em without even *trying* to beat 'em.

The Pacific States: The Lesser of Evils?

What about the Japanese totalitarians? In the novel, Dick appears to softball Japanese fascism. According to Dick critic Darko Suvin, Dick's assumption that a victorious Japanese fascism would be radically better than a German one is "the major political blunder" of *The Man in the High Castle* (Olander and Greenberg, p. 76). Suvin also writes that "Dick repeatedly hints that the atmosphere of the USA is the antithesis of that found in the PSA. This dichotomy is embodied in Mr. Tagomi. In the novel, Tagomi—realizing that there's no balance between the powerful evil and the saintly weak—exclaims, "There is evil! It's actual, like cement. Evil is not a view." Dick frequently has the understanding that political people and their power (be it military, economic, or industrial) are evil in contrast to his heroes, who tend to be ordinary people like Juliana and Frank. Although he stretches the mold a bit because of his political position as Trade Minister, Tagomi is a prime example of this kind of evil-fighting hero.

According to critic Patricia Warrick, "the totalitarian spirit, implemented by techniques and machines, creates this evil. It is evil because it destroys the authentically human spirit" (p. 188). For Dick, Satan acts through the Fascists, and Tagomi refuses to partake in their evil by declining to sign the form that will send Frank to a certain death in Germany. Dick implies that the world would be just if it was ruled by a man like Tagomi. Why does Dick place so much faith in this character? The answer may lie in a traumatic episode from Dick's biography

In an interview, Dick tells the story of seeing a World War II newsreel as a child which showed American soldiers killing a Japanese soldier with a flamethrower. The audience, Dick said, laughed and cheered. As the soldier was running and burning to death, Dick was "dazed with horror at the sight of the man on the screen and at the audience's reaction" and thought, "something is terribly wrong" (*Dream Makers*, p. 154). Coupling this story with Tagomi's moral compass, Dick takes sides in the novel on behalf of the Japanese. This favoring of the Japanese is thoroughly demolished in the TV show, where the Japanese have an uneasy alliance with the Reich that culminates in the murder of Juliana's sister, and, even worse, in the Nazi-like execution of Frank's sister and children. Whatever moral high ground Tagomi might possess as a Phildickian hero is smashed by the actions of his countrymen, and the Pacific States of America is no better than the Reich.

Why wouldn't oppressed white people flee the PSA for the Neutral Zone, which resembles what John Locke, Thomas Hobbes and other philosophers call the "state of nature"?

Maybe, as Hobbes argues, any kind of government—even an oppressive one—is better than the anarchy of the state of nature because at least your fellow citizens are intimidated by the same government you also fear and therefore provides security against one another. This is a scary idea: because the threats to your security by other governments or from your own neighbors are worse than the threats from the government itself, any government—even a really, really bad one—is better than no government at all. In that case, the loss of privacy is outweighed by the gain in security.

F is for Fascist and Fake, but not Fake Fascists

Dick loved to play with the idea of the fake, and *The Man in the High Castle* is full of fakes including Frank's gun and the phony Sitting Bull artifact. But although the violence is real, the explanation for it is fake. Thanks to Tagomi's mystical vision at the end of the story (it's roughly the same in both novel and the show) and to Juliana's encounter with *Grasshopper* novelist Hawthorne Abendsen (he's the filmmaker in the series), we discover what it must have felt like for Charlton Heston's character at the end of the original 1968 version of *Planet of the Apes*: we're home, and we never left it.

What's fake in *The Man in the High Castle* is the claim that the pre-Reich USA lost the war. *Grasshopper*, both film and book, is true: the United States won the war. Or, more accurately, *part* of it won: the absolute worst features of American culture—racism, violence, the violation of basic human rights—are the ones that triumph in the *Reich* government that 'replaced' the US government. The leaders themselves, aided by men like John Smith, always wanted a fascist, racially-pure USA, but knew it wouldn't play in Peoria. So the US won, or could have won, but faked a loss: the important, powerful, and evil people threw the fight and collaborated with the losers to bring the losers' ideology to the States from within.

The Germans aren't the victors: the *American* Nazis are. Recall John Smith's chilling portrayal of a loving suburban father cheerily wishing his neighbor Harry "Sieg Heil" on VA day—in Nazi America, Victory in America Day has replaced the Fourth of July—and then urging his thugs to torture a helpless prisoner until he dies. He supposedly fought for us, and now he's running the show against us. He won.

Dick's subtext is that the United State was already morally evil and capable of implementing political evil, but the takeover by Nazis would need to be pulled off as a trick or a fake because even the Americans wouldn't have capitulated to the 'enemy.' America won—it's right there in *Grasshopper*'s novel and newsreels—then fabricated a loss in order to ease the transition to the ideology many Americans, or at least the ones who run the government and the corporations, *really* believed in. Not only can *it* happen here, but I've got news for you: it *already* happened here.

In the alternative world of *The Man in the High Castle*, America fought against racist fascists (and won) but in doing so it fought against its own racism and military aggression—and lost. It fought against a version of itself as many wished it to be: racially pure and highly efficient, with no jazz or rock music and no gender equality. *The Man in the High Castle* is, according to Suvin, "the high point of Dick's explicitly political anti-utopianism," partially because it reveals the "affinities between German and American fascism, born of the same social classes of big speculators and small shopkeepers." The alternative history depicted in the story is that of a minority view—fascism—that becomes the mainstream.

"Sunrise" and the Triumph of Evil

In "Sunrise," Frank is in the custody of the Kempeitai and is tortured. He meets Randall—the resistance member Juliana met at the train station—and learns about the revolution. Frank wants no part of it. Randall says "Evil triumphs only when good men do nothing." Frank screams. Randall's words are inspired by a quote from the Anglo-Irish political writer,

Edmund Burke, whose actual words were, "The only thing necessary for evil to triumph is for good men to do nothing." Burke was a conservative who disapproved of the French Revolution's radical changes because they disrupt established social harmony (though he was more favorable to the American Revolution). Burke would probably have shrugged his shoulders at the Pacific States: revolution would be too costly with little chance of winning, and life's better there than in the Neutral Zone or the Reich. In fact, that's Frank's take on revolution—until he's tortured and released, of course. Then he becomes a revolutionary and a failed assassin.

With a slight twist to Burke's quote, Dick once said that "ethics may far more involve an abstention from evil than a commission of good. We tend to regard ethics and morality as motivations to do good, good works. It may be actually more identifiable authentically with a balking and a refusal . . . to do something, from some kind of innate perception that this is not done" (*Philip K. Dick: In His Own Words*, p. 144). This was the case with Tagomi, who refuses to do evil by refusing (in the novel) to authorize Frank's deportation to Germany.

In *The Man in the High Castle*, too few people refused, too many people acted, and when they acted they violated people's rights. But there's little hope for totalitarianism if nobody shows up to the torch-lit midnight rallies. Libertarianism means less law and more liberty. It uses the basic idea of freedom to put constraints on the state when it tries to use law to promote the kind of racism, loss of privacy, and violence saluted by Obergruppenführer Smith's "Sieg Heil!"

Dick's fear—and it's a fear shared by anyone who can grasp the humanitarian message of the story—is that here in the United States, maybe even in our own neighborhoods, someone is watching Obergruppenführer Smith with admiration and thinking the world would be a better place had Dick's alternative history been the true one.

The alternative to the alternative history is reality. And that's not science fiction at all.

6
The Self-Willed and Ignorant Law

MARC W. COLE

> But we see law bending itself more or less towards this very thing; it resembles some self-willed and ignorant person, who allows no one to do anything contrary to what he orders, not to ask any questions about it, not even if, after all, something new turns out for someone which is better, contrary to the prescription which he himself has laid down.
>
> —PLATO, *The Statesman* (lines 294a10–c8)

Obergruppenführer John Smith's face was contorted in agony, as if his father's heart was torn out. The doctor told him that his son had a disease that, under Nazi law, required his son's death.

This scene is loaded with philosophically interesting material, including the nature of statecraft. Why does the state control who lives and who dies? Why is the law blind to this father's love of child? Presumably, the Reich wants the best possible society for those it deems worthy. Who got to say that this sort of law was best for citizens? The Reich as well as Japan in *The Man in the High Castle* are often called fascist regimes. Undoubtedly. However, the structure of these governments was discussed favorably by Plato 2,400 years ago. Let's call the template "Plato's Republic" after the name of his book, *The Republic*.

I'm not saying that Plato would have looked favorably on the Reich or Japan. He has very strong views on bad laws and dictatorships. All I'm claiming is that the governmental shape of the Reich and Japan are very close to Plato's *Republic*.

The Art of Statecraft according to Plato

According to Plato, the art of political expertise has at least two, but possibly three components. At any rate, political expertise requires:

1. **an excellent knowledge of human psychology.**

This means, in part, knowledge about different personalities, and general knowledge of human behavior, as well as knowledge of the capabilities of citizens. And it also means being able to figure out the kind of person you're dealing with in day-to-day business.

2. **The political expert must also be able to manage the day-to-day affairs of the state.**

This includes not only doing government-related stuff, but also controlling the day-to-day shenanigans and goings on of citizens, including employment, education, and relationships.

3. **Finally, the political expert must be really good at legislation.**

At one point, Plato did not think this third component was properly part of the art of statecraft because law cannot attend to particular circumstances. Later, he seemed to think it was part of the art of statecraft.

The political expert should use her superior knowledge of human psychology, her managerial expertise, and her legislative expertise for the good of the state and the subjects therein, mixing and blending together the various sorts of personalities and lifestyles therein. How?

Plato's "Republic"

You might be thinking: "Hey, that sounds wicked awesome! If only more political leaders were like that, things would be better." Ha, ha. You say that, but things are about to get cra-cra.

Because of the political leader's expertise in human psychology, management, and legislation, the political leader should control all the aspects of day-to-day life in the state. So unlike an actual republic where supreme power rests with the people, supreme power rests with the political expert in Plato's ideal "republic."

What should the leader control? Well, according to her superior psychological knowledge, she can determine what kinds of people there are in her realm. Due to her management expertise, she knows not only what the state needs (such as farmers, blacksmiths, and lumberjacks), but how and when these tasks should be performed. Combined with her psychological knowledge, she also determines who does what jobs.

You read that right. She determines who does what jobs. But this is just the beginning. According to Plato, the political expert should control breeding and who breeds with whom. The aim here is to control the number of personality types suited for particular tasks. Marriage is also done away with and breeding simply occurs how and when the state directs it. Children are not raised by parents, but by the State. Also, the political expert controls education and music in order to inculcate in the population the right sort of morals and right attitudes towards life. This is just some of what the political expert would control. The perfect states controls their citizens from the cradle to the grave: where they work, what their job is, whom they reproduce with, the timing of reproduction, and the sort of education received and even music listened to.

Her expertise in legislation enforces how and when the activities of the land are done, and ensures people are all doing what they're supposed to be doing. The consequence, of course, for breaking laws is a punishment of some sort, presumably also determined by the political expert. Suppose I am ordered to breed with someone. If I refuse, I am punished.

What justifies this? In part, it's the superior knowledge of the political expert. They know what's best for the state and for its citizens. It is very important to remember that when the political expert is doing his job correctly, there is a harmony and balance in the realm.

Of Emperors, Führers, and Laws

There are a number of parallels between Plato's ideal republic and the main governments in *The Man in the High Castle*.

Japan is governed by an Emperor. The Emperor conducts the affairs in his realm in accordance with his own judgment, probably also taking into account reports from his advisors about the state of affairs in the Empire. He has enacted numerous laws, especially laws about anything that threatens, or is perceived to threaten the state. And the laws around this are very harsh.

Recall the incident in which Frank Frink was arrested, imprisoned, and beaten by the Kempeitai. This treatment was justified by law because Frink was accused of having information about something deemed dangerous or important to the Japanese government. Recall also that Frink is Jewish. To further press him, Inspector Kido authorizes Frink's sister, Lauren Crothers and her children to sit in an actual gas chamber. Kido threatens to kill them if Frank does not co-operate. And indeed they die at Kido's command. The will of the state is absolute, and they have the means to make laws and policies . . . and enforce them.

The Reich is similar. All the power rests with the state, headed up by the Führer. He has constructed a society where everyone has a place, and there is a place for everyone (provided, of course, you are white and free of debilitating diseases, or other conditions the state doesn't recognize). Laws and policies are devised and enforced to ensure that the aims of the State are achieved. One of the horrible policies supported and enforced by the law is of course the wholesale slaughter of an unfathomable number of human beings.

Both Japan and the Reich are examples of forms of government where the power rests in the hands of the political leaders. They are supposed to conduct the day-to-day affairs of citizens, determine how and when jobs are performed, and in general know how to use their knowledge of psychology to integrate the various sorts of persons under their rule. This is the key point of comparison I wanted to draw from Plato's *Republic*. It is not to the point that Japan and the Reich show, in several areas, that they do not have a superior knowledge of management, psychology, and legislation. What is to the point is that we have two forms of government that, in several important ways, look like Plato's *Republic*.

In some regards, Plato's favored government seems even more "extreme" than Japan or the Reich. For example, people in Japan and the Reich can have families and raise their own children. Presumably they can marry who they want to as well. Undoubtedly, there are class restrictions or some such that make some matches "suitable" or "unsuitable." But Plato's *Republic* abolishes family completely. Just how far should the state reach into the lives of citizens?

Law clearly plays an important and even critical role in enforcing the will of the state. And this is something Plato wrestled with and changed his views on. Let's take a look.

Plato and the Legislative Skill

Plato held two very different views on the art of legislation and the political leader. In *The Statesman*, Plato thought that the art of legislation did not belong to the art of statecraft; that is, the statesman was an expert in human psychology and management only. In fact, he thought law was contrary to the aims of the political expert! Why? The law was simply too general. Law could never account for all the particular circumstances that arise in human affairs. Further, the law purports to hold absolute authority and does not countenance actions contrary to its demand, nor does it allow for thinking about whether or not it's just. This is where the quote I opened with comes in. The law behaves like a self-willed and ignorant person always demanding his own way. And it cannot do otherwise. Because of law's ineffectiveness in particular circumstance, Plato thought that political leaders should not be bound by law at all because it would hinder their ability to exercise their political craft. Law, by its nature, is insensitive to particular circumstances, wherever they occur.

Obergruppenführer Smith finds out his son must die according to the law. No exceptions. No consideration of particular circumstances. No appeals. But consider Smith's position in the scheme of things. He's a very high-ranking Nazi with ties to the Führer himself. He knows a lot about the inner workings of the government and is therefore potentially dangerous. You would think it would behoove the Führer to ensure his most trusted advisors remained happy, so he might make an exception to the law in order to preserve the stability of his government. Or can't he do that? Is the Führer also bound under this law?

For a less dark example, suppose the law required x number of farmers, x number of engineers, and so forth. But suppose a terrible drought hit, killing all the crops. Presumably, the sensible thing to do would be to increase the number of both engineers and farmers to attempt to find a solution, possibly in irrigation. To do this, the law would have to be changed because there is nothing in the law that allows for a different course of action.

You might think this is weird. You might think: "Yeah! Change the laws when they become outdated, or when it suits to keep the peace. What's wrong with that? What's all this business about law's being like a belligerent person?" But the point is that when a law is in place, its "will" is absolute and allows no consideration of particular circumstance. One example is of course the required death of citizens with certain congenital illnesses in the Reich. No particular circumstances are considered. The tears of countless mothers and fathers, including Obergruppenführer

Smith, are effectively invisible to law. And laws can only be changed by the political experts who deem it necessary. If the Führer does not count the agony of mothers and fathers as a circumstance that requires a change, the law remains in effect.

Laws cannot have built-in wiggle room. Laws, unless changed by the political expert, must demand that citizens obey . . . even if they know better. The citizen cannot recognize the outdatedness of the law and go against it. For example, laws are of the form: murder is illegal. And murder is defined in a particular way. The law does not say, in most cases murder is illegal. Wait, you might say, it does! Crimes of passion are a thing. Yes, but by definition they are supposed to fall outside the category of murder. Laws cannot be of the form "in most cases, this or that is wrong" because it leaves judgment up to private citizens as to what the particular circumstances demands. So the murder law can't be of the form: murder is illegal, unless you, the citizen, consider it necessary in a particular circumstance. For this is the realm of the political experts only. Only the political expert should act as arbiter among particular circumstances.

By the time Plato wrote *The Republic*, he had changed his mind about legislative expertise. He not only thought that it belonged to the skill set required by the political expert, but also that it was the most important part of political expertise, even more than expertise in human psychology or managerial skills. It went from no place to first place! Why? How? Plato perhaps thought that well-constructed laws, based on the political expert's psychological and managerial expertise, could keep things running smoothly, and help to weave together the various personalities.

The key point is this. Whatever Plato thought about the legislative skill—whether it belongs to the political skill or not—the law still behaves in the same way. That is, citizens do not get wiggle room to decide when particular circumstances merit ignoring or breaking a law. Moreover, the political leader must be above the law in order to correctly attend to particular circumstances. Whatever the law prescribes must be adhered to on pain of punishment . . . even for such a high-ranking individual as Obergruppenführer Smith.

Notice, the Führer has the power to think about Obergruppenführer Smith's case and make an exception if the particular circumstances merit this. But, of course, this would involve letting the Führer know and awaiting his decision, which could turn out to be no.

Plato's *Republic* and Fascism

What's the difference between Plato's *Republic* and Germany and Japan? Not much, really. Structurally, they are very similar. All three have leaders who control the law and are above the law. All three are aimed at weaving the various personalities together through psychological, managerial, and legislative expertise. All three aim at controlling the lives of citizens from the cradle to grave. Though, in some ways, Plato's *Republic* is even more extreme (abolishing marriages and civil unions, and raising children apart from families).

"Wait!," you might protest, "There *is* a significant difference between Plato's *Republic* and Japan and the Reich! Plato's *Republic*, although extreme, insists that the ideal government should have political experts aimed at the good of society. But the Reich and Japan seem to have corrupt leaders and policies."

That's true as far as it goes. But it doesn't go far enough. Whether or not the leaders and policies are corrupt or good, the structure is the same. The government has a monopoly on legislation and management. Let's put this point another way. Traditionally, fascism is hallmarked by a governmental leader and system having complete power over law and infrastructure. It also has strong connotations of that governmental leader and system employing unjust, often racist, and frequently nationalistic laws and policies. Presumably, Plato's idealized republic would not have evil or bad policies by definition. But take that away, and what remains? A governmental leader and system that holds all the power. *That* is the issue. Should such a governmental form be accepted or not?

What is the argument for having such a governmental form? Well, we could compare the political expert to a doctor. The doctor, because of his superior knowledge in health, can tell me that I need to eat less fatty food and exercise more. He knows what's best for me, even better than I do. Similarly, if we got the properly trained political expert in power, she can control education, infrastructure, and daily affairs much better than any of the citizens due to superior knowledge. She knows what's best for me and my life, even more than I do.

But the ideals of democratic republics stand against this.

Plato's *Republic* versus Democratic Republics

The ideals behind democratic republics are different. One key idea is that people should be free to determine the course of their own lives. But, just saying this doesn't address the argument from the last section.

What a champion of democratic republics might say to it is this. The comparison between a doctor and political expert fails. In order for it to work, citizens would have to be completely, or close enough to completely, ignorant of all things psychological and managerial . . . like I am about doctor stuff. Really, though, most people do have an idea about psychology and management: they have relationships, friendships, are part of a community. To get along in it they have to know something about persons. Moreover, people can run households and perform jobs. There is competency in managerial stuff as well. The comparison, then, might be between a fully-trained doctor, and a student in medical school. But if this is right, the student in medical school should be afforded a say in matters because they are not completely ignorant of the craft of doctoring. Similarly, people should have a say in government and running their own lives. Even if they are not total experts like the political expert, they do have enough relevant expertise to be afforded a say in their affairs.

The Man in the High Castle, both the TV show, and especially the novel, have this as a subplot. What many of the characters yearn for is the freedom to breathe, to run their lives without interference from the government. For example, in the show, Trudy Walker felt so stifled by the government, she was willing to risk her life for the promise of something better (in this case, the stuff surrounding those newsreel films). Indeed, the grasshopper lies heavy, if we reinterpret "grasshopper" to mean the government and assume it lies heavily on its subjects, pinning them and their aspirations down. I know, I know. I repurposed this.

Anyway, who's right? Plato, or the democratic republicists? There are, of course, more arguments on both sides, but this should get us thinking.

Final Thoughts

These days, so many people are clamoring for better laws, more laws, important legislation, enforcing key policies. Let's linger on this a moment. Laws are binding and insensitive to particular circumstance, by their nature. And if they allow for wiggle room, they are not really laws because they allow the thinking citizen to follow it or break it according to circumstance. We need to be very careful where we apply law, therefore.

Laws which dictate how citizens are to live, what they can and cannot say, or watch, or wear, are laws that restrict personal liberties. But it is not just laws about personal liberties that require reflection.

The more we want the government to manage infrastructure, markets, and the more we desire better laws to goad us on, the closer we get to Plato's republic. Where is the line drawn? Sure, we like the idea of state-controlled education, perhaps. But why not state-controlled breeding?

The whole reason we want a government-controlled education system is to ensure a certain standard, right? We don't want kooks in education. But, you know, a lot of people get into toxic relationships, and raise children badly. Shouldn't there be state-controlled standards for relationships and breeding? You see the point. Where do we draw the line between the political expert and the non-political expert?

Historically, the aim of Western-styled democracy has aimed at making as few laws as possible, and these largely aimed at enforcing contracts. This allowed for the maximum amount of personal liberties. But the more we in democratic republics hand over control of infrastructure to the government, and the more we use law to govern human behavior, the closer we get to Plato's republic, or worse, the Reich.

If we value personal liberties and having a say in how things are run, then we need to insist on fewer laws and legislation, and get power back in the hands of people. If we value Plato's republic, we should insist the more on an increase in just laws and policies. Of course, it's not as simple as all this.

What should the state do about hungry children or corporate corruption? This is a difficult question, indeed; especially in a democratic republic. In Plato's republic, you just make more laws and policies. Actually, for the one who values democratic republics, the question is not first and foremost what the state should do, but what the citizens should do about hungry children and corporate corruption. Personal liberty comes with responsibility for communities and the persons in them.

Nothing has been settled, but there's plenty to think about![1]

---

[1] Many of the ways I interpret Plato are debated. I am very grateful to Antony Hatzistavrou. My interpretations of Plato and government are heavily influenced by him, though any mistakes are entirely my own, and the claim that Plato's Republic is not ideal is my claim, not Antony's. I would also like to thank Will Gamester and Erika Hawkins for helpful comments and criticisms.

7
What if Your Hero Is a Fascist?

BRUCE KRAJEWSKI

> Thus, my real idol is Hitler.
>
> —PHILIP K. DICK, *In Pursuit of Valis*, p. 140

The marker for a cultural moment took place on *The Late Show* in November of 2015 when the host of that program, Stephen Colbert, brought out a blackboard to illustrate something about the presidential candidacy of Donald Trump. Colbert ended up drawing a swastika on the blackboard.

Swastikas in New York City had caused a stir a few months earlier when Amazon's show *The Man in the High Castle*, based on the Philip K. Dick novel, was about to appear. The people at Amazon decided to place posters in the subways of New York City, and those posters advertising *The Man in the High Castle* led to complaints. According to a 24th November 2015 article in *The Guardian*, the mayor of New York City requested that Amazon remove the advertising. Mayor de Blasio said the advertising was "irresponsible and offensive to World War II and Holocaust survivors, their families, and countless other New Yorkers." Immediately after the mayor's request, the posters were pulled.

Everything "Alt" Is New Again

Based on that quotation, what disturbs de Blasio is not the repackaging of Nazism and totalitarianism in a capitalist context in which a company is aiming to make a profit from an ongoing entertainment series about National Socialist domination during a time when groups friendly to the ideology of National Socialism are finding new welcome mats in the United States. De Blasio's complaint is rooted in some notion of PTSD—that seeing such old symbols will bring back memories, mainly to groups of people who might have suffered during World War II. De Blasio's reaction seems blind to the appeal of National Socialist ideology to another audience—those with no first-hand memory of World War II.

Numerous reports from a variety of sources in the past few years have chronicled the rise of far right groups in the United States, and mainstream media outlets have been willing to comment that part of that rise can be linked to Donald Trump's participation in the presidential election. Colbert's use of a swastika to provide a map of how we arrived at Trump is no accident, nor is it a cultural oddity. We are now in the era of the alt-Right. That's appropriate in its German meaning, because "Alt" means old in German, so we are really talking about the return of the repressed, the old Right, a Right that has threatened before.

While the swastika was not invented by the National Socialists, its multiple meanings can have an unsettling effect. Its use by people both for and against right wing ideology means that all concerned parties need to be careful with any analysis of its symbolism. Part of my purpose for using that symbolism as a starting point is to encourage recognition of the swastika as a capitalist tool. It has been unquestionably used in the promotion of a television series called *The Man in the High Castle*. It's also employed in the promotion of this book, *The Man in the High Castle and Philosophy*.

Capitalism has colonized the swastika, and made it a brand, a product, a tool that helps to sell something, in this case an ideology. This was also the case during the National

Socialist period in Germany, as we can learn from the research of Pamela Swett at McMaster University. Fascism is not a separate entity, apart from capitalism. The two have a brotherly relationship that goes mostly unacknowledged, especially by people who depend on capitalism for a livelihood, and who have been prevented from imagining an alternative. With *The Man in the High Castle*, Philip K. Dick has contributed to that prevention.

Danger, Will Robinson!

Despite novels like Katharine Burdekin's *Swastika Night*, published in 1937, which offers an alternative world with many similarities to Philip Dick's *The Man in the High Castle*, Burdekin's work has remained marginal in comparison to the continued posthumous surge in interest that Philip Dick's works enjoy. Dick is a Hollywood pet. My thesis can be injected here. The spinoffs from Dick's works, from *Blade Runner* to *Minority Report* to Amazon's *The Man in the High Castle* have been viewed almost universally in the same celebratory light as Dick's primary texts. In short, people miss the evidence that Dick and his works promote fascism rather than provide a warning about its return. Dick aligned himself and his works explicitly with fascism. It might matter to some that the Italian strain of fascism via Mussolini attracted Dick's admiration. Here's the proof text in Dick's own words:

> Lem & the party experts saw correctly that in my writing I was handing over weapons (secrets) of power to the disenfranchised of the capitalist west; their appraisal of me is correct. Over & over in my books (1) power is studied; (2) who has it; & (3) how those denied it manage to get it. Although not appearing left wing my training is really Fascistic—not "Fascistic" as Marxist rhetoric defines it but as Mussolini defined it: in terms of the deed & the will, with reality de-ontologized, reduced to mere stuff on which the will acts in terms of deed. Since few living people correctly understand (genuine) Fascism, my ideology has never been pejoratively stigmatized by the left, but those to whom I appeal are in essence the

> core-bulk of latent masses, the fascist mob. I speak of & for the irrational & the anti-rational, a kind of dynamic nihilism in which values are generated as mere tactics. Thus my real idol is Hitler, who starting out totally disenfranchised rose to total power while scorning *wealth* (aristocracy) plutocracy to the end. My real enemy is plutocracy; I've done my [fascistic] homework . . . my fascistic premise is: "There is not truth. We *make* truth; what we (first) believe *becomes* objectively true. Objective truth depends on what we believe, not the other way around." This is the essence of the Fascist epistemology, the perception of truth as ideology imposed on reality—mind over matter. (*In Pursuit of Valis*, p. 140)

As Geoff Waite has noted about this passage from Dick, regardless of whether defenders of Dick wish to invoke "irony" or "insanity" to protect Dick here, the content of Dick's message is to transform any Left for the sake of an actual Right. My sense is that the vast majority of Philip K. Dick fans do not view themselves as crypto-fascists, but they might want to rethink the matter. Stay with me. More shocks are on the way.

Now You See It, Now You Don't, but It's Still There

Part of the Fascist homework that Dick has done includes Fascism's fear of communism, and that's a structuring absence in *The Man in the High Castle*. If you're not familiar with what a structuring absence is, you actually do know what it is, but perhaps not by that phrase.

At Thanksgivings past, my grandmother would set a place at the dining room table for my grandfather, only my grandfather had been dead for over a decade. My grandfather was a structuring absence in that our Thanksgiving table was literally set for a missing person, some might say *by* a missing person. Some missing entity (thing or person) influences how the future gets put together, how it is lived. In many cases, structuring absences are not as easy to see as the Thanksgiving place setting for my expired grandfather. Another way to think about a structuring absence is as a central matter that goes unspoken, because the point is to avoid that matter. It's like a by-pass, a road constructed specifically to avoid a place, but which only exists because of that place (Cormack, *Ideology*, p. 31). What we have, according to most accounts of *The Man in the High Castle*, is a projection of a fascist future for the United States, and a structuring absence in communism. Think of the Russians during World War II as one of the main forces fighting against fascism. For my purposes, it is important to recall the virulent hatred many fascists had for communists during that time.

Projection needs to be addressed before a structuring absence. Projection in a psychoanalytic sense might best be understood through its analogy to Plato's Cave and to our experience with movies. As Slavoj Žižek relates in his book *Looking Awry*: "Fantasy space functions as an empty surface, as a kind of screen for the projection of desires." This sounds like a version of "We see what we want to see," and that might be an accurate accounting of what Žižek wants us to learn. I might illustrate this better by temporarily putting aside projection and turning to the concept of the overlay. A shifting of ideological positions might occur more smoothly if the imagery doesn't need to be altered in a way that draws attention to itself.

The very first object to appear in the opening credits to the Amazon show is a functioning projector. Later in that same montage of opening credits, the American bald eagle is overlaid with the National Socialist eagle as if they were a match, as if interchangeable. Note also the earlier poster used for advertising the series, in which capitalists at Amazon decided that the raised arm of the Statue of Liberty might as well be a case of mimicking the Nazi salute. The people at Amazon had ads for *The Man in the High Castle* with such an image. They also had one in which an electronic billboard in Times Square displays a swastika. The advertising spaces in Times Square are overlaid with National Socialist symbols and propaganda. The Times Square image reinforces the notion that Fascist ideology is similar to capitalist advertising. Other examples of overlaying can be found, including the shadows of what looks to be a military operation involving paratroopers superimposed on one of the figures of Mount Rushmore, and a map of the United States that has on top of it both the Japanese flag and the National Socialist eagle perched on top of a swastika.

Perhaps the most important overlay is a musical one, a new version of the tune "Edelweiss" made famous in *The Sound of Music*. While the original music exists in many viewers' memories, *The Man in the High Castle* version of "Edelweiss" sung by the Swedish artist Jeanette Olsson gives the song a quite different mood with her raspy rendition along with some key changes to the lyrics. There's an utterly incoherent account of the song used for the Amazon series in *The Atlantic* magazine. At one point in the article, the author claims the song is one of desperation, and then by the end of the article, the new version of "Edelweiss" is part of some triumphant vision of homeland, in which the US is the homeland. You can't miss the German-ness of the title "Edelweiss." You can't miss the whiteness of "Edelweiss," even if you didn't know that "Weiss" is "white" in German. And for those who keep the layer of *The Sound of Music* in mind, "Edelweiss" conjures up a story about a conflicted, wealthy Austrian who doesn't know what to do about his homeland in the face of a takeover by Fascism. Sound familiar? No one can miss that the "homeland" line raises the problem of nationalism that partially makes National Socialism what it is. In the play and movie *The Sound of Music*, the character of the Captain uses the song as a way to focus nationalistic feeling. You might think of the way "La Marseillaise" is used in *Casablanca*.

The structuring absence of communism is anti-nationalistic and does not involve a God or anyone else who will provide a blessing, as the lyrics in "Edelweiss" suggest. "We'd be living under Red rule now, if it wasn't for Germany. We'd be worse off," says Joe Cinnadella in the novel *The Man in the High Castle*. While Communists were the primary enemies of fascism before and during World War II, economically and politically, Dick's novel makes it clear that life under communism is imaginatively a worse proposition than the oppressive occupying force of the Greater Nazi Reich in the former USA. In the Amazon series, suburban life on the East Coast has easily morphed into Aryan *Gemütlichkeit* (coziness—and this before there was COZI TV). The fascist option is merely a version of the capitalism that already ruled the day in the United States at the time of the Second World War. SS Obergruppenführer John Smith's neighborhood as depicted in Amazon's series could just as easily be substituted in as the setting for a *Leave It to Beaver* episode, or an installment of *Desperate Housewives*.

The Desperate Hours

According to one famous definition of fascism, it is merely capitalism in desperation. It is in a sense, even without Thomas Piketty's recent book, the world we have now in the United States. We live in a time of a declining middle class, a small wealthy class wanting more political control, and a growing fear that what was great about America has been lost (the slogan of the 2016 Republican presidential campaign). Many Americans live in fear of foreign workers and immigrants as potential colonizers who will change the American way of life.

The success of *The Man in the High Castle* TV series serves as evidence that Philip Dick's projected world in that novel has, in important ways, come to pass in the United States, as some parts of the populace become entrenched in white supremacy, nationalism, and attempts at identifying "outsiders" who provoke fear. This led recently to Newt Gingrich's suggestion that the House Un-American Activities Committee be resurrected. While Gingrich himself seems confused about the purpose of that committee, its main purpose was to investigate people's connections to communism. Dick himself identifies his audience as "the fascist mob" (*In Pursuit of Valis*). Is it surprising then that Amazon has produced a work in which the fascists have come to power in the United States?

What ought to be disturbing is Dick's popularity with the Left in the US, while his esoteric, or secret, philosophy, of which *The Man in the High Castle* counts as a major installment is engaged for the benefit of a fascist Right. Part of the evidence for the secrecy can be linked to the way characters deal with *The Grasshopper Lies Heavy* in Dick's novel.

What awaits us is not a version of what Zeev Sternhell has labeled "Spiritual Fascism." Sternhell uses that phrase for French fascism before and during World War II. Sternhell goes out of his way to combat a view of fascism as an outgrowth of capitalism. In short, Sternhell does not provide us with any tools to deal with Dick's fascism in any of its manifestations—movies, graphic novels, TV series. When thinking about Philip Dick, it is important to remember that Dick's admiration for fascism is not rooted in France, but in Italy, particularly Benito Mussolini. Dick writes:

> In some ways I was quite an admirer of Mussolini . . . I think Mussolini was a very, very great man. But the tragedy for Mussolini was he fell under Hitler's spell. But then so did many others. In a way you can't blame Mussolini for that. (*Philip K. Dick: In His Own Words*, p. 153)

Mussolini might have been a better Hitler, from Dick's viewpoint.

Geoff Waite, an academic who has been careful about his reading of Dick's works, calls Philip Dick "America's greatest science-fiction writer." Given that "fascism" is a now a common word in North American political conversations, due to the events surrounding the 2016 presidential runoff, it seems we are at an opportune moment to address the greatest science-fiction writer in a new way, and to provide a response to the question of why Amazon's *The Man in the High Castle* is making its appearance in America now. Peter Schmidt, who teaches at Swarthmore, has done some of the preliminary homework on the novel and the television series. He writes: "*High Castle* was Dick's counter-factual history experiment, imagining what might have happened if Japan and Germany had won World War II and divided up the US. It was inspired in part by postwar sources like William L. Shirer's *The Rise and Fall of the Third Reich*, as well as by events like the McCarthy era's paranoid inquisitions to root out traitors. Inspirational too for Dick may have been another literary precedent, Sinclair Lewis's best-selling, scathing prewar novel about America's romance with fascism, *It Can't Happen Here*."

I'm Shocked, Shocked to Find that Gambling, I Mean Fascism, is Going on in Here!

Some overt elements of fascism in the past few years have "shocked" some US citizens, who behave as if the Right had nothing to do with fascism prior to the presidential candidacies of Donald Trump and Ted Cruz. (People forget the attempted fascist overthrow of FDR, as described in Sally Denton's *The Plots against the President*. That coup was intended "to save the capitalistic system.") For others, the 2016 presidential season made public what had been hidden in America before, such as the episode in the previous election when Mitt Romney's "forty-seven percent speech" was secretly videotaped and made public. Of course, WikiLeaks documents addressed by *The New York Times* in the fall of 2016 reveal that Hillary Clinton thought out loud in front of Wall Street backers about the necessity of having "both a public and a private position" on politically contentious issues. In other words, capitalism has been conducted in a way that we have our leaders speaking in public (exoterically) as if one set of policies is in place while secretly (esoterically) carrying out quite the opposite. It's not as if democracy has been the guiding light for our leaders in the US.

The Man in the High Castle has a world divided between the Germans and the Japanese, but generally leaves out the Russians, as if they had no role in the post–World War II future. Some capitalists go out of their way to insist that capitalism is the best we can hope for. One psychological consequence of that is that the average person is hard pressed to imagine an alternative to the alleged free market. Yet, a virulent hatred of communists persists in a context in which capitalists insist that there is no alternative to capitalism. Why despise something, like communism, you imagine is not a possible position to hold?

In a 1975 notebook entry, Dick puzzled over his popularity among both Western and Soviet Marxists. Dick explains in that notebook entry that the Marxists believed that Dick was having a subliminally critical impact on capitalism. Dick says that he later realized the reverse was true, that he had subliminally injected a Christian ideology into the thoughts of the Marxists, who did not understand what Dick was up to with his esoteric Christian and Gnostic writings. Dick was happy to program his readers and the reception of his texts. Dick's happiness over the reversal ought to be the catalyst for Dick's fans to revise their view of Dick as some kind of praiseworthy author.

Despite the provocative title of this chapter, my purpose takes note of the late historian Tim Mason's warning about dealing with fascism through individualism. "Methodologically individualism simply cannot work as a way of giving a coherent account of social, economic and political change" ("Intention and Explanation," p. 219). When it comes to National Socialism, for instance, "'Hitler' *cannot* be a full or adequate explanation, not even of himself." While Dick should be held accountable for his own works and words, Dick will never be the prime cause of any resurrection of fascism, but he might turn you, his reader, into an unwitting accomplice.

III

Captives of Unchance

8 Is It Free Will if You Pay for It?

JOHN V. KARAVITIS

"Everyone knows the part they play." That's the counsel that the propaganda film gives in the beginning of the first episode of *The Man in the High Castle*. Joe Blake is in that theater, watching, and waiting to be told the identity of his contact in the American Resistance. If anything could set the tone for the lives of those in this alternate world, it would be this simple statement.

It's a sobering message. It implies that you can't change your situation. That you have to live your life on anyone's terms but your own. That you have no control over your life. That you're like a cork, bobbing up and down in the water. This message seems to be the underlying theme for both the TV series and the Philip K. Dick novel on which it's based.

Many Books Are Actually *Alive*

With the takeover of the western part of the former United States by Imperial Japan, many aspects of traditional Japanese culture have taken hold. In the novel, we see this most clearly in the use of the *I Ching*. This is a three thousand-year-old book; the title means *Book of Changes*. Referred to as "the oracle," it's consulted when anyone wants to know how the future will unfold. Through a sequence of six random throws of either yarrow stalks or coins, the practitioner creates a hexagram which "pictures . . . the *situation,*" and results in the selection of a corresponding passage in the *I Ching*. This seemingly ambiguous and obscure passage is then interpreted by the practitioner asking the question.

Examples of characters relying on the *I Ching* abound. When his supervisor Ed McCarthy proposes that they go into business crafting contemporary jewelry, Frank consults the oracle. "Should I attempt to go into the creative private business outlined to me just now?" In the midst of setting up their new business, Frank wants to know "How are things going to turn out?" Even when things do not turn out as expected, the oracle is never to blame. When Ed McCarthy points out that the oracle gave Frank incorrect advice, Frank rationalizes this. "Then the oracle must refer to some future consequence of this. That is the trouble; later on, when it has happened, you can look back and see exactly what it meant."

After the SD agents have been neutralized in their attempt to seize Captain Wegener at the Trade Mission, Tagomi turns to the oracle. "He wondered if in this instance the oracle would be of any use. Perhaps it could protect them. Warn them, shield them, with its advice." Tagomi has absolute faith in the *I Ching*. He views the oracle as being intelligent and *alive*, because "As so often, the oracle had perceived the more fundamental query . . ." He expresses how confused he is by the Nazis and their view of reality. Tagomi thinks, "The oracle will cut through it. Even weird breed of cat like Nazi Germany comprehensible to *I Ching*."

Juliana uses the oracle "all the time to decide. I never let it out of my sight. Ever." As she flees the hotel in which she has just killed Joe Cinnadella, she reflects, "Too bad I didn't consult the oracle; it would have known and warned me. Why didn't I?" Later, she tells Caroline Abendsen, Hawthorne Abendsen's wife, "Listen . . . the oracle told me to come to Cheyenne." For Juliana, the oracle is a source of wonder. "She scanned the text ravenously . . . It depicted the situation exactly—a miracle once more." Upon finally meeting Hawthorne Abendsen, Juliana quickly surmises that the oracle wrote his novel. She then asks the oracle why, and what it expects them to learn. The implications of its answer—*that not only did Germany and Japan in fact lose World War II, but that their world isn't real*—do not faze her one bit.

Throughout the novel, the passages of the *I Ching* which are used to predict how a new situation will unfold are selected at random. Yet practitioners treat the results of the *I Ching* procedure as being inescapable. Indeed, the oracle is perceived as being intelligent, infallible, and *alive*. The main characters in the novel look at the world in a fatalistic manner and do not believe that they have free will.

Free Will? Really? You Mean It's *Free*?

Free will is a subject that's hotly debated even today by philosophers and scientists. In trying to define free will, you run into a paradox. A paradox is a conclusion that appears to contradict itself. The paradox of free will comes from French mathematician Pierre-Simon Laplace (1749–1827).

If the exact positions and velocities of every particle in the universe are known for a given point in time, then, given the laws of physics, both the past and future positions of every particle can be determined for *any* point in time. Imagine a frictionless billiard table with a number of balls on it, all moving about. Knowing their exact positions and velocities at one point in time would mean that their positions could be calculated for any other point in time. Thus, since everything that *will happen* is determined by what *has happened*, how could free will exist?

The challenge to this is that there is a lot more uncertainty in the world than Laplace was aware of. This is because the laws of physics with which Laplace was familiar were the laws of *classical* mechanics, not *quantum* mechanics. There is no way to know the positions and velocities of every particle in the universe at any given time. For example, some atoms are radioactive, and you can't predict exactly when an atom will break apart. From the work of German physicist Werner Karl Heisenberg (1901–1976), the

Uncertainty Principle states that you can't determine *both* the location *and* velocity of a particle at any given time. This is the German scientist after whom the Nazis' atomic bomb —the "Heisenberg device"—is named. With modern physics as we know it, our future is indeterminable, as is theirs.

Laplace's argument requires a situation that could never exist in the real world. It's a simple, naive view of how the world works. We do *not* live in a deterministic, billiard ball-type universe. We do live in an orderly universe with laws of physics, and with events subject to cause and effect. The alternative would be to live in a chaotic and totally indeterministic universe. In such a universe, there would be no cause for anything, and nothing would make sense. It's misguided to confuse a universe you can understand and make your way in with a universe where everything is predetermined. You would want to live in a universe where you could, to some degree, predict how your actions will affect events.

Objections to free will have also arisen in modern psychology. Neurophysiologist Benjamin Libet (1916–2007) determined that your decision to take a specific action occurs *before* you are consciously aware of it. The implication is that free will plays very little, if any, part in how we decide what to do. At least some of our decisions to act are made unconsciously. We are also creatures of habit, as Frank acknowledges while thinking about Juliana, and how she has fared since their divorce. "Her vanity probably as great as always. She always liked people to look at her, admire her . . . I could pretty well figure out what she was thinking, what she wanted."

Free will implies the ability to choose. But choices do not occur *ex nihilo*—out of nothing. Given that events are subject to cause and effect, choices cannot arise out of nowhere. It is this view of what free will *should* mean that leads to so much consternation. But where possibilities for action exist, a choice can be consciously made. Characters in the novel do make choices. Curiously, they also seem to believe that the future is predetermined. Although, as Robert Childan reflects, the oracle was "forced down our throats" by the Japanese, using the *I Ching* in important situations must mean that they feel that their future is out of their control.

So, it's curious why they would even bother asking the oracle anything. If the oracle could foretell the future, then knowing the future should mean that you would be able to act to change it. But if you could change the future, then the oracle would always be wrong! And if it were not possible to change the future by "knowing" how it would turn out, then it would be meaningless to ask the oracle anything in the first place! In the novel, no one ever repeats the *I Ching* process for the same question. Surely the characters must realize that they would get different answers to a question every time a hexagram is randomly cast! However, they act as though it would make no sense to cast a hexagram more than once.

Can You Tell the Fake from the Reel?

In the TV series, the *I Ching* plays a less prominent role. Here, only Trade Minister Tagomi uses it. Rather, the main plot line deals with mysterious newsreel films labeled *The Grasshopper Lies Heavy*. The Nazis, the Kempeitai, and the American Resistance pursue them. There is an obsession to collect these newsreels, regardless of the cost in time, money, or lives.

Juliana's half-sister, Trudy Walker, runs into her in a Chinese herbal shop. Trudy cryptically tells her, "I found . . . the reason . . . for everything." That evening, Trudy again runs into Juliana, and gives her a newsreel moments before she's shot dead by the Kempeitai. "What is this?" she asks. Trudy replies, "A way out." Juliana plays the film at Frank's apartment, and he realizes what it is. "Jesus, I know what this is. The Man in the High Castle." Juliana is convinced it is real. "They look real 'cuz they *are* real." Frank, however, is not convinced.

While imprisoned by the Kempeitai, Resistance member Randall Becker tells Frank "That film can change the world." The authorities want the film reels "Because they know that that film shows the world not as it is, but as it could be . . .

They're scared. Scared this film will bring the whole thing tumbling down."

"The films are more important than you know," Resistance leader Karen Vecchione tells Frank at their first meeting. Lemuel Washington reinforces the importance of the film reels, but disregards their content. Juliana asks, "Have you seen the films?" Lemuel replies, "It's not my job to see 'em. I just pass 'em along." "Then you don't know what they mean," Juliana challenges. "I just know they help kill Nazis," Lemuel responds. We later learn that the film reels are exchanged for information. "All we know is we get them to him and he passes back intelligence that we can use against the 'Pons' . . . If you came here looking for answers about the films, you'll be disappointed," Karen admonishes Juliana.

Not all of the film reels are of *our* history. The film reel that Joe Blake viewed in Canon City has Soviet propaganda for Joseph Stalin from 1954; whereas, in their history, Stalin had been executed in 1949. In *our* history, Stalin died on March 5th, 1953. Toward the end of Season One, Frank and Juliana view a film reel that appears to show a *future* where San Francisco will be nuked, and Joe, wearing a Nazi uniform, will execute Frank. In the final episode of Season One, we see that Adolf Hitler has a large collection of these film reels! Hitler remarks to Colonel Wegener, "Most days I watch these films, and every time I learn something."

The film reels are perplexing. They don't just show alternate histories. The latest film reel shows a horrific future. By the end of Season Two, we still don't know who has created them, or why, or how exactly they are being released into the world. But the search for these film reels reveals the view on free will of those who hunt for them. The world is full of uncertainty, but *people* actively shape the world. We're constantly faced with uncertainty. So we plan, make choices, and take action, as in the TV series. And even though he relies on the *I Ching*, Minister Tagomi succinctly, yet perhaps unwittingly, expresses this position on free will when he tells Colonel Wegener, "Fate is fluid, Colonel Wegener. Destiny is in the hands of men."

The Reason for Everything

By the end of Season Two, we've witnessed a number of curious events that make us question the reality of this alternate world. Juliana's mother, Anne Crain Walker, has a premonition that Trudy is dead. "But then I woke up . . . and it was gone. Just like that. I feel her again, just like nothing ever happened." A short time later, Juliana sees Trudy in the outdoor marketplace! She tells Frank, who does not believe her. Through information that Minister Tagomi provides, Juliana finds Trudy's body in an open mass grave. Even after Juliana reveals that Trudy is dead, Anne persists in her belief that Trudy is still alive. She tells Juliana, "Your sister is here, I can feel it." Yet in the final episode of Season Two, Juliana is reunited with Trudy by Hawthorne Abendsen!

Tagomi's assistant Kotomichi, who is from Nagasaki, briefly exposes his right wrist and forearm while helping Juliana. We see burn scars reminiscent of those received by many people during that city's atomic bomb blast. After failing to convince General Onoda that they should be more cautious in their catch-up nuclear program by showing pictures of the aftermath of the bombing of Washington, DC, Tagomi notices the similarity between the burn scars on Kotomichi's forearms and those of the survivors of the DC blast. Tagomi later confronts Kotomichi, and learns that he is not the only one who can transport himself to an alternate world. Kotomichi was a survivor of the atomic bomb blast that leveled Nagasaki in *his* world. Lying in a hospital bed, in pain, he found himself in a "happier" world by accident. Tagomi, in trying to come to grips with the injustice and evil of the world that he's seen and experienced, did so too.

Do these curious events strike a familiar chord? I think they should.

These events and the revelation that you could transport yourself to an alternate world by just wishing it sound a lot like what it must be like to write a novel! Only in this case, you're writing your way out of a situation in your life that you do not like. It seems as though we're being told that you can take control of your life, and write the story of your life, as long as you're willing to make a voluntary choice to do so. As long as you're willing to take control of the direction of your life. To set goals, to plan, to choose, to act—to express your free will.

In the novel, Juliana learns the truth behind Abendsen's novel. The oracle wrote *The Grasshopper Lies Heavy*, and it is true. *Germany and Japan did in fact lose World War II*. But this also means that their world is just a story, and not the "real" world. It's a mass delusion. This idea is reinforced by the American antique replicas sold to Japanese collectors; the Zippo lighter once owned by President Franklin Roosevelt; and Tagomi's experience of the alternate reality implied by the oracle's answer to Juliana's question. The novel also has the main characters accepting the futility of changing their lives, and we see this expressed most prominently in the persistent use of the *I Ching* to make decisions about the future. They are trapped *in* a novel.

In the TV series, the theme of free will is repeatedly expressed. It's what people believe that creates reality, and so it's what you decide to do with your life that creates *your* reality. You have free will to direct your life, as long as you believe that you can. Childan takes a moment to explain to Frank a similar idea about belief—here, the suspension of disbelief—required in the antiques trade. "That's your point? It's all a giant racket?" Frank asks Childan. "And they're playing it *on themselves*," Childan replies. "It's all in here. In the mind." Here, the characters actively write *their own story* of their lives. In a sense, they are the authors of their own novel.

Your Actions Define You

In the TV series, we see the characters rebelling against their situations and laying claim to their free will. But the most prominent and indeed most illustrative example is not any of the characters that would first come to mind. I believe that the best example of the expression of free will is found in the actions of SS-Obergruppenführer John Smith. John

Smith was born to a prominent family that lost it all during the Great Depression. He became a US Army intelligence officer who fought bravely in World War II; and yet, after the war, he rose through the ranks of the SS to become the equivalent of a general, and to be trusted by Adolf Hitler.

We see John Smith continuously taking actions that expose him to the possibility of arrest and execution. He murders Hauptsturmführer Connolly, who, by order of Heydrich, had leaked details of his travel route to work to the American Resistance, by pushing him off of the SS Headquarters building in New York. Smith kills the doctor who knows about his son's incurable multiple sclerosis, and then he makes sure that the doctor's body is cremated, contrary to the demands of his widow for an autopsy. Smith maintains a line of communication with Inspector Kido of the Kempeitai, which could be construed as conspiring with an enemy agent. At the end of Season Two, Smith disobeys a direct order from Acting Chancellor Heusmann to stay at his post in New York. Doing so results in averting a final world war, and brings him to the height of respect and prominence in the Nazi Party. John Smith has continuously challenged the hands that fate has dealt him, and has always taken charge of his own destiny. As Acting Chancellor Heusmann counseled his son, Joe Blake, "Your actions define you . . . and they do not lie."

The Way Out

Regardless of any doubts of its existence, we behave as if we do have free will. We set goals, take chances, learn from our mistakes, and remember both the good and the bad that we experience. Given options, we even have the ability to do otherwise than we have ever done before.

So, maybe the best thing to do is simply to acknowledge that free will is very important to us, and view the world as built to guarantee this. We do not live in a deterministic, billiard ball-type world. To some degree, we do have control over our lives. *We should act as though we are awash in free will, and that we can't escape being the authors of our own futures.*

In the novel, Robert Childan rejected the path that Paul Kasoura had expected him to take regarding the mass production of Edfrank Custom Jewelry pieces. Faced with a situation that "did not fit any model he had ever experienced," he made a novel *choice*, one at odds with his previous behavior. Thus, he created "an entire new world" for himself. When Captain Wegener returned to Germany, he was immediately taken into custody. He reflected on his situation. "We go on, as we always have. From day to day . . . It is a sequence. An unfolding process. We can only control the end by making a *choice* at each step." In the TV series, after VA dinner, Mrs. Smith counsels Joe Blake. "You know, John believes that a man determines his own worth."

In the final episode of Season One, Frank and Juliana talk about their future, right before she is to go to the Nazi Embassy to find Joe Blake and lure him into a trap. Juliana is anxious and despondent, full of regret at the path she chose. "I got on that bus, with Trudy's film, because I thought it meant hope for the future . . . There is no hope. There is no future," she laments. Seeing her dismay, Frank points out to Juliana the only possible *choice* they have.

"But we have to go on. What else is there?"

9
Could the Axis Have Won the War?

MIGUEL PALEY

In one of the most harrowing scenes of the very first episode of *The Man in the High Castle*, Joe Blake finds himself by the side of the road talking to a cop who fought in the war. Casually eating an egg sandwich as the ashes of "cripples and the terminally ill" rain down on them, the two men briefly talk about the war. "We lost the war didn't we?" says the cop with a chuckle, "Now I can't even remember what we were fighting for."

Of the many shocking things going on in this scene, the officer's resignation to his fate stands out. How could he, "a soldier so fierce he'd kill a rose," have become such a carefree Nazi officer? How could he possibly act like this, as if everything was okay?

In asking ourselves these kinds of questions, a fundamental presupposition of our everyday thought comes to light. The cop's attitude may bother us because we believe that things could be different from how they are. The disabled don't *have* to be burned, the man didn't *have* to become a Nazi officer. We usually think that our actions matter and that our world is whatever we make of it. If there's something we don't like about our world, we are free to try and change it. But what if that's not the case? What if the cop realizes something we don't? What if the entire history of the world is already written in stone and there's nothing we can do to change it? What if, in the end, we are not free at all?

Questions such as these have been asked by Western philosophy for hundreds of years and the resulting debates have led to three main theories about freedom and the nature of our reality. Some think freedom is just a weird illusion, while others hold that it exists and is maybe the most important feature of human life. In the dystopic world of *The Man in the High Castle*, these questions and issues can be seen everywhere: In the actions of Frank and Juliana, in the wise words of Tagomi, and even in the brutal actions of Obergruppenführer Smith. It's as if the very theme of the show were this debate itself!

We're talking about "freedom" here, but the freedom we're talking about is *metaphysical* freedom, not political freedom. *The Man in the High Castle* takes place in a world where the Axis powers severely limit the kinds of things people can do and where they can go, and that curtails their political freedom, such things as "freedom of religion," or "freedom of speech." But here we're looking at freedom in the metaphysical sense.

As philosophers use the word, *metaphysics* doesn't mean things like clairvoyance or poltergeists. The word simply refers to those things which are the most fundamental aspects of reality. *Metaphysically* then, the question of "freedom" is whether or not human beings really have the power to choose anything at all.

When asking if the Nazi cop is free, metaphysically speaking, the question is about whether, given his circumstances, he had the power to do something other than become a cop in the Reich. Perhaps he could've joined the resistance or maybe he could have run away to South America. If human beings are not metaphysically free though, then we would say that the former soldier had no choice in the matter and that he simply *had to* become a cop.

How Is a Nazi Like an Apple?

I'm going to kill you now, and there's nothing you can say or do about it.

—MARSHALL

It's probably not a coincidence that one of the most intense discussions of freedom in *The Man in the High Castle* happens behind bars. Sitting in his cold, dark prison cell, Frank talks to Randall, who is in a cell next to him. "Who are you?" Frank asks. "I am a man who wants to breathe freedom . . ." Randall responds. Immediately cutting him off, however, Frank interrupts, "Spare me the propaganda bullshit! I don't want your type of freedom! I don't want anything!"

Frank's answers are those of an old fashioned *determinist,* he seems to act as if we humans were not ultimately free. Instead, Frank seems to believe that the only principle behind our actions is survival. "I'm all for keeping my head down and my mouth shut." Frank says, speaking like a classic determinist.

This theory has several variants, but the most basic one is called "causal determinism." It says that our sense of freedom is an illusion. Causal determinism comes from the scientific observation that all things in nature behave according to the laws of cause and effect. As Newton famously observed, our world is governed by certain principles like the law of gravity. These things are called "laws" because there's simply no way of getting around them. Just as the apple fell on Newton's head, so did Connolly, the man Obergruppenführer Smith pushed off a building, fall to his death. This is cause and effect. This law is so basic that it would be crazy to doubt it. Obergruppenführer Smith doesn't need to look over the ledge to see if the body floats instead of hitting the pavement. Unfortunately for Connolly, that's just how matter works!

Perhaps the most basic of these laws however is Newton's famous third law, which says that for every action there is an equal and opposite reaction. Since the world is made up of bits of matter, and since matter strictly follows these laws, then in order to know where any piece of matter is at any moment, we would just have to know where it was the moment before and how it was moving. If I tell you Smith pushes Connolly off a building, you would know that he would then fall to the ground. Again, this is cause and effect.

From this basic fact however some scary conclusions follow. Imagine now that we had the ability to know where *every single* piece of matter was and how it was moving at any instant. If we knew this, then by simply following the law of cause and effect *we would know everything that ever has happened and everything that ever will happen!* This idea of a superintelligence that could know everything was first described by a philosopher called Pierre-Simon Laplace in his essay *A Philosophical Essay on Probabilities.* Philosophers today call this "Laplace's Demon."

> We may regard the present state of the universe as the effect of its past and the cause of its future. An intellect which at a certain moment would know all forces that set nature in motion, and all positions of all items of which nature is composed, if this intellect were also vast enough to submit these data to analysis, it would embrace in a single formula the movements of the greatest bodies of the universe and those of the tiniest atom; for such an intellect nothing would be uncertain and the future, just like the past, would be present before its eyes.

If the world does behave like this, then we shouldn't say that we have free will! Everything that will happen is just determined by what happened before.

"Okay, well that's an interesting idea," you may say, "but we aren't just apples or Nazis falling off buildings. We human beings have souls, or at least minds, we have something that escapes these simple physical laws!" This is a great point, and one determinists have to deal with if we're to find their theory convincing.

A French thinker, Baron d'Holbach, in *The System of Nature*, understands this and argues that although we might think our minds or souls might escape the physical laws of cause and effect, they in fact do not. The mind, d'Holbach argues, is tied to the physical world just as much as poor Captain Connolly's body was.

Think back to *The Man in the High Castle*. In trying to figure out who betrayed them, the Nazis arrest several resistance members and subject them to torture and interrogation. One prisoner is given LSD in hopes that he will feel relaxed enough to not care about betraying his co-conspirators. Although the ploy doesn't work, the whole experiment is very telling. The prisoner is given LSD and suffers a radical change in perception and ways of thinking. Much to Obergruppenführer's dismay, the prisoner undergoes an "oceanic experience." As this shows, the mind is not really free from the influences of the physical world. Like everything else, mind or soul are themselves subject to the unrelenting Reich of causality. This is the idea behind d'Holbach's definition of determinism.

> Man is unceasingly modified by causes over which he has no control, which necessarily regulate his mode of existence, give the hue to his way of thinking, and determine his manner of acting . . . In all this he always acts according to necessary laws, from which he has no means of emancipating himself.

But what are these laws? What is the formula that determines all our action? According to d'Holbach, the simple law that determines all human behavior is the desire for conservation. Just as a Nazi will always fall of a building when pushed, so a human being will always "choose" based on a desire to survive.

In *The Man in the High Castle*, Frank often plays the role of determinist, illustrating these ideas through his actions and attitudes. When Juliana first shows him the *Grasshopper* newsreel for instance, he immediately tells her to get rid of it, to go and deliver it to the Kempeitai. Having Jewish ancestry, Frank is scared for their survival. This is what he was saying to Randall in jail. Plus, he doesn't seem to believe in what the reels show, as a good determinist he thinks the world is what it is and couldn't be different.

If the determinists are right, though, then why do we feel like we're free? We have this feeling, they say, because unlike the simplicity of the falling apple or Nazi examples, the mechanisms of our day to day lives are just too complicated for us to fully understand them. This is why Laplace's hypothetical being is called a Demon, because understanding all of the things that contribute to our actions would require superhuman intelligence. Since we cannot understand the complexity of what's going on, we come up with the illusion that we're free. In the end however, that's all freedom is, a pure illusion.

I Am Not an Apple! Freedom Is Real!

> You ever think of how different the world could be if you could change just one thing?
>
> —JULIANA

Determinism isn't the only game in town. In spite of the pretty strong arguments we just saw, many argue that it's ultimately wrong and that *we do have free will*. This theory is called libertarianism (not to be confused with political libertarianism, which means something different) and can also be illustrated by looking at *The Man in the High Castle*.

If Frank embodies determinism, then his partner Juliana is the perfect example of the opposing theory, libertarianism. Unlike Frank, Juliana's acts don't seem to follow the law of preservation. In fact, she constantly places herself in great danger because she believes that the world could be different. This is a core belief of libertarians like Juliana, they think that we are actually free and that our actions can and do shape the world. Some of the best arguments for this theory were summarized by the American philosopher Corlis Lamont in a short piece called "Freedom of the Will and Human Responsibility."

Freedom, says Lamont, is much more than just some curious philosophical problem. We *feel* we are free. This intuition is what motivates Juliana to say in the third episode that, "things don't have to be this way, maybe the world can change!" Now, of course just because we *feel* free doesn't mean that we necessarily *are* free. What this feeling does mean however is that when it comes to arguments about metaphysical freedom, the burden of proof lies with the determinists. Deciding who has the burden of proof matters because this is what allows us to be confident in the truth and, more importantly, tells us what to believe and how to act whenever the truth is up for discussion.

Think of the situation of Inspector Kido at the end of Season One. He knows it was a German officer that shot the prince but he's also aware that this fact might cause a war. He would like to arrest Frank for the shooting instead but, since the burden of proof lies with him, he can't just arrest Frank without evidence. If Kido is to prevent a war, he must find a pistol and frame Frank. This is a basic principle of most modern justice systems, where people are "innocent until proven guilty."

In the same way, Corliss Lamont argues that since we feel free, then we should think of ourselves as "free until proven determined." And here, the determinist argument that says that this feeling is an illusion resulting from too much complexity is just not convincing. Why would we have this illusion? According to Lamont, d'Holbach's argument is just a desperate frame job. We know we're free and, until proven otherwise, we remain unconvinced by the determinists.

More importantly though, libertarians argue that they actually have convincing arguments that prove we are free. One of these comes from the fact that we constantly find ourselves deliberating over some choice. Think of Colonel Wegener here on the day the Japanese prince was shot. Wegener was supposed to secretly pass along a microfilm to a Japanese minister but a last-second change in seating arrangement made his task very risky. Noticing this, Wegener doesn't just stretch his arm to give the microfilm away anyways. He hesitates. He deliberates, not sure of whether or not to go for it. He looks at Tagomi, unsure of what to do. Tagomi shakes his head. The whole scene is tense and filled with uncertainty.

If everything was already determined however, then this whole episode would be nothing but some kind of useless play-acting. What would be the point of this fake deliberation? Why would there be feelings of hesitation? Why would he sense danger or nervousness? If everything was determined then Wegener would simply pass the microfilm along or he wouldn't, there would be no point in this play-acting as if he were deliberating. As Lamont points out, there is just too much left unexplained by the determinist theory.

Perhaps the best argument in favor of free will however, and one beautifully demonstrated by *The Man in the High Castle*, is about the nature of the past itself. The "past," says Lamont, doesn't really exist in any meaningful way except as being part of the present.

This may sound weird but the idea is quite simple. The determinists say that cause and effect rule the world, so, the present is the result of the past and the future is the result of the present. They speak of time and of causality as if it were a moving arrow, where the direction of the tip of the arrow results from the direction of line leading up to it. If that's how time and history worked, then, of course, the past would determine the present like the line segment determines where the arrow is pointing. But that's just not how life works according to the libertarians!

As we go about our day, we don't experience *all of our past*, we just experience the present. The "past" exists only as whatever is in *this* moment. In experience, there is no line segment; there is only a point which is the present. This means that the past doesn't determine our actions; it just provides the present conditions from which we freely act. Whatever we do with the present, is up to us.

Consider again Colonel Wegener and his old friend Obergruppenführer Smith. As they reveal in Smith's living room, they both lived the same past. They both did horrible things for the Reich. In spite of their shared history however, they turned out very different men. Smith is the highest ranking Nazi officer in the American states and fiercely loyal to Hitler. Wegener on the other hand is a traitor to the Nazis and is trying to undermine their expansion.

This kind of possible difference is what the libertarian argument is hinting at. The past only exists as the present. Of course the past does present a specific situation from which we can act, but it does not decisively *determine* what we can do. This is what Wegener's character points out. At any given moment, because we have free will, even a Nazi can change his ways.

What if, however, we didn't actually have to choose between these theories? What if there was a way for both of them to be true at the same time?

What's with All the Fuss? Both are Right!

Fate is fluid, destiny is in the hands of men.

—TAGOMI

In the crazy world of *The Man in the High Castle*, the one place of peace is usually Trade Minister Tagomi's office. In that world, where East and West meet in the most macabre of circumstances, Tagomi offers us an interesting third alternative to our debate on free will. This is the stunning theory known as *compatibilism*, which claims that both determinism and libertarianism are right and that there is no conflict between the two. As Tagomi tries to make peace between dueling empires, so do compatibilist theories attempt to reconcile philosophical enemies.

The idea of compatibilism is that the whole debate between determinists and libertarians is just one big misunderstanding. They both think that the word 'freedom' means "to act without a cause," but this is just plain wrong. As philosopher W.T. Stace says, it doesn't even take a whole lot of sophisticated philosophical trickery to show this. All we have to do is just look at how the word "freedom" is normally used and all our metaphysical problems will disappear.

Take these two examples:

1. **Juliana gets on a bus to go to the Neutral Zone**
2. **Frank gets naked in his prison cell**

Which of these are free acts? Well, it's quite obvious that Juliana acted freely. Nobody forced her to get on that bus.

Reasons aside, she believes that going to the Neutral Zone can accomplish something, so she got on the bus. What about Frank? Well, it's also very clear that this was not a free act. The Kempeitai beat him and forced him to take his clothes off. He didn't really have any choice here.

Even though we say that Juliana's is a free act and Frank's isn't, *both of these acts have causes*. Juliana says, "I got on that bus *because* I thought there was hope for the future." Frank of course got naked *because* he was being beaten. Since both free and unfree acts are caused, then, Stace says, "The only reasonable view is that all human action, both those which are freely chosen and those which are not, are either wholly determined by causes, or at least as much determined as other events in nature."

What these simple examples show is that freedom has nothing to do with whether or not an event is caused! Remember, this is the crux of the determinist argument. They said that everything is just the result of causes, which means we aren't actually free. But, as Stace shows with examples like the ones we just saw, even free acts such as Juliana's are the result of causes!

What then is the difference between a free act and an unfree act?

Well, if we look at our examples again, the only difference has to do with the source of the cause in question. The cause behind Juliana getting on the bus is an internal or psychological cause. She got on the bus because of a belief she had. It is her belief, and not something imposed from the outside. On the other hand, the cause behind Frank's undressing is external. He didn't decide or believe that getting naked would make the prison cell more comfy. It was the Kempeitai who forced him to do it.

What is freedom then? According to compatibilism, freedom is acting according to an internal or psychological cause. Since the world has both types of causation, since they can both exist together, and, since we're regularly affected by both, compatibilists say that we're both free and determined, and that there is no conflict in holding both ideas.

Minister Tagomi is keenly aware of this. In a scene that might have seemed quite random until you, dear reader, realized that this debate is what *The Man in the High Castle* is about, Tagomi is told, "You're such a good gardener! What's the secret with flowers?" Knowing that we live in a world of causes, Tagomi says, "No secret. You plant them, they grow. Of course, you must water them." Cause and effect. The determinists are right. And yet, so are the libertarians! When talking to Wegener about their plot to stop the war, Tagomi then says, "Fate is fluid, destiny is in the hands of men."

That is to say that Tagomi has recognized that the world will present us with all kinds of situations. Perhaps the science minister will bump into a friend and end up sitting somewhere other than planned. This was simply the fate Tagomi and Wegener had to deal with. This is the external causation of the world. But, like a poker player freely choosing how to play the cards he's been dealt, it's up to Wegener to decide whether or not to risk it and go ahead with his plot. That is now a matter of internal causation.

We're both free and determined, then, the compatibilists say, and there is no conflict in maintaining both theories at the same time. Everything has a cause. Deciding whether we are free at any given moment is then just a matter of understanding what kinds of causes are responsible for our actions.

Okay, So Are We Free or Not?

> Do you believe in fate, Rudolf?
>
> —ADOLF HITLER

Well, are we? Unfortunately, philosophy isn't always great at providing definitive answers. Unlike science, philosophical theories don't have the benefit of being proved by looking through a microscope. This is certainly the case with our debate on freedom. Whether or not you believe we're free is now, ironically, completely up to you!

And yet, there's much we can learn about both ourselves and the world by thinking these things through. This is why philosophers are often fond of saying that questions are more important than answers. It's also one of the many reasons we find *The Man in the High Castle* fascinating. Thinking about these situations, about what we might do or how we might act in such a world, gives us the opportunity to learn about ourselves, about what the possibilities of human action are, and about how we would like to judge our world.

Maybe the most important consequence of this debate is how we then look at morality and punishment. If we decide the world is completely determined, then should we still hold criminals or Nazis responsible for their actions? Is punishment justified at all?

What about if we're free? Would your morality fit a compatibilist world?

10
Defying Fate

BENJAMIN EVANS

"You ever think how different life could be if you changed just one thing?" This is the question Juliana Crain asks Joe Blake towards the end of the third episode of *The Man in the High Castle*. At the time, she was thinking about how different things might have been if her father hadn't died during the war. Yet in a way, Juliana is also asking one of the big questions posed to us by the entire show: How different would things be today if only one detail of the past were altered? Not only that, but *could* things have been different?

It isn't too hard to imagine: If it had been a bit windier on February 15th, 1933, the bullet fired by Giuseppe Zangara might well have been blown just an inch to the right, where, instead of killing Chicago mayor Anton Cermak as it actually did, it would have killed Franklin D. Roosevelt. If that had happened, Roosevelt would never have been president, and perhaps the Americans wouldn't have had the leadership necessary to successfully enter the war when they did. Perhaps as a result they wouldn't have been so quick to develop the atomic bomb, leaving the Nazis to acquire such technology first. And if *that* had happened, it isn't too hard to imagine them bombing Washington to oblivion and then conquering the United States. An entirely different world would have resulted, and all because a bullet went an inch to the left instead of to the right.

Some of us are quite happy to nod our heads to comforting platitudes like "Well, if it was meant to be, it was meant to be." When we say things like this, it is as though we believe in the existence of "fate," some mysterious force of nature or God that directs the universe to unfold as it's supposed to. *The Man in the High Castle* plays with this common enough idea by presenting us with the troubling thought that perhaps the world as we know it is not in fact inevitable, that our fate could have been otherwise. The strange films which form the basis of so much of the action reveal glimpses into different potential realities, suggesting to many of the characters that life could have been (and one day again might be) quite different.

This theme of fate has a rich history in Western philosophy. Theologians have wondered if god's omniscience means that our actions are therefore predestined, and modern secular philosophers have worried that a purely mechanical understanding of the universe might lead to the conclusion that there is no free will.

So, if there's such a thing as fate, what is it and how should we react to it? And if there's no such thing as fate, what role can the mere *belief* in fate play in shaping our behavior and influencing the future?

Fate in the Greater Nazi Reich

The Man in the High Castle gives us several answers to the first question. While it does present an alternative universe (suggesting that fate is flexible and could have created a very different world), it also sometimes presents fate as totally inescapable, or at least beyond the ability of the characters to influence.

Some, like Frank Frink, seem to be blown around by forces way outside their control. He starts off the story as a relatively contented guy with a decent job, but then the discovery of the first film quickly turns his life upside down, leading him to prison and eventually a firing squad. Then, seemingly through sheer coincidence, he is suddenly pardoned just as he's about to be executed.

Later on, the assassination attempt on the Crown Prince by the German agent coincidentally thwarts Frank's own assassination plan. Later still, just as he is about to flee forever, his friend Ed happens to drops the murder weapon at work, gets arrested, and ends up falsely confessing to the Kempeitai. It seems that no matter what Frank does, fate has other plans for him, as he keeps on narrowly escaping death through "coincidences" unrelated to his own actions.

Other characters actively attempt to fight against fate. Juliana begins the story just like Frank, relatively content to make the most of life under Japanese rule. Like the *aikido* she practices, her attitude is one of non-aggression, and she seeks harmony with the world around her. Again, the arrival of the film throws her life into upheaval, but she seems to be somehow more in control of what happens to her than Frank is in control of what happens to him. The film gives her a glimpse of another possible world, and as a result she says to Joe, "Maybe things don't have to be this way. Maybe the world can change."

The chance arrival of the film is out of her control, but how she decides to react to it is not, and she's soon launched from her complacent life and onto the wild and dangerous path we watch her follow. Yet later on, fate gets more complicated for her. For much of the second season, she's attempting to prevent the destruction of San Francisco depicted in another of the films. This involves tracking down George Dixon in New York to warn him of his possible involvement, but it turns out that her actions threaten to bring about the very thing she's been struggling to avoid. In one of the films she saw a man lying in an alley, killed by gunfire, and this is exactly what takes place later on in New York. Yet it wouldn't have taken place if it hadn't been for her own interference, which leads to the very situation she hoped to prevent.

An even plainer case of fate's inescapability is that of Trade Minister Tagomi. More than anyone else, Tagomi is interested in the question of fate, as throughout the show he continually consults the *I Ching* (an ancient book of Chinese divination) for guidance as to what might happen in the future. Yet his attitude towards fate is complicated—while he takes the *I Ching* seriously and thereby must believe that the future is at least somewhat decided, he also tells Rudolph Wegener in the very first episode "Fate is fluid. Destiny lies in the hands of men." With this attitude, he teams up with Wegener to try to prevent the catastrophic destruction that would result from a war between the Nazis and the Japanese. Together they slip secret documents about hydrogen bomb technology to the Japanese science ministry, thus hoping to ensure that both sides are on an even playing field and can maintain their nuclear *détente*.

Yet just like Juliana, it seems he might end up becoming responsible for the very thing he was trying to prevent. Instead of working for peace, the Japanese decide to make use of the technology he helped supply to develop an attack on the Nazis. At the end of the first season and well into the second, Tagomi reflects on his attempts to direct the course of history, and becomes increasingly pessimistic. No matter what action he takes, the web of human activities is just too complicated to see how any particular action will end up affecting the future. At one point he concedes that he is just a foolish old man, unable to make an impact on the fate of the world.

Just Deal with It

This idea of the inevitability of fate became a cornerstone of the philosophical school called Stoicism. Stoicism originated in the work of Zeno of Citium in the third century B.C.E., and then Stoic thought continued through the work of Greeks like Seneca and Epectitus, and Romans like Marcus Aurelius.

The Stoics didn't think that fate was some separate and mysterious supernatural force, but instead simply took "fate" to mean the system of unbending rules that governed the natural world. Since there was nothing anybody could do to change the fixed laws of the universe, it made no sense to waste time and energy trying. So much suffering and misery, they thought, was caused by the futile attempt to struggle against things that cannot be changed. We might be able to prepare for such things as disease and natural disasters, but there is nothing we can do to entirely eliminate them and so should just accept that they are part of the fate of being human.

While the Stoics realized that they couldn't do much to control the workings of nature, by contrast they believed that we can control our own minds. It might take some effort, but through a process of mental conditioning (what they called *askesis*) we can learn to direct our thoughts, control our emotions and shape our desires. In other words, we're not in control of whether it will rain tomorrow, but we are in control of how we react to the rain if it appears. For a Stoic the trick is to learn to control our responses to life's inevitable problems, to condition ourselves so as to be in harmony rather than opposition with the sometimes harsh world of nature. Only by attaining the necessary level of emotional control can we find peace of mind.

Refrigerator Magnets and Philosophy

Several characters in *The Man in the High Castle* illustrate Stoic ideas at different levels. Consider Ed McCarthy at the show's start. His strategy for life under Axis rule seems to be to keep his head down, take care of those close to him, and not rock the boat. Ed's attitude might be summed up by a slogan found on inspirational posters and refrigerator magnets all over the world: "Grant me the serenity to accept the things that I cannot change, the courage to change the things I can, and the wisdom to know the difference." Though often attributed to Reinhold Niebuhr, this sentiment (sometimes called "the Serenity Prayer") can be traced back all the way to the ancient Stoics

Throughout the show, Ed tends to sees the political order he has inherited as unchangeable, and the best thing anyone can do is to simply get on with living as decent a life as is possible in the circumstances. He is certainly willing to put his life on the line for those he cares about, but even in

Season Two when he becomes more actively involved with the resistance, he remains cautious, and skeptical about how much he can really change things.

Examples of Stoicism on the Nazi side, however, look quite different. Here the idea of emotional detachment in the face of a hostile world presents a very sinister picture. Consider the character of SS-Obergruppenführer Reinhard Heydrich. This real-life figure was so ghoulish even Hitler called him "the man with the iron heart." For Heydrich and other members of the Nazi elite, the "natural order" so esteemed by the Stoics just meant the domination of the strong at the expense of the weak. Wolves eat sheep with no emotional interference, and clearly it is much better to be a wolf than a sheep.

Pity, mercy, and empathy were taken to be signs of weakness and considered irrelevant to the smooth ordering of the natural way of things. Remember Hitler's words to Wegener: "Your only sin is your weakness." According to Hitler, Wegener's problem is that he allowed his emotions to get in the way of progress. Even Obergruppenführer Smith eventually wrestles with this harsh attitude. Though able to kill others with chilling detachment, he still cannot detach himself sufficiently to allow the rules against terminal illness to be applied to his own son. Instead, he contrives a plan to send him to South America, but again fate has other plans. Because he provided such an excellent model of loyalty and devotion to the Nazi cause, his son is ultimately inspired to turn himself in for almost certain execution.

Stoic Sticking Points

These examples highlight different problems with aspects of Stoicism. First of all, in the case of Ed, it's all well and good for him to follow the serenity prayer and accept the things he cannot change, but his central problem is trying to decide what those things are! Without "the wisdom to know the difference" between what can and cannot be changed, the whole idea falls apart, and obtaining that wisdom is precisely the hard part.

Can the Nazis be stopped? Is their power really like an unchangeable law of nature? Is there some way to realize an utterly different world? It might well be useless to struggle against things that cannot be changed, but unless we try we can't easily find out what those things are. Consider all the things which humans once thought could never happen: manned flight, splitting the atom, or walking on the moon. Perhaps a Stoic would have assumed all of these things were in the "cannot be changed" category, and would never have made the effort of trying.

We should ask whether the Stoic is correct in thinking that external "nature" cannot be changed, while internal "emotions" can be. Frank found it pretty easy to take care of the external, physical injuries he suffered from his beating by the Kempeitai, but much harder to switch off the powerful mixture of emotions he felt as a result of the death of his sister and her children. Even though the history of human advancement has involved the gradual increase in our ability to manipulate natural laws through increasingly sophisticated technological intervention, we don't seem much better than our ancestors at controlling our emotions, at least not if numbers of people with clinical depression are anything to go by.

Another related problem with Stoicism is deciding just what counts as "natural." Just because wolves happen to eat sheep doesn't mean that we can draw the general conclusion that it is "natural" for the strong to dominate the weak. There are also lots of examples of animals, including wolves that take care of each other, nurture their young, and even play for apparently no reason other than for the fun of it. Does this suggest that if Stoics like Heydrich want to act in accordance with natural laws, they ought to be loving and nurturing rather than cruel and emotionless? By viewing our emotional lives as somehow unnatural, the Stoics seem to have a very selective understanding of what nature is all about.

The Stoic idea of accepting fate clearly has a certain appeal, since we can all likely agree that it is better to accept rather than fight things that we are certain can't be changed. At the same time, it's equally clear that we ought to be very careful when deciding just what those things are! Rather than asking whether or not we should accept our fates as the Stoics suggest, maybe we would do better move on to our second question and ask how our belief in fate can affect the decisions we make.

Hitler and Horoscopes

One philosopher to have asked this kind of question is Theodor Adorno. Like that of the Stoics, Adorno's work is directly relevant to *The Man in the High Castle*, as he was a German intellectual who witnessed the rise of Nazi fascism and eventually was forced into exile in 1934. Adorno was keen to try to understand the roots of fascism and how authoritarian personalities could be so successful in spite of centuries of "enlightened" rationality. Most of his work is deliberately dense, difficult, and engaged with the writings of many other thinkers. However, in his short writings on astrology columns and the occult, Adorno describes how fate plays a role in the development of authoritarianism.

This shouldn't be too surprising—in the show Hitler himself recognizes the usefulness of fate as a political tool. When Wegener repeats Tagomi's belief that "Fate is in the hands of men," Hitler quickly responds by claiming that fate is only in the hands of *some* men, only those who have the courage and strength of will to bend it to suit their desires. Hitler recognized that what matters most is not the actual existence of fate, but that people *believe* in such a thing. For he knows that if people see the victory of the Third Reich as a matter of fate they will put up less resistance to it since it becomes a matter of historical or even natural necessity. Just as American colonizers had used the idea of "manifest destiny" to claim that their program of expansion was simply a matter of inevitable fate, so too did Hitler want people to accept the domination of the Third Reich as an irresistible force of nature.

Adorno identifies this as one of the big problems with believing in fate. Instead of taking responsibility for the way things are in the world, we all too easily put up less resistance to things because of the mistaken impression that we have no control over them. Wegener knew that the idea of fate can be dangerous, which is why he insisted on delivering the microfilm to the science minister himself, rather than simply letting Tagomi pass it along. Even though they got along well, Wegener couldn't completely trust the trade minister, because he might suddenly be convinced by a prophecy in the *I Ching* to abandon the plan at the last moment. Wegener saw Tagomi as too reliant on his attempts to see into the future, and worried that he might let an ancient book of what he saw as hocus-pocus dictate his decisions.

The Authority of Stars

Adorno doesn't talk about the *I Ching*, but he did write about the seemingly innocuous newspaper horoscope. Even though the everyday readers who consult such things are typically not hard-core believers in astrology, Adorno sees their eagerness to catch a glimpse of the future as a small sign of their willingness to give up control of their lives to the dubious authority of star charts. His analysis of astrology columns suggested to him that deep in the modern Western psyche there is a demonstrable tendency towards authoritarianism, a capacity to give up responsibility for our actions and place it in the hands of a higher power, even where there is not much rational reason to do so. It didn't matter much to him whether this power was religious, occult, or political. What mattered was that people were quite happy to let themselves be guided by irrational forces (like astrology columns or ancient Chinese books) that often went directly contrary to their own best interests. Rather than doing the difficult and complicated work required to achieve the results we want, we all too easily give ourselves over to anything promising quick and simple solutions.

Looking at a horoscope doesn't make you a fascist, and Adorno didn't think that. Few people actually guide their lives by what the astrology columns say. Nevertheless, their presence in all our newspapers is evidence of their ongoing popularity, and our ongoing acceptance of the idea of fate. Even if we don't take them very seriously and only read them for fun, Adorno still sees in this activity the tiniest seeds of what can develop into devotion to irrational forms of authority. In fact, their very lack of seriousness, their seeming unimportance is exactly what makes them interesting. While we might not support such things at a conscious, "serious" level, the fact that we continue to take an interest in them at an "unserious" level is itself a serious issue! Part of his point was to argue that the rise of authoritarianism in Germany was not because of fate, nor because the Germans were more "evil" than anyone else, but because in all of us there is an almost subliminal willingness to accept easy answers and ideas like "fate," which can be exploited by people hungry for power.

Juliana's Heroism

The Man in the High Castle provides an excellent illustration of some of Adorno's ideas. Juliana starts the show as a bit of a Stoic. She's willing to just go with the flow, and rather than resisting the Japanese empire she even adopts some of its traditions. Then, the first film presents her with hope that things could somehow be otherwise, and as other films materialize she begins to allow the possible futures they represent to guide her actions. But in the last scenes of Season One, she totally reverses direction when she decides to let Joe Blake escape on the boat to Mexico. Here she decides to *ignore* the prophetic film that portrays Joe as a murderous Nazi and instead believe in her own impression of the man himself. This is my favorite part of the show, because at this moment she abandons her belief in the importance of the films, and reasserts her belief in her own powers of judgment. Regardless of whether this turns out well, we can still see Juliana's action here as heroic in Adorno's terms, since she has decided to give up striving for the "destiny" presented to her by the films and start acting according to her own sense of what is right and wrong. At the start of the show, the world depicted by the films means everything to her, but at that moment she has decided that fate is in her own hands.

Whatever you believe about fate—whether you think it is inescapable, or can be shaped by exceptional people or events, or is just a myth that people believe in to comfort themselves sometimes, *The Man in the High Castle* reminds us that the world we live in could have been very different, had it not been for the actions of both powerful people and ordinary folk who don't always see how powerful their actions can be.

Even if there is some form of irresistible fate in the universe, the show reminds us that we have to be very cautious in believing anybody who claims to know what our destinies might be. We should never put our lives into the "hands of fate," for we never know whose hands those actually are.

IV

Flow My Tears, the Ethicist Said

11
Is Resistance to Fascism Terrorism?

COREY HORN

September 11th 2001 started out like any other calm day, people heading to work without a care, traffic filling the streets, and businessmen slinging stocks left and right. No one that morning could have anticipated that one of the largest ever attacks on US soil was about to occur.

In the aftermath of 9/11, as first responders ran from building to building trying to help, one question came to Americans' minds: who was responsible? After learning that those responsible were a terror-linked group named Al-Qaeda, President George Bush took to the podium to declare the "War on Terror." Years later, we find ourselves still fighting terrorism. Many argue this is a war that can never be won; this may be true. The current threat has changed names but not form. Today we find ourselves fighting the militant group called "Islamic State for Iraq and Syria," or as it's more commonly known, ISIS.

Yet we seem to be fighting an entity that cannot be beaten; no matter how much force the US and the rest of the world employs, terrorism always seems to push back. The question for today is no longer, "Who is responsible?" but rather "What is responsible?" Many groups like Al-Qaeda and ISIS claim they are only fighting a war of faith, while others call them terrorists.

In Amazon's *The Man in the High Castle*, an interesting, parallel dynamic develops. In an alternative history, the new rulers of the United States, the Nazis and Imperial Japanese, find themselves fighting those they believe to be terrorists, the Resistance. However, the Resistance is not exactly parallel to Al-Qaeda or ISIS: they never exhibit the aggression of the latter, and they have been recently conquered by outsiders.

Can *The Man in the High Castle*'s American Resistance be considered terrorists—or are they simply fighting a just war against the occupying Germans and Japanese?

Defining Terrorism

The United States government distinguishes between two types of terrorism, domestic and international. It defines domestic terrorism as any act that "involves violent acts dangerous to human life that violate federal or state law" and "appear to be intended to intimidate or coerce a population" or "government," or "affect the conduct of government by mass destruction" (United States Department of Justice). International terrorism is when these same actions take place outside the United States territory. The actions of Al-Qaeda on 9/11 are an instance of domestic terrorism since they happened on US soil, but not every attack by Al-Qaeda has been domestic terrorism. For example, attacks on US military bases are considered international attacks. Using the Department of Justice's definition (admitting that in *The Man in the High Castle*'s Nazi-occupied US the domestic-international distinction does not matter), can we consider the American Resistance group terrorist?

We first meet the Resistance in the opening scenes of episode 1 when Joe Blake receives a package that he must deliver to the "Neutral Zone" (land that is mutually agreed to be neither Germany's nor Japan's). In this first instance the group operates out of a local business. When Joe signs up for his first mission, we learn what the Nazis do to members of the Resistance: pull fingernails out and other forms of torture. The Nazis raid the business when Joe attempts to leave, and we see that the Germans use brutal and deadly force when dealing with the Resistance or people associated with it.

In this first example, the American Resistance breaks laws of the occupiers, conspiring against the regime, but doesn't act against the civilian population or cause destruction of property. With this first example, the Resistance may be a criminal organization, but not a terrorist one. A second example from the first episode deals with Juliana Crain's stepsister. Trudy Walker is a member of the Resistance, also transporting a reel to the Neutral Zone. We see Walker running from the Kempeitai, the Japanese police force, when she is gunned down unarmed. At no point, does she seem to meet any of the criteria brought forth by the Department of Justice definition of a terrorist.

However, we can also hold the Greater German Reich to the same set of standards as well. In the first example, we said they have recently occupied the US and have begun forcing the citizens to adopt their ways. Throughout the first episode, many characters allude to the use of an atomic bomb which forced the hand of the US government. The Germans broke many old federal laws, and in the process coerced the civilian population into fear, and the government into giving the Germans what they want. When the bomb was eventually dropped on Washington, DC, this could be seen as an act of domestic terrorism.

Under the definition of terrorism from "our" Department of Justice, the American Resistance would not necessarily fall into one of the two categories of terrorists. In the first instance, they may have broken laws set forth by the Nazis, but they did nothing to coerce or cause damage to the Greater German Reich. In the second instance, the Resistance can't be called terrorists merely for transporting cargo unarmed. The United States definition seems to be too broad, since someone who commits homicide could be considered a terrorist under it. Put another way, "terrorism is any form of unlawful violent . . . act intended to intimidate . . . government or populations."

Corey Horn

Four Conditions of Terrorism

Terrorists use violence in a particular way, aiming at certain kinds of intermediate results en route to their ultimate ends.

—JEREMY WALDRON

In order to consider more thoroughly whether the Resistance is a terror organization or just a band of survivors continuing the war their parents had unsuccessfully fought, we need a better standard by which to determine whether a group or organization can be accurately called "terrorist."

Jeremy Waldron has written on an array of political issues from constitutional rights to torture and security. In his essay, "Terrorism and the Uses of Terror," we find a helpful definition of terrorism. Waldron gives four conditions for the definition to apply, using the language of "coercers" and "victims":

1. **The coercer gets the victim in his power so that he can communicate the threat and impose the threatened harm if he must.**
2. **The coercer demonstrates the threat, by imposing harm of the kind that he is threatening.**
3. **The coercer by making the threat affects the decision-making of the victim; or**
4. **If the victim defies him, the coercer inflicts the harm.**

We can apply these conditions both to Al-Qaeda and ISIS, as well as to the American Resistance and the Nazi party. Throughout the series, we get glimpses into the actions of both the Resistance and the Germans; for example, the Resistance operates quietly and primarily within the Neutral Zone, while the Nazis are very prominent in their providence and seem to ignore borders where they see fit. In the first episode, as Juliana is on the bus headed to the Neutral Zone, she's approached by a stranger who speaks of a Nazi agent who travels the Zone in search of members of the Resistance. What is important to point out here is the fear tactics used by the Nazis and the quietness exhibited by the Resistance.

There is one instance where the Resistance shows hostility towards others, when Juliana and Joe are in the woods. In this scene, Joe and Juliana are walking with Lem Washington, a member of the resistance, to turn over the film they transported from their respective zones. When they arrive to the meeting place, Lem turns a gun on both of them and demands the film.

At this moment Lem has acted as the coercer and has his victims under his control in order to communicate his demands. Although Lem does demonstrate condition #1, he never harms or shoots anyone to display his willingness to carry out any action if Joe and Juliana do not comply, so Lem fails to meet condition #2. By pointing a gun in their faces, Lem is attempting to make his victims panic and make a rash decision based on fear, which meets condition #3, but since condition #3 works, Lem never has to carry out condition #4. In the circumstance, the Resistance exhibits two of the four conditions Waldron set forth in order for a group to be considered a terror organization.

When we turn to the Nazis, however, we see a group that demonstrates all four conditions. In the very first episode, we see this when the Germans capture and torture the Resistance member from the factory Joe had left. The Nazis got the gentleman under their control (condition #1), and proceeded to beat him to the brink of death (condition #2), and threatened to continue beating him unless he gave up the truck's destination (condition #3). When the Resistance member refused to give up the information they demanded, the Nazi soldiers continued to beat him savagely (condition #4). Using our conditions, we see that the Nazi party in their conduct to promote state security exhibited all four measures, yet the Resistance, which is actively called a terror group throughout the show, only showed two and they were the *less* extreme two of the four actions.

This leaves us with the question, what examples today fit the script of terrorism by our new definition, and how do they compare with the American Resistance and Nazis?

Modern Instances of Terrorist Acts

Terrorism has been in the forefront of newspapers and social media especially since the events of 9/11. With the recent emergence of ISIS in Iraq and the Middle East, and domestic attacks by those in the name of some cause, a deeper question can be asked: how many different instances of terrorism are there?

Jürgen Habermas is a German philosopher who has written on matters of cosmopolitan issues, political theory, and topics that deal with terrorism. In an interview Habermas gave shortly after the events of 9/11, he addressed the questions of what kinds of terrorism there are, and the difference between acts of war and those of terror.

Habermas distinguished two versions of terrorism; political and global. An example of political terrorism is the situation in Palestine, while global terrorism is highlighted by the events of 9/11. The key differences between the two types of terrorism are the reasons behind them. In the first instance, Palestine and Israel, actions are motivated by religious and political goals, the ends of which are to assert the one side's agenda. In global terrorism, these terrorists lack an end goal, so in Habermas's view their acts are largely criminal ones.

These two distinctions allow us to see both the resistance and the Nazis as either political or global terrorists. As we have seen, the Resistance seems to be fighting back against the Nazi Party in order to take back their country. They use force, but only when necessary, and only against the Nazi soldiers, never against the native population. The use of force against non-combatants is also a distinct feature of terrorism, according to Habermas. Terrorism is typically named as such by the group being terrorized; so for example the Germans quickly name the Resistance "terrorists," or the US occupying forces in Iraq name the Iraqi freedom fighters terrorists. What is important to highlight is both the Resistance and the Iraqi freedom fighters are fighting to take back control of their home country, and exclusively target the occupying forces (in some cases there are civilian casualties, but the question is whether those were intended or not).

The Nazis are hard to pin down. One can make the case that their motives are driven by a political agenda, domination of the entire globe, but on the other hand, after taking control of another country, it seems that the systematic eradication of specific groups of people is no longer a political motive but a fear tactic. Many characters throughout the show fear the occupying government because they believe that if they speak out or step out of line, they will be killed. An interesting point Habermas makes is that global terrorism exclusively targets civilian populations in order to instill fear. We see this with the events of 9/11, as well as the recent attacks by ISIS on westerners. Although these terror organizations have political motives in the Middle East, their motives towards the West is to cause destruction and instill fear whether it is through explosions or beheadings.

In the two distinctions that Habermas lays out, one type can be seen as constituting acts of war while the other is purely terrorism. Political terrorism can be viewed as acts of war since it has an end goal that justifies the actions. In other words, terrorism that has political motives can also be viewed as acts of war. Global terrorism is purely motivated by fear-based coercion, as highlighted by the events of 9/11. In the words of Habermas, "I cannot imagine a context that would . . . make the monstrous crime of September 11th an understandable . . . political act."

Keep Calm and Fight On

Using Waldron's criteria, we established that the Resistance met two of the four conditions: getting victims under their control, and affecting their judgment. If we consider these two conditions enough to define a group as a terror group, then we can move on to what type of group the Resistance resembles, political or global terrorism.

As we've seen, the Resistance has political motives that are geared towards a certain end, which makes them political terrorists. So, the Nazi claim that the Resistance is a terrorist group appears to be valid, but as we have also pointed out, political terrorism can also be an act of war, or can occur during war.

The Nazis, though, satisfy all four conditions of Waldron's criteria, so this is clearly enough to call them terrorists. The Nazis appear to exercise both types of terrorism, political and global. If we speak in terms of Nazi soldiers systematically killing conquered civilians and using death camps as fear tactics, then it would be fair to call them political terrorists. However, if we speak about the Nazis who are fighting to expand the Third Reich's boundaries, then it is equally fair to call them global terrorists.

With these two distinctions, it would be fair to assume that the Resistance are terrorists, but of a distinctively political nature. They are people who have lost their homes and are fighting back, to secure what was lost. Just like the colonists in revolutionary America, when you fight the established system you're marked as terrorists. It's not until you prevail and establish your new regime that you're generally viewed as fighters for justice.

12
Are We Really Sure They're Wrong?

TIMOTHY HSIAO

If you're reading this, then you probably think that there's something deeply wrong and unjust about the way the Japanese and German governments are operating within the universe of *The Man in the High Castle*. But why? What do we mean when we say that something is "wrong" or "unjust"?

There are two basic ways of approaching this question. According to what we may call *moral relativism*, the truth of moral statements is dependent on either the individual or the individual's culture. So if something is right or wrong, then it is right or wrong for *me* or my culture, but that doesn't necessarily mean that it's the same for *you* or your culture. There is no "higher" morality to which everyone is subject. Morally speaking, one view is as good as another.

On the other hand, *moral objectivism* asserts that the truth of moral statements are independent of what individuals or cultures believe. If something is objectively wrong, then it is wrong because it violates some higher moral law, and not because it is something on which an individual or culture has a negative opinion. Where does this moral law come from, you might ask? Answers vary, but popular ones include God, reason, and human nature. The one feature that all of these answers have in common is that morality is not something that we get to decide or make up.

Which view is more plausible? I submit that upon reflection, nearly everyone is in some way implicitly committed to the truth of moral objectivism. Although many people like to pay lip service to moral relativism, it is deeply inadequate in explaining what we know to be true about morality. Consider just one example: When Joe Blake is travelling from New York City to make initial contact with the Resistance, he interacts with a highway patrolman in the Midwest who assists him in changing a flat tire. During the course of his conversation, he asks the patrolman about ash that he notices is falling from the sky. The patrolman casually responds, "Oh, it's the hospital. On Tuesdays they burn cripples . . . the terminally ill. Drag on the state."

We're rightly horrified at this revelation. There's no doubt that such a practice should be condemned and resisted. But *why*? It can't be that it violates a societal or cultural norm, for the very values of a Nazi society are such that those with disabilities should be put to death because they are "life unworthy of life." Accordingly, if cultural relativism is true, then it's morally permissible—and perhaps even obligatory—for those in a Nazi society to put the disabled to death because they are disabled. The *real* bad guys turn out to be the Resistance fighters, because they're the ones working actively to undermine Nazi values!

But we rightly dismiss this as absurd. Nazi values are objectively corrupt, even to those who accept them. If it is ever possible for a society to make moral mistakes, then society cannot be the barometer of moral truth.

The appeal to personal opinions or tastes fares no better: if individuals can ever err in making moral judgments, then individual attitudes cannot be the source of moral truth. Not all opinions are created equal. Someone who believes that it is morally permissible to put the disabled to death because they are disabled is just as wrong as the person who believes that 1 + 1 = 3. Without a standard of morality that is independent of our say-so, we cannot condemn anything as being *truly* evil. At best, all that we could say is that we personally disapprove of their actions, and nothing more.

When it comes down to it, we all seem to recognize that there exists an objective moral law that is independent of our personal beliefs or preferences. This "natural law" is what provides us with a basis for saying that individuals and even whole cultures can err in their moral thinking. Many philosophers, echoing St. Paul's remark that this law is "written on the hearts" of man, think that there are a set of fundamental moral truths that are known to anyone with properly functioning rational faculties. Consider Obergruppenführer Smith's reaction to the news that his son has an incurable congenital defect that requires mandatory euthanasia. He finds it unacceptable that his own son should be put to death simply because of his condition. And yet, he must surely recognize that this runs counter to the Nazi values of his culture. This, we might think, is his knowledge of the natural law tugging away at his conscience.

Granted, there is reasonable disagreement on the finer points of morality, but the mere fact of disagreement doesn't prove relativity. Disagreement can be found all the time in the sciences, but nobody thinks that disagreement there shows that there is no fact of the matter about biology, chemistry, or physics. The fact that there is disagreement only shows that the deeper you get into a subject matter, the more difficult the questions become. But it would be a mistake to focus on the hard cases while ignoring the clear ones.

So what's the point of all of this? The point is that there is an objective moral law that governs human behavior, and that this objective moral law is being violated by the Japanese and German governments in *The Man in the High Castle*. If we want to say that these governments are acting wrongly in any meaningful sense, then we must presuppose the existence of a moral standard that is independent of human opinion. As C.S. Lewis put it, you can't call a line crooked unless you have an idea of what a straight line should be.

Resisting a Tyrannical Government

Unless there is a standard of morality that is higher than any nation or group of nations, there can be no basis for saying that what the Nazis did was wrong. It is for this reason that, in the actual world, American Supreme Court Justice Robert H. Jackson argued in the Nuremberg Trials that the Nazis could be held morally accountable for their actions because they violated the "natural and inalienable rights in every human being." Even though the Nazis were just following the laws and norms of their own society, their actions were nevertheless in violation of a higher law to which all societies are subject.

Thus, St. Augustine famously stated that "an unjust law is no law at all." Augustine argued that law should reflect morality, and therefore any civil law that contradicts the natural moral law is null and void. This distinction between just and unjust laws is what provides us with a basis for justified civil disobedience.

But there is a difference between mere disobedience and active rebellion. It is one thing to refuse to obey an unjust law, and another to take up arms against a government that has passed an unjust law. Governments are in general a source of social stability that should not be abolished without a good reason, so the mere fact that a government might make a mistake does not by itself justify its overthrow. .

An armed rebellion is a type of war, and so the rules of war must apply to those who wish to take up arms against the government. On this point, many philosophers, again following Augustine, have argued that a just war can only be initiated if the following five conditions are met:

1. **Proper authority**
2. **Just cause**
3. **Reasonable chance of success**
4. **Proportionality**
5. **Last resort**

Does the American Resistance movement's fight against the Axis governments satisfy these conditions? Let's consider them one by one.

Proper Authority

The proper authority requirement is tricky, at least when considering the American Resistance movement. Normally, wars are conducted by *nation states*. Why? Because nation states are responsible for maintaining social order within their respective domains, they carry with them the mantle of *authority*. This social authority is what allows a nation state to organize a military to fight on behalf of the common good.

Since the purpose of a just war is to restore the balance of justice to a given society, only those with the responsibility of maintaining social order can initiate such a just war. Here we run into a problem: the Resistance movement is clearly not a nation state, but an entity within a nation state. So how can the Resistance movement wage a just war against the Axis governments if it lacks the authority of a state?

Before we proceed any further, it's crucial to distinguish between *de facto* authority and *proper* authority. To have de facto authority is to be in a position where you have the actual power to impose your will on society, whether or not your will is morally licit. The Nazi and Japanese governments certainly exercise this kind of authority (and they do so ruthlessly), whereas the resistance movement obviously lacks it.

Proper authority, by contrast, consists of the power to enforce the natural moral law. To have authority of this kind is to be in such a position where you are able to carry out what the moral law requires. The Axis governments obviously lack this kind of authority even though they possess a great deal of de facto authority.

While the Resistance movement lacks de facto authority, it nevertheless possesses proper authority in the sense that it acts in a co-ordinated way so as to restore the natural moral law. That is to say, in working together to overthrow an unjust government, the Resistance is acting as a representative of a social order rooted in the natural moral law. True, it may not wield the all-encompassing de facto authority that the Nazi and Japanese governments have, but the Resistance does function as a single entity with a certain kind of authority (even if weak and minuscule) that unites its members for the sake of a common goal.

Just Cause

The goal of a just war should be to re-establish a just peace. While we're never really presented with an explicit declaration of what the Resistance seeks to accomplish, it's not unreasonable to assume that their ultimate goal is the re-establishment of a legitimate and peaceful social order. The newsreel-style footage of the films may offer some insight, as they depict the Allied powers victoriously fighting for a just cause. At the very least, we can be sure that this is why Juliana is participating in the Resistance, given that the films had a transformative effect on her. Trade Minister Tagomi's mystical experience of what a peaceful San Francisco could have looked like might offer another glimpse into the social order Juliana and the others hope to bring about.

Reasonable Chance of Success

Why must there be a reasonable chance of success before we can initiate a just war? Well, the rationale is easy to see: it is wrong to cause unnecessary suffering. Accordingly, the amount of suffering that you're prepared to accept should at least be proportionate to the benefits that are being sought. Even if you're fighting for a noble cause, engaging in a futile conflict will only result in unnecessary casualties and damage to the social order. This is not to say that it's sometimes obligatory for us to submit to an unjust government. Rather, the point is that if we're going to fight, then the fight must be "worth it," so to speak. For instance, even if you are fighting an evil enemy, it would be immoral for you to gather a bunch of your comrades to charge a machine gun with pitchforks only to get mowed down.

Nobody doubts that the German Nazi and Japanese imperial governments are evil. But can the insurgency against these governments be morally justified given the seemingly insurmountable odds faced by the American resistance movement?

We can't help but be initially skeptical, especially given the ruthless efficiency of Chief Inspector Kido, Obergruppenführer John Smith, and their respective agencies at infiltrating and hunting down the resistance. The fact that Joe Blake is secretly working for Smith doesn't exactly provide much reassurance either. This skepticism presumably explains why Frank wants nothing to do with the Resistance when he learns that Juliana has become involved.

This skepticism is reinforced when we consider that the Resistance movement itself doesn't seem to have much to offer in terms of a reasonable prospect of success. They are out-organized, outgunned, underfunded, and are no match for the intelligence services of the Nazi and Japanese governments. The extent to which the Nazis have infiltrated the Resistance (both with Joe Blake and the undercover SD agent in Canon City) doesn't generate much confidence in their ability to make a meaningful dent in the Axis regime. True, they might've had some small successes—the near assassination of Obergruppenführer Smith, for example—but their overall efficacy has so far been questionable. Indeed, the botched assassination attempt was possible only because Smith's enemies—Oberst-Gruppenführer Heydrich and Captain Connolly—provided them with the necessary information.

However, there seems to be something to the mysterious newsreel films from the Man in the High Castle that might very well give the resistance the moral justification required to mount a just rebellion against the Axis governments. The almost magical content of the films, combined with Hitler's peculiar interest in finding them and the willingness of Resistance members such as Trudy Walker to die for them, suggests that the Resistance may very well have a fighting chance after all. The films may not offer complete assurance of success (indeed, at least one film depicts the nuclear bombing of San Francisco along with Frank's execution at the hands of Joe!), but they do seem to offer at least a reasonable basis for believing that a Resistance victory is possible.

Proportionality

Proportionality is an attempt to balance the scales of justice. For a rebellion to be proportionate, the goal that is sought must not exceed the harm that was incurred, nor must the force used to achieve this goal be excessive. In this case, the harm incurred was the violent destruction of the legitimate American government and the corresponding evils that were forced upon the population. Considered in this light, this goal of the American Resistance is clearly proportionate, as what they are seeking is the destruction of the illegitimate Axis governments. What's more, given the extremely limited resources of the Resistance, excessive force is simply a non-issue for them—at least for the time being. If anything, the Resistance needs to use *more* force!

Last Resort

Armed rebellion is only justified when a government as a whole becomes incorrigibly corrupt. This is tricky to cash out in precise terms, but one way to think about it is in terms of a corrupt value system. Lawmaking is never completely arbitrary. Laws are commands or ordinances that are based on reasons. These reasons reflect a core value system from which the government acts to promote its agenda. If this core value system is diametrically opposed to the natural law, then any government that adopts that system does not have the common good in mind.

These criteria are obviously met by both the Nazi and Japanese governments, as depicted, insofar as genocide, racism, and deprivation of due process are institutionalized as part of their core value systems. The dictatorial form of government makes it practically impossible for these worries to be addressed via democratic or legislative means, leaving force as the only option.

The Practical Application

You might be wondering what the point of all this is. After all, isn't it just plainly obvious that the American Resistance movement is fighting the good fight? I of course agree. But there is a difference between knowing *that* something is obvious and knowing *why* it's obvious.

What I've attempted to do here is to carve out a foundation for thinking about unjust laws, civil disobedience, resistance, and insurgency, so that when it comes to the cases that are not so obvious, we have a way of approaching them.

When we look at these issues within the imaginary universe of the *Man in the High Castle*, we can get a sharper picture of the way we naturally think about right and wrong.

13
But Why Is Our World Better?

TIM JONES

When our leading lady Juliana writes back to Frank from the Neutral Zone, she's pretty clear that the images she's seen in the newsreels show not just "another world" but "a better world."

This belief is what led her to abandon her partner and family. It's what leads her to put her life in the hands of strangers and risk murder by undercover assassins and psychotic bounty hunters like the Marshall. And given that it concerns a world where the Third Reich is a distant memory, this belief might be perfectly understandable no matter how much danger it brings her way, not only to her but to myself as a viewer and, I'd imagine, to the vast majority of my readers too. But what if she's wrong?

Imagine living in a reality so horrible that your only hope is a mysterious series of videos that promise an alternative world where the source of your problems never happened. A video that offers you a way out through showing that life could've happened differently. That life can *still* happen differently, since this other world might even exist, just beyond a thin threshold separating it from your own nightmarish realm. This video would probably be the most important thing you'd ever heard of and you might even devote your life to tracking down as many copies as you could find, to make sure they got out there into the world for all the other people suffering like you to watch and be inspired by.

"Hang on a sec," you might well be thinking right now. "Isn't this just the premise of the show? It's about a bunch of people in a parallel version of America, hunting down film reels showing a wonderful alternative reality where the Nazis lost World War II and the Allies won. Is this guy just going to repeat the plot of what I've already watched?"

Yes and no. I'm not actually referring to the specific situation in the show itself, but a mirror of the show's central plot that could exist in the world you and I live in right now.

Imagine an alternative version not of our history, but of *The Grasshopper Lies Heavy*. Imagine a series of newsreels secreted throughout *our* world that show the Allies losing and the united forces of Germany and Japan winning and occupying the United States. And imagine how normal, regular folk like you or I might very easily come to see these film reels exactly like Juliana sees the *Grasshopper* reels. As their only beacon of hope in a living nightmare. A beacon for a better world.

Good Guys and Bad Guys

I'd not be surprised if the majority of you think that I'm starting with a pretty indefensible premise. *Our* world is the world in which the Nazis lost. They're the ones who gassed tens of thousands of disabled Germans to death and then engineered the Holocaust, who murdered entire villages of innocent Czechoslovakians in reprisal for the assassination of Reinhardt Heydrich, to name just two of their numerous atrocities. How can I possibly imagine any right-meaning folk in our reality dreaming of their having won the war? I'd bet you're thinking that if anyone you knew in this world celebrated the existence of a video showing a reality where the people behind these atrocities were victorious, then at best you'd want nothing more to do with them. At worst you might punch them in the face.

The show itself works to encourage the incredulity you might be feeling at what I'm suggesting now. It's not just

Juliana who's pretty clear that the images she's seen in the film-reels show "a better world." The huge smile that Trade Minister Tagomi has throughout his trip to the world of the newsreels in the closing moments of Season One shows how strongly he'd agree with her. And I reckon the smile is for more than just his family being alive there, as we find out in Season Two.

Throughout Season One, he's shown to be a far more sympathetic guy than the rest of the ruling Japanese. Witness his apology to Juliana in "Truth" for the violence of the Kempeitai and his refusal to sacrifice Rudolf Wegener to meet his goals for a nuclear Pacific States. Even this goal (the only real black mark against his softer nature) attests in part to his character, since he sees it as the only means by which the Japanese Pacific States can be secure from an otherwise inevitable German attack. It's a defensive necessity, rather than a weapon of attack. Before you denounce his nuclear ambitions, consider that the reason that the Germans cancel their attack on Japan in "Fallout" is their believing that the Japanese possess a Hydrogen bomb. Sure, this might be a hydrogen bomb that the Germans don't realize is actually from an alternative future, but peace between the two nations enduring because of the presence of weapons of mass destruction ironically backs up Tagomi's genuine belief in their necessity for his country's security.

So the good guys of the show prefer our world to their own. The only people in the show who'd disagree with Juliana or Tagomi on this are people that the majority of the audience would recognize as "the bad guys"—SS or Kempeitai agents who torture prisoners to death, for example. Or antique shop owner Robert Childan, who's at best a casual racist and is happy with what happened to the Jews. So the people whom the show wants us to root for desire the world shown in the *Grasshopper* reels, while the people we hiss at would much prefer their status quo, thank you very much.

None of this is that surprising, right? When we look at what the Nazis got up to before and during the Second World War, it's easy to see that a future under their control would be a living hell for anyone who cherishes democracy, human rights and personal freedom over a totalitarian dictatorship. (If you're reading this and would prefer to live under Nazi occupation because their manifesto just sounds totally swell—you might be one of the two hundred people who The Atlantic tells us gathered at an alt-right conference in Washington and celebrated Trump's election victory with Nazi salutes—then I'm personally sorry on your behalf that you don't live in Juliana's reality instead of our own. You'd love it there.)

But my own horror at the world that the Nazis could have created doesn't mean that it's impossible for me to imagine a person who I'd be happy hanging out with hating the fact that *our* reality is the one they're forced to live with. And even if you share my view that Nazis = bad news, I bet that if you spoke to these people with an open mind, you might even end up understanding exactly where they're coming from.

Better for Whom Exactly?

Don't get me wrong. I'm writing this chapter in an English city called Norwich (roughly in the middle of the big bit that bulges out to the East, about half-way up). When I'm not playing at being an academic, I work at Norwich City Hall. Hitler desperately wanted to invade England during the early stages of the Second World War and rumor has it that plans for the occupation were so advanced that he'd already scheduled a victory speech from Norwich City Hall's balcony, to deliver to his newly conquered people sometime in the summer of 1942.

When I watch the show, I like to imagine that Wolf Muser's Hitler actually did this and still pops over to my city of residence from time to time. He'd love the market. In the real world, I'm incredibly glad that he never got the opportunity. If he had, then I could've grown up in one of many territories of the Third Reich and life would likely have been horrible. If I lived in the world of the show, I'd definitely be siding with Juliana and Tagomi in preferring the world of the *Grasshopper* newsreels.

But here's some stuff that's also pretty horrible and that happened in our world, the world that Juliana and Tagomi would rather live in. In the world that *I* would rather live in and which the majority of people reading this chapter would probably rather live in too:

- In April 1945, the Soviet Army invaded the German capital Berlin, leading towards Hitler's suicide on April 30th. While this in itself would be an entirely reasonable part of their counter-attack against the Nazis, the actions of its soldiers towards German civilians were often not. Civilian casualties are estimated at 125,000. It's also estimated that 100,000 German women were raped by Red Army soldiers, many of them multiple times, by multiple men.

- On August 6th 1945 the US air force dropped an atomic bomb on the Japanese city of Hiroshima. Three days later, they dropped a second bomb on Nagasaki. Over 200,000 Japanese people are estimated to have died across both attacks. The argument goes that more civilians would've died as a result of the war dragging on, had the US not taken this unprecedented step. The lingering effects of the radiation across the following decades have been held accountable for numerous cases of birth defects and cancer in survivors.

- At the end of the Potsdam Conference on 2nd August 1945 it was officially decreed that all German residents of Czechoslovakia could be forcibly deported from that country, in retaliation for the actions committed during the Nazi occupation throughout the war. Many of these German residents and their familial ancestors had been living in Czechoslovakia long before the Nazis' rise to power. It's conservatively estimated that around 15,000 people died during the expulsions. German residents were also interred in concentration camps. Czech President Edvard Beneš didn't seem to care about these potential similarities to the actions of his country's occupiers when he called in October for a "final solution" to the Czechs' "German problem."

I'm definitely not trying to convince you that both sides are as bad as each other—I'm not sure that would be useful, even if it were remotely possible. But imagine being one of the German women who suffered at the hands of the Russians (and who then would live the rest of her life in the Soviet-controlled East Germany); imagine being one of the residents of Hiroshima dying a lingering death as a result of an illness caused by the bombs, or nursing a child deformed for the same reason; and imagine being one of the innocent Germans uprooted from his or her home in Czechoslovakia, purely for having the wrong genetic background.

These hypothetical people would live in our world as perfectly nice, lovely folk who want the best for everyone they know; entirely tolerant and unprejudiced towards minorities. Not brutal torturers like the Kempeitai's Chief Inspector Kido, or casual racists like Robert Childan, who'd both clearly prefer to live in the show's own reality because it allows their baser characteristics to be indulged. They could be your neighbours and you'd never think a single bad thought about them. They'd live a normal life as much as they could, carrying the huge physical and emotional burdens forced onto them by the historical events of this world, fighting every day not to let it grind them down.

I reckon that if one of them were to stumble upon a newsreel called *The Grasshopper Lies Heavy* that shows the Axis forces winning the war—and if this person then copied Juliana and wrote a letter to his or her partner gushing about having seen on this reel "a better world"—it would be entirely understandable.

A Worse World

So it's possible that sympathetic people in our reality might disagree with Juliana's faithful description of the world in the *Grasshopper* newsreels as "better"—and that if these people were to find reels of their own, then they might just as readily assign Juliana's evaluation to the world it would show them, in which the Allied powers were defeated by Germany and Japan. We shouldn't simply dismiss these people as evil, since they've lived through horrible events in our timeline and so their longing for the world they see in our world's equivalent of the *Grasshopper* reels would deserve our understanding and empathy. It would be a world in which they could live without carrying the legacy of sexual violence, terminal illness or forced displacement.

But even though I'd not condemn any of these people, *I'm* still incredibly glad that I live in this world and not Juliana's. I agree with her pretty much unconditionally that the world she sees in the film reels is "better" than her own. And I bet you do too, even if you agree with what I've just said.

Is this simply because it's extremely unlikely that anyone reading this book will have experienced any of the historical events I mentioned earlier? Perhaps. That'd mean that my agreeing with Juliana comes from an element of privilege I get just from my own country having been on the winning side of the war. None of the bad things happened to me, *not* because our version of history is unconditionally great for everyone involved, but because I'm lucky enough not to have lived in any of the situations I described. I'm not a woman who lived in Berlin during the Russians' occupation, nor a resident of Hiroshima, nor a displaced Czechoslovakian German. If I hadn't been so lucky to have avoided any of these fates through the sheer lottery of birth, then I might well find Juliana's perspective on which world is best harder to agree with.

A Better World for the Most People

But I'm not entirely happy with the conclusion that thinking our own world superior to the world of the show *is* entirely down to the thinker's good fortune. To say that one bunch of people suffer in one version of history while another bunch of people suffer in the other, and that any evaluation that one world is "better" than the other depends entirely on which bunch you happen to belong to. One of the main reasons for my dissatisfaction with this line of thinking is the fact that one bunch is almost certainly way bigger than the other.

Without being ghoulish enough to count up every single victim, it's highly likely that many more people across the world suffered in Juliana's version of history during and following the Second World War. At least two of the horrible events from *our* world that I described earlier will have comparable incidents in her reality. The alternative world of the show has its own equivalent of Hiroshima, when a German atomic bomb called the Heisenberg Device was dropped on Washington D.C, just like we see in a flashback in "Fallout" at the end of Season Two. So in Juliana's world there'd be an equivalent group of people to the Japanese survivors I described earlier, who've suffered equivalent trauma. The psychological trauma for America as a whole could conceivably have been even worse than it was for Japan, considering the impact of the capital itself being attacked in this horrifying new way. And going by real-world evidence about the actions of the German SS units in Russia towards the women they encountered there in the early 1940s (in blatant contradiction to their own supposed codes of "racial purity"), I can't imagine that the German's subsequent occupation of American cities would've been any less terrifying than the Soviets' occupation of Berlin.

Added to these equivalents of the people in our reality who might reasonably long for Juliana's version of history, we have the people subjected to fresh brutalities as a result of the Nazis' victory that don't have an obvious parallel here. The TV show hasn't gone into too much detail about what happened to the rest of the world after the war, but if you read Philip K. Dick's original novel, there's lots of hints about how the brutality the Nazis showed towards the Jews was directed towards new targets following their victory, including the extermination of most of Africa. And thanks to the Nazi rule consolidating itself across Europe and the Americas, millions more people in Juliana's present live under the daily stresses of totalitarian rule than do so in our world.

Sure, there's places today like North Korea where life for regular folk is comparable to life for Americans and Europeans under the Nazis. A United Nations report in 2014 on human rights in North Korea, written after listening to over 320 testimonies, including those from prison camp survivors and former guards, concluded that the regime employs "systematic, widespread and gross human rights violations" in order to "dominate every aspect of its citizens' lives and terrorize them from within" (United Nations Human Rights Council). It's fair to say though that the extent of totalitarianism's reach is far more limited in our world than in hers. Life in Soviet Russia was pretty horrible under Stalin, but he died in 1953 and none of the following Soviet leaders were anything like as hell-bent on mass murder as he was. Much of Russia gets destroyed in Juliana's reality anyway, so I think it's pretty unproblematic to argue that this part of the world has a relatively easier time of it in our reality than in hers.

Since 1945, the United Nations has worked in our world to foster human rights and prevent another outbreak of world war. It's definitely not perfect and has missed opportunities where it could have saved many, many lives, particularly in the Balkan conflicts of the 1990s, but it's much better than the status quo in the show, where the peace that exists seems likely to collapse the moment Hitler dies. The best thing that can be said in the regime's favor is that everyone is safe from another world war as long as Hitler stays alive and well—which is a pretty shocking point of reassurance, if you think about it!

So Juliana's world has its own equivalents of many of the people who suffer as a result of our version of history, as well as millions more whose suffering is a direct result of that world's own historical events happening instead of ours. This is one quantifiable, if perhaps a little cold, way of suggesting that Juliana would be objectively correct to say that the world you and I live in right now is "better" than her own. Even if her evaluation is motivated by how she imagines her own life would have turned out differently, it's not just Juliana who'd personally suffer far less as a result of history running the way it has for us, but a greater number of people overall across the world.

Whether or not Juliana and I agree over which world is best because *we*'d both be better off here than in her reality, the numbers are on our side either way.

A Better World's Victims

So yeah, I for one strongly believe that the world you and I live in *is* the better world, in spite of some of the people who share this world with us having sympathetic reasons for finding hope in the existence of Juliana's alternative reality.

We still have to acknowledge the people whose suffering is written in stone as historical fact—as an inevitable part of our better world coming into being. The victims of our better world. If these people need any additional evidence beyond the numbers game that the world of the *Grasshopper* films is better, despite what it's done to them, then perhaps it's our duty to provide this evidence through the way we act towards them. Through the ways in which we empathize with what our world has done to them and commemorate the events they wish had never happened. Through the ways in which we work to ensure those events don't happen again.

In May 2016, President Obama, on a visit to Japan, refused to apologize for the US bombing of Hiroshima. But he did embrace survivors, place flowers at the foot of a cenotaph dedicated to the dead and call for countries to work together to forge a world without nuclear weapons. I can't see the most powerful person in Juliana's world making a similar overture towards the victims and survivors of the Heisenberg's detonation in Washington DC. This isn't to mitigate the suffering of Hiroshima. But if the equivalent event happens in both worlds, and one recognizes it as a tragedy, expresses sympathy for its victims and puts effort into minimising it happening again, while the other one does none of these things, then I think we can agree with Juliana's evaluation that the first is better than the second, however distasteful it might be to point this out to those whose emotional and physical scars will never heal.

What'd be even better than a *better* world is a perfect world. A world that never experienced either the bad stuff that followed the Allied victory, or the bad stuff that we learn happened in the show. Neither Juliana's reality nor the reality of the *Grasshopper* newsreels is that world. Perhaps Juliana already knows this and that's why she chooses the particular word "better" when she writes to Frank from the Neutral Zone, rather than one that's even stronger. I wonder if there's a set of film reels out there that shows this perfect world. Perhaps not. Perhaps a world whose history is entirely innocent is too much to hope for. If so, then even though better can't mean perfect, better might be the very best there is.

14
Reel Lucky

ELIZABETH RARD

We typically assess the moral character of people largely based on their actions. If a person gives their time and money to a charity, abandoning personal goals in an honest attempt to make the lives of others better, we deem them of high moral character, and we say that their actions are morally good actions. Likewise, if a person engages in actions that cause harm to others, such as stealing from those in need, or ending innocent lives, we say that the person is perhaps of a lower moral character, and that their actions are morally bad.

Yet we do not always blame a person simply because their actions cause harm, or praise a person whose actions are beneficial. The intentions behind an action matter, sometimes even more than the outcome of the action. Hence if I bump into you unintentionally, causing you to fall and scuff your knee, we would not want to say that I was a bad sort of person in that instance, although perhaps we would want to say that I had been thoughtless, maybe even negligently so. If my actions had unintended beneficial consequences (perhaps I borrowed your car without asking, not knowing you planned to use it in a bank robbery that same day) we would not praise me based on the good outcome of my actions.

Now here's the rub. There are many, many events that are beyond my control that contribute to each and every one of my actions. We are all constantly being judged because of actions that only come about because of the way the world is.

In the TV show *The Man in the High Castle* people live in a world that's very different from the one we're familiar with. The events of World War II unfolded in such a way that Germany and Japan were able to seize joint control of the United States. The characters in this world face choices and pressures that are very different from those faced by people in our United States. Nazi soldiers are a constant threat. An underground Resistance has sprung up in order to fight against the Nazi regime. A tenuous alliance between Germany and Japan is seemingly all that stands between the country and total Nazi domination.

Along with these extreme circumstances come opportunities to act in ways that show either moral strength or moral deficiency. Juliana is swept up in the Resistance and engages in many actions that we would consider heroic. We feel we should praise her for her efforts to fight against the Nazis, at great risk to her own personal safety. Yet she becomes involved in the Resistance, and seems to be pushed forward at almost every turn, by situations that are entirely beyond her control.

Joe is a duplicitous agent working undercover for the SS in an attempt to infiltrate the Resistance. We would judge both his actions and his character to be morally bad, yet Joe has been placed in extreme circumstances. He becomes a Nazi agent largely due to situational pressures, even a desire to protect his girlfriend and her child. And Joe's luck is not all bad. After meeting Juliana—a chance meeting to be sure—he begins to question his own actions and starts to move towards redemption. It seems that Juliana has been morally lucky, whereas Joe has been, at least initially, morally unlucky.

In our world we evaluate people based on what they actually do. We can reason about what they might have done had situations been different, but we're always making an inference from their actual actions when we do this. In the universe of *The Man in the High Castle* there is another avenue of investigation. *The Grasshopper Lies Heavy* newsreels make it possible for us as outside observers, and even for the characters within the fictional universe, to gain knowledge of the way various people would have acted had situations been different. Joe may have acted poorly, engaged in actions we would evaluate as bad, but we can now compare his actual actions with the way he acted in other situations by looking at his actions on various film reels. In this way we can construct a moral evaluation of Joe, which is largely immune to luck, because we can potentially access information about his actions across a wide variety of circumstances.

Shaped by Our World

The world we live in, the circumstances we are faced with, go a long way towards shaping our character and our actions. There are many characters in *The Man in the High Castle* whose lives, character, and actions are shaped by the circumstances they find themselves in. When Juliana witnesses the death of her half-sister Trudy at the hands of the Japanese military police she comes into possession of a film reel and learns of her sister's involvement in the Resistance. She's placed in extraordinary circumstances and has an opportunity to act bravely by finishing her sister's mission. In a certain sense Juliana is morally lucky. Events have transpired around her in just the right way to afford her the opportunity and motivation to act in a morally exemplary way. Had her sister merely disappeared, rather than being killed in front of her, it is doubtful that Juliana would have begun down such a heroic path. She engages in actions that warrant our assessment of her as a good person, an exceptional person even, but the events leading to her actions are largely beyond her control.

Joe is both morally unlucky and morally lucky over the course of Season One. He grows up in a Nazi German–occupied portion of the United States, a situation that in itself is unlucky, morally speaking. Joe is in a situation where there is danger to himself and his loved ones if he does not work for the current regime, and opportunity for advancement and success if he does. These circumstances lead him to become an undercover agent for the SS, working to infiltrate and undermine the Resistance, leading us to evaluate Joe as a morally bad character at the beginning of the story. But Joe is also morally lucky. Early on he meets Juliana. He seems to be immediately emotionally attached to Juliana, which causes Joe to repeatedly engage in actions that are contrary to his superiors' commands. Often Joe directly intervenes in order to help save Juliana's life.

Poor Frank also gets a bit of both good and bad luck, morally speaking. Early on he and his family are taken into custody and imprisoned while Frank is interrogated about the whereabouts of Juliana. Frank is released but unfortunately his family has already been executed. In addition to being a horrific outcome for Frank and his family, it is also morally unlucky for Frank as it directly motivates him to seek revenge. Frank decides to assassinate the crown Prince, an individual who is painted in the show as being at the very least the lesser of two evils, an important figurehead in the struggling Japanese government, which may be all that is preventing total domination of the former United States by Nazi Germany.

Had Frank assassinated the crown prince he would have engaged in an action that would be considered morally wrong by most measures, and he would have done so primarily due to a situation that was both extreme and beyond his control. Frank seems to fully intend to assassinate the Prince. He acquires an illegal gun and ammunition, which he brings to a public appearance by the Prince. He then removes the gun from his coat and appears to prepare to fire at the Prince. At this point Frank's moral luck takes a turn for the better. A small Japanese child, attending the appearance with his father, makes eye contact with Frank. Something in that child's eye, some look of hope, and perhaps confusion or fear at the visible gun, causes Frank to hesitate. Whether or not Frank would have gone through with his plan we cannot know, for during his hesitation someone else fired a shot, killing the Crown Prince. Had Frank fired he would have done something very wrong. He was lucky that someone else killed the Prince first, because it prevented him from engaging in a morally bad action.

John also lives a life that is influenced by moral luck. He is born a German in a world where a Nazi German regime wins the Second World War and takes control of a large chunk of the United States. He's raised to believe that the way you succeed and demonstrate your loyalty to the country is to enforce the Nazi regime, often times through violence and intimidation. John is old enough that he would actually have been in the military during World War II, and so even had he grown up in a world where the Allies had won the war, he would have most likely been morally blameworthy for actions committed during the war. Yet it seems that simply being born in Germany some twenty years before World War II is very morally unlucky. Had John been born in Canada he may well have lived, at the very least, a morally neutral life, never having had the opportunity to become a Nazi agent, nor the same pressures to live a life where he harmed and killed so many other people.

The more we look at the specific circumstances of each character, the more it becomes clear that to a large extent their actions, good or bad, are caused, or at least strongly influenced, by events that are entirely beyond their control. We want to be able to give a moral assessment of the characters, not just of their actions, but at the same time we hesitate to judge people for actions that are largely outside their control.

The Problem of Luck

To understand the problem clearly let's look at what happens when we try to compare our various characters. Assessing the moral status of actions is a complex business, and at the very least it seems that not all bad actions are equally bad. Joe lying to Juliana does not seem as bad as Joe executing Juliana and Frank. Likewise not all good actions are equally good. Juliana bringing a flower to Tagomi might be considered a good action, but not as good as Juliana rescuing Joe from the Resistance.

But to keep it simple let's limit ourselves to three possible moral ways of evaluating actions: good, bad, and neutral. Intuitively a good action will be one that we would praise the acting person for, an action that makes the world a better place in some way. A bad action is one that we would blame the acting person for committing, and a neutral action would be one that is neither morally positive nor negative.

In addition we will also simplify our discussion of moral luck. Moral luck comes in several different forms. The luck someone has when they grow up in a home where their parents teach them never to murder people is a different type of luck than the luck someone has when their gun jams, preventing them from committing murder. Moral philosopher Thomas Nagel has actually identified four distinct types of moral luck, but here I'm just going to assume that luck exists, and I will disregard the different types.

Moral luck is not all or nothing. At different points in a person's life, to different degrees, they might be morally lucky or morally unlucky. Again, I'll simplify this and simply consider what the situation might be if people overall were either morally lucky, morally unlucky, or neutral with regard to moral luck. We can think of neutrality with regard to moral luck as a situation where circumstances place little to no pressure on the acting person to act in either a morally good or morally bad way. Growing up in the suburbs of a relatively just and affluent society might be considered neutral, depending on the status of the rest of the world. We would not be pressured into harming others, but at the same time there would be few opportunities to act in a truly heroic manor.

Juliana is an individual who acts largely in a morally good way, whereas John can be considered someone who acts in a morally bad way. Both Joe and Frank can be considered morally neutral because at times they act in better or worse ways. We can assign each value judgment a numerical judgment for easy comparison:

Good = 3

Neutral = 2

Bad = 1

This assignment allows us to rank our acting persons from best to worst, where an acting person with a higher score will be ranked morally better than an acting person with a lower score:

Juliana (3)

Joe/Frank (2)

John (1)

The problem with the above ranking is that it does not take moral luck into account. I'm ignoring the differences in situation between our acting persons. Juliana is rewarded in our assessment because she's lucky, and John is punished because he's morally unlucky. Let's say that Juliana is lucky, John is unlucky, and Frank and Joe are neutral with regard to luck. We can represent the data we have so far as follows.

	Unlucky	Neutral	Lucky	Average
Juliana			Good (3)	3
Joe		Neutral (2)		2
Frank		Neutral (2)		2
John	Bad (1)			1

We can here see the issue represented visually. Across the top we have the three different types of luck an acting person might have. We then fill in the assessment of their actions under the appropriate column for each person's circumstances. While we know how the persons actually acted in the circumstances they found themselves in, we don't know how they would have acted if things had been different.

We feel that people should not be blamed for actions that are beyond their control, and we think that sometimes people can be morally lucky or unlucky, engaging in good or bad actions because of situations beyond their control. Therefore we can't fairly compare the moral quality of persons based on actions engaged in, where moral luck played a part in the actions. As it stands we cannot compare these persons, other than to say that Frank and Joe seem to get the same moral assessment, since they have the same action assessment in comparable circumstances.

Finding the Reel Answer

In our actual world this would be the end of the story. We can only infer to how people might have acted in other circumstances, based on how they act in the circumstances they actually find themselves in.

But in the universe of our fiction there is another source of information, one that promises to fill in some of the missing information for our moral assessments. *The Grasshopper Lies Heavy* newsreels are films that show up throughout the series, and seem to depict alternate histories. The first reel that we see shows a timeline in which the Allies won the Second World War. This timeline might be similar to, or even identical to, the one that we the viewers take to be the way things actually happened.

In another film shown much later in the story we see a timeline in which Germany seems to have conquered all of the U.S., including the west coast (which is occupied by Japan in the main timeline of the series). In this timeline Joe is seen executing Juliana and Frank. It's revealed near the end of the series that Hitler is in possession of a large number of these newsreels. He has in fact become obsessed with them. The final reveal of Season One is that Tagomi can apparently move between these timelines. The final scene shows him sitting on a park bench in a United States that looks much more like the history we as the viewers remember, as opposed to the alternate history of the show. The upshot is that we can take the film reels to depict actual alternate timelines that we (and some of the characters) now have access to.

This opens up the possibility that we can learn how various characters actually acted in different situations, rather than simply inferring what their actions might have been. We learn that in another timeline, one in which Joe was truly morally unlucky, he was a Nazi soldier who executed Frank and Juliana. Returning to our above simplified assessments we can say that in unlucky circumstances Joe acted in a way that was morally bad. In addition we see that in these circumstances Frank and Juliana both acted in a way that was largely neutral, although we may not have enough information from the film reel to determine if Juliana and Frank were placed in morally lucky or unlucky circumstances.

For the sake of seeing how our assessments can benefit from the information made available in these reels let's fill in some possible information that could be found on the newsreels, beginning with John. Imagine we pore over hours of footage and find that, in addition to acting badly when he's unlucky, John also acts badly when he is in morally neutral circumstances. For example we find that in all the histories in which John grows up in a boring suburb he decides to embezzle money from a local charity. When we look at John in timelines where he is afforded an opportunity to act truly heroically we find him acting in a way that is mostly neutral, neither helping nor harming those around him.

We already have values for Joe when he has bad and neutral luck. Let's imagine that in all the realities where he is given the opportunity to be heroic he actually rises to the occasion. Joe's not really a bad guy; he's just very susceptible to moral luck. Frank, on the other hand, let's assume, is slightly less susceptible to moral luck. In the universes where he is unlucky he engages in bad actions.

Suppose that in the timelines where Frank is born a German he becomes a Nazi soldier. But let's also suppose that Frank is not as heroically disposed as Joe and Juliana. When placed in a situation similar to Juliana's he chooses to go home and read books rather than join the resistance, hence we evaluate him as acting neutrally when he has good moral luck.

Lastly we turn to our heroine Juliana. She has the benefit in the show of getting many opportunities to act in good ways, and for the most part she does not disappoint. Let's suppose that trend towards moral praiseworthiness carries across timelines and that even when she finds herself in morally neutral circumstances she still engages in good actions. For example perhaps in the timeline where she grows up in a boring suburb she spends all her spare time doing charity work. Alas, Juliana is not actually perfect, though, and in the timelines where she's morally unlucky the most she can muster is neutral behavior.

Equipped with this new (hypothetical) information about our characters we can fill in the rest of the details from our previous chart:

	Unlucky	Neutral	Lucky	Average
Juliana	Neutral (2)	Good (3)	Good (3)	2.7
Joe	Bad (1)	Neutral (2)	Good (3)	2
Frank	Bad (1)	Neutral (2)	Neutral (2)	1.7
John	Bad (1)	Bad (1)	Neutral (2)	1.3

Once we know how the various actors will behave in different timelines, where their moral luck is different, we can give an assessment of them across timelines that is relatively immune to moral luck. By seeing how every acting person behaves in every type of situation we get a comparison of acting persons that is not susceptible to any particular person getting an unfair advantage or disadvantage. Given the values that we assumed for the persons, and the values we originally assigned to the various assessment levels, we can get an average score for each person, allowing us to compare them.

When we compare averages we get a more accurate ranking, with Juliana still getting the highest evaluation and John getting the worst, but we can now distinguish between Joe and Frank. Even though Joe and Frank acted the same in neutral circumstances, they may become dissimilar when we look at how they behave in better and worse circumstances.

With the values we filled in we did not see much change in our original ranking, Juliana was still ranked highest while John was still ranked lowest, but we can imagine situations where our assessment would change more dramatically upon consideration of reel footage. Imagine we check all the newsreels and discover that John devotes his life to building homes for the poor in every single timeline except the actual one, or that Juliana is a high school bully in sixty percent of the timelines, or that Frank is worse than Hitler in eighty percent of the timelines.

This sort of information would cause our final rankings to look very different from our initial single-timelines assessment. How much of this sort of result we should expect may depend on human psychology, on how susceptible we are to our moral circumstances for our actions. How representative my actions in one timeline are of my character across timelines might tell us something about how closely we resemble our counterparts across various timelines.

The Reel Lesson

The characters in *The Man in the High Castle* exist in a timeline that has significant differences from the history we're familiar with. National Socialist German and Imperial Japanese control over the United States places people in extraordinary circumstances, leading to situations that are both morally lucky and unlucky for various characters. The existence of the newsreels allowed us to assess the quality of the characters without worrying that our assessments (and their actions) were caused by this luck. In a sense we leveled the playing field for our characters.

Yet extreme circumstances are not limited to fictional worlds. Without the benefit of information about alternate timelines we out here in the real world might be trapped in a situation of incomplete information, unable to separate a person's character from their actions, and many of these actions may be caused by circumstances beyond their control.

V

A Maze of What-ifs

15
Farts, Butterflies, and Inner Truth

FRANKLIN PERKINS

Frank Frink has decided to quit his factory job and go into business making jewelry. He knows his life will change. He throws the yarrow stalks to get a reading from the *I Ching*, the *Book of Changes*. From the contradictory results, he concludes that his decision will not only change his life but will impact all of humanity, leading to the Third World War. He struggles to make sense of this:

> What's happening? Did I start it in motion? Or is someone else tinkering, someone I don't even know? Or—the whole lot of us. It's the fault of those physicists and that synchronicity theory, every particle being connected with every other; you can't fart without changing the balance in the universe. It makes living a funny joke with nobody around to laugh. (Orion edition, pp. 54–55)

Frank raises one of the fundamental ideas of chaos theory and complexity science, more often known as the butterfly effect. The claim is that a butterfly fluttering its wings in some distant part of the world might set off a series of events culminating in a hurricane. While the fart also involves a small movement of air, its implications differ radically, and not just because butterflies are pretty. The butterfly effect emphasizes the complexity of the world around us, showing that it exceeds the grasp of our finite minds. The fart effect places our actions within that complex system. The terrifying point is that the butterfly that causes the hurricane might be me. That the cause might be a fart, an action both trivial and involuntary, pushes the point into the realm of absurdity. It makes life into a joke, but if the result might be a world war, who could laugh?

Living with the Fart Effect

Frank's worry that his career change might cause a world war seems far-fetched, but *The Man in the High Castle* shows us that it's not. The Third World War is precisely what is at stake in the negotiations among Tagomi, Baynes, and Yatabe. What will determine if they succeed? Frank asks this question:

> Can *anyone* alter it? he wondered. All of us combined . . . or one great figure . . . or someone strategically placed, who happens to be in the right spot. Chance. Accident. And our lives, our world, hanging on it.

Baynes (a.k.a. Rudolf Wegener) might be the great figure who saves the world, or it might be the strategically placed Italian Foreign Minister they hope to approach. What we know is that if Tagomi did not have his 1860 Colt .44, the whole thing would have failed. And that pistol came from the antiquities dealer Bob Childan and was probably made at Wyndam-Matson Corporation, perhaps even by Frank. So Frank may be the one who has saved the world. All of history unfolds in this way. We're told that the decisive event leading to German and Japanese victory was the assassination of Roosevelt in Miami. If that had been averted, as in the alternative history of *The Grasshopper Lies Heavy*, the allies would have won. And what might have averted the assassination? Perhaps a great hero or someone strategically placed, but perhaps a late bus, a piece of jewelry, or even an ill-timed fart.

We constantly shape and are shaped by circumstances beyond our comprehension. When Frank is arrested and later released, he can only see these events as inexplicable. Is it a miracle, or a fluke? Is there someone to thank? Tagomi made the decision, but had he not received Frank's jewelry, he would not have been in the right place or frame of mind to intervene. So should Frank thank himself, or Childan (who gave it to Tagomi), or the Japanese connoisseur Paul Kasoura (who awakened Childan's appreciation for it), or his ex-boss Wyndam-Matson (whose actions pushed Frank into the jewelry business in the first place)? Human beings occupy an absurd position, compelled to act without knowing why things happen or where our own choices will lead. As Tagomi puts it:

> We're blind moles. Creeping through the soil, feeling with our snouts. We know nothing. I perceived this . . . now I don't know where to go. Screech with fear, only. Run away. (p. 97)

But there's no escape, nowhere to run. Even flight has consequences.

What is the mole to do? How do we live with this kind of world? The problem of living with complexity has been central to Chinese philosophical traditions from the start. The basic approach crystallized in the Han dynasty with what has come to be known as "correlative cosmology." While specified in different ways by different philosophers, the most fundamental ontological principle is life or vitality (*sheng* 生) as spontaneous growth, generation, and differentiation. The ground for this growth is formless and hidden but infinitely productive. It is labelled as the *dao* (Tao) 道, the way or guide. It could also be described as empty, absent, or indistinct, *wu* 無, which literally means to lack or not have. As Paul Kasoura says, *wu* has vitality but no distinct form, intention, or design (p. 170). The *dao* is described well by Childan:

> *The Tao is that which first lets in the light, then the dark.* Occasions the interplay of the two primal forces so that there is always renewal. It is that which keeps it all from wearing down. The universe will never be extinguished because just when the darkness seems

> to have smothered all, to be truly transcendent, the new seeds of light are reborn in the very depths. That is the Way. When the seed falls, it falls into the earth, into the soil. And beneath, out of sight, it comes to life. (p. 106)

The world that arises is differentiated on many levels, but the most fundamental distinction is between *yin* (the dark, yielding, soft, hidden, feminine) and *yang* (bright, forceful, hard, evident, masculine). The ceaseless interaction between these forces is the direct cause of life, renewal, and cyclical change.

Many specific strategies emerged in the Chinese tradition as ways of living with complexity. Some of these appear in the novel. The most central is awareness of the concrete details of our situation, which requires attentiveness, patience, and adaptability. As Childan puts it:

> The Moment changes. One must be ready to change with it. Or otherwise left high and dry. *Adapt.* The rule of survival, he thought. Keep eye peeled regarding situation around you. Learn its demands. And—meet them. Be there at the *right time* doing the *right thing.* Be yinnish. (p. 146)

The mutual implication of all things means that sometimes good can only arise from bad and sometimes bad arises from good. We must be ready for that. Realizing that both good and bad are inevitable leads to a degree of equanimity. Frank's ex-wife Juliana says she learned this attitude from the Japanese: "Imbibed placid attitude toward mortality, along with money-making judo. How to kill, how to die. Yang and yin" (p. 35). At the same time, the darkest moments cannot last. From the fullest yin, there must be yang. That hope appears most of all in the stirring of new life expressed in the *wu* of Frank's jewelry.

The Changes: A Guide for Moles

The most prominent element of Chinese philosophy used to deal with complexity in the novel is the *I-Ching*, more commonly written now as *Yijing* (易經) and translated as the *Book of Changes* or *Classic of Changes*). The earliest layer consists of divination statements that usually include a concrete image and then some indication of whether you will succeed or fail. That is the level quoted in the novel. Another layer consists of brief explanations of these lines, sometimes extrapolated to give ethical guidance. The *Classic of Changes* is formed with the addition of commentaries that build a cosmological and philosophical system around these divination statements. While the origins probably go back to the early Zhou dynasty (founded in the eleventh century B.C.E.), the classic as a whole represents the correlative thinking that developed later. In that form it becomes a self-conscious manual for living with complexity.

The commentaries say that the *Changes* mirrors the structure of nature. That requires that the text itself be complex. The basis is the determination of a single line as either yin (represented by a broken line) or yang (a straight line). Grouping three lines forms the eight possible trigrams. Those are then paired to form sixty-four hexagrams. On top of that, any number of lines in the hexagram can be in the process of change, allowing for 4,096 possible outcomes. The complexity of the text goes further, though, as it brings together commentaries and explanations from different periods and perspectives. Aside from those constituting the classic, some of the greatest philosophers in the Chinese tradition, both Daoist and Confucian, added their own commentaries.

Philip K. Dick's encounter with the text is even more complex. The Chinese text and commentaries passed through the German translation and commentary of a Christian missionary, Richard Wilhelm, and then into English through Cary F. Baynes, supplemented with an introduction by Carl G. Jung. That introduces some distortions, as in Wilhelm's introduction of God in relation to hexagram fifty-one. Tagomi refers to it as "God appears in the sign of the Arousing," but the original Chinese makes no mention of God. The proliferation of new meanings, though, is at the heart of the *Changes*. The classic itself is a distortion, making a profound philosophical system out of a collection of statements that sound like they could come from a fortune cookie.

How does the *Changes* work as a guide? It is explained the first time Frank uses it:

> Here came the hexagram, brought forth by the passive chance workings of the vegetable stalks. Random, and yet rooted in the moment in which he lived, in which his life was bound up with all other lives and particles in the universe. The necessary hexagram picturing in its pattern of broken and unbroken lines the *situation*. He, Juliana, the factory on Gough Street, the Trade Missions that ruled, the exploration of the planets, the billion chemical heaps in Africa that were now not even corpses, the aspirations of the thousands around him in the shanty warrens of San Francisco, the mad creatures in Berlin with their calm faces and manic plans—all connected in this moment of casting the yarrow stalks to select the exact wisdom appropriate in a book begun in the thirtieth century B.C. A book created by the sages of China over a period of five thousand years, winnowed, perfected, that superb cosmology—and science—codified before Europe had even learned to do long division. (pp. 19–20)

The whole universe is implicated in this one moment and the casting of the yarrow stalks. The *Changes* gives us a starting point for making sense of that complexity.

What makes the *Changes* so important in the context of the novel is that it provides guidance through the concrete. That contrasts the madness to which Tagomi almost succumbs. It contrasts the assassin Joe Cinnadella, who admits that "it's all darkness" and yet argues for decisive action (pp. 158–59). Most of all, though, it contrasts the flight from the real into abstraction. That is the greatest evil in the novel. Baynes tries to pinpoint the particular form of German insanity, coming to this conclusion:

> Their view; it is cosmic. Not of a man here, a child there, but an abstraction: race, land. *Volk. Land. Blut. Ehre.* Not of honorable men

> but of *Ehre* itself, honor; the abstract is real, the actual is invisible to them. *Die Güte*, but not good men, this good man. (p. 45)

This move to abstraction attempts to evade our finitude. The Germans, as Baynes says, "want to be the agents, not the victims, of history." That's impossible, as we have seen. It's also destructive. One of the most profound philosophical points in the novel is that meaning can only originate in the concrete. Juliana sees this: "We have no value, she said to herself. We can live out our tiny lives. If we want to. If it matters to us" (p. 35). It can matter, but only to us. The move to abstraction culminates in nihilism, because abstracted from concrete human concerns—looked at from a cosmic perspective—nothing human matters. Humanity is just a temporary stage, the blink of an eye. Dust returns to dust.

If there is to be life, it must be mole-like. When Frank gets the reading he interprets as predicting another world war, he finally concludes:

> I should take my tools, get my motors from McCarthy, open my shop, start my piddling business, go on despite the horrible line. Be working, creating in my own way right up to the end, living as best I can, as actively as possible, until the wall falls back into the moat for all of us, all mankind. That's what the oracle is telling me. Fate will poleaxe us eventually anyhow, but I have my job in the meantime; I must use my mind, my hands. (p. 54)

We will all die eventually, even the whole human species. Yet we must find meaning in the here and now. Tagomi comes out of his crisis in the same way, just returning to work. Baynes gives the same view in ethical terms:

> Evidently we go on, as we always have. From day to day. At this moment we work against Operation Dandelion. Later on, at another moment, we work to defeat the police. But we cannot do it all at once; it is a sequence. An unfolding process. We can only control the end by making a choice at each step.
>
> He thought, We can only hope. And try. (p. 236)

Baynes longs for a world in which "morality is easy because cognition is easy," but that is not our world.

Purple Knee Bands and Falling into the Moat

How does the *Changes* come in? We might worry that it is a way of evading complexity, a *deus ex machina*, a divine voice that reveals the truth. It is sometimes spoken of that way, particularly when personified as "the Oracle," but that isn't how it works, in the story or in real life.

A reading from the *Changes* doesn't just express the complexity of the moment—it participates in that complexity. The meaning emerges from the interplay among the question asked, the statements from the text, and the situation we face. All three are open to interpretation and those interpretations are interdependent. The result is a complex process in which we view our situation in terms of the hexagram but also interpret the hexagram in light of the situation, and in all of that we also come to a clearer understanding of the concern that led us to do the reading in the first place. The entire process works through the concrete.

Consider the reading that leads Frank into the reflections with which we began. His question is straightforward: "Should I attempt to go into the creative private business outlined to me just now?" (p. 53) He receives hexagram 11, Peace (Tai 泰), with a changing line at the top. The hexagram statement is:

> PEACE. The small departs,
> The great approaches.
> Good fortune. Success.

The line statement is:

> The wall falls back into the moat.
> Use no army now.
> Make your commands known within your own town.
> Perseverance brings humiliation.

Although the first is positive and the second mostly negative, these bits of text (just seven and thirteen characters in the Chinese) give no clear answer, even in light of Frank's specific question. While we might say that the first is vague (so many things could count as small or big), the issue with the second is its utter concreteness. What in Frank's situation is the wall? What counts as his own town, and what would a command be? Frank focuses on the tension between the two outcomes, one good and one bad. His first insight is on how the two might relate:

> Hell, he thought, it has to be one or the other; it can't be both. You can't have good fortune and doom simultaneously.
>
> Or . . . can you?

Of course you can, and if all things are interconnected, you must! There's no pure good or pure evil, no pure success or pure failure. So he immediately learns a basic lesson about complexity. But it isn't just an abstract principle, as the question is: Which part of the situation is good and which bad? Frank's first interpretation is that the jewelry business will succeed, but the very same actions will lead to a Third World War. Later, though, he brings about a different reading by returning to the complexity of the *Changes* itself. If the line at the top is changing, then the hexagram is on its way to becoming hexagram twenty-six, the Taming Power of the Great (Daxu大畜). That too is a good outcome. The difficulties appearing in the line statement are necessary for transition to a better position. Good things arise through difficulties, just as difficulties arise from good fortune. Another lesson for living with complexity.

The meaning of the *Changes* results from active and creative engagement with the text, the concrete world, and our own mental state. The message we take from it can be revised again and again as the situation changes. When asking about the prospects for their business, Frank receives hexagram forty-seven, Oppression—Exhaustion (Kun 困) (p. 102). The hexagram judgment is not quoted but it says:

> Oppression. Success. Perseverance.
> The great man brings about good fortune.
> No blame.
> When one has something to say,
> It is not believed.

Tagomi receives the same hexagram at the same moment but finds nothing specific in it, just a general ill-omen (p. 102). Frank's reading includes a moving line in the fifth place:

> His nose and feet are cut off.
> Oppression at the hands of the man with the purple knee bands.
> Joy comes softly.
> It furthers one to make offerings and libations.

What in Frank's world is the man with the purple knee band? Who is punished by having his nose and feet cut off, and who gets the joy? Frank first decides that they will not get the money they need for the business. Then the money arrives. Frank reinterprets the situation and the lines. He concludes that it refers to some future trouble, but one he might not be able to recognize ahead of time. Childan receives the same hexagram and changing line, but in contrast to Frank or Tagomi, he is put at ease (p. 106). He has just given a gift to Paul and he now sees that making an offering will be helpful.

If the *Changes* is so open to interpretation, how does it guide? On the one hand, the *Changes* encapsulates general principles for dealing with complexity—bad results might come from what is good, outcomes lie not in our actions alone but in relationships, success can only come when the moment is right, the most important factors in a situation are often hidden. On the other hand, the process of interpretation requires attentiveness to the concrete complexity of the moment. The *Changes* forces us, as Childan says, to be *yinnish*. The characters ponder their situations, seeking the missing details that might map onto the images of the hexagram's message. The interdependence of the question, situation, and hexagram requires continually attempting to construe the moment from different angles and with different frameworks.

Part of what we gain is self-knowledge. In the first appearance of the *Changes* in the novel, Frank asks how to deal with Wyndam-Matson and then whether or not he will see Juliana again (pp. 18–19). On the surface, neither outcome is helpful. The first is obvious and the second evades the question, telling him only that Juliana is wrong for him. Neither of these hexagrams are so explicit, though. The meaning is his own—the first hexagram confirms that he already knows what he needs to do and the second prompts him to recall something he tries to suppress. This conjunction of multi-perspectival reflection on the complexity of a situation along with widely applicable advice allows the *Changes* to function as a practical guide, even if we see the determination of the hexagram as just random. It gives no definitive answers, but definitive answers are more than we should expect.

The Inner Truth

One key point in the story might throw this interpretation of the role of the *Changes* into question. In the end we learn that the alternative reality depicted in *The Grasshopper Lies Heavy* was generated by the *Changes* itself. When Juliana asks the *Changes* why it did this, she receives hexagram sixty-one, "Inner Truth" (Zhongfu 中孚) (pp. 246–48). The hexagram statement is never quoted in full, but is the following:

> Inner truth. Pigs and fishes.
> Good fortune.
> It furthers one to cross the great water.
> Perseverance furthers.

Juliana sees the message as unambiguous. It says the reality depicted in Abendsen's novel is the truth, his alternative reality is the true reality. Are we to trust her? Juliana ignores any element of interpretation and evades the need to pause and ponder, but the function of the *Changes* in the novel and in practice shows that its messages are never so clear. Who are the pigs and fishes? What is the body of water that she (or we) should cross? Tagomi receives the very same hexagram, but, reflecting in the immediate aftermath of a heart attack, he sees its ambiguity:

> What had the oracle last said? To his query in the office as those two lay dying or dead. Sixty-one. Inner Truth. Pigs and fishes are least intelligent of all; hard to convince. It is I. The book means me. I will never fully understand; that is the nature of such creatures. Or is this Inner Truth now, this that is happening to me?
>
> I will wait. I will see. Which it is.
>
> Perhaps it is both. (p. 231)

Dick himself said that he used the *Changes* in writing the novel (*Vertex* interview). Did he ask the same question and get the same answer? Which then is the truth—the alternative reality of *The Man in High Castle* or that of *The Grasshopper Lies Heavy*? Both? We never know the meaning of the *Changes* with final certainty. What the *Changes* reveals, though, is the contingency and complexity of any given world.

Our reality, the alternative reality of *High Castle*, and the alternative alternative reality of *Grasshopper* are all possible. That we ended up in exactly this one depended on a complex web of seemingly insignificant events, including farts and butterflies, ultimately beyond our grasp or control.

The Inner Truth is that our world arose with the same contingency as the throwing down of a bunch of yarrow stalks. Under such conditions, the best we can do is crawl slowly onward, trying to be as attentive, creative, and adaptable as possible.

16
How Close Is That World to Our World?

BRETT COPPENGER

The Man in the High Castle asks us to imagine a dystopian world. Dystopian worlds stand in stark contrast to utopian worlds: places where things could not be better. A dystopian world is supposed to strike us as frightening or scary (as opposed to the bliss of utopia).

If the Second World War had not gone our way, if the evil Axis had won the war, what scary world would we be living in? *The Man in the High Castle* aims to explore this scenario. The premise of the show is not what's true in the real world (our world, where we defeated the Nazi scum), but what the world *would* look like *if* the Nazis had won.

The Man in the High Castle and Possible Worlds

The Man in the High Castle is an exploration of what philosophers call a possible world.

As I write this chapter I am sitting at a bar, typing on my computer. That I am sitting at a bar typing on my computer is what is true of the actual world (our world: the real world).

However, that these things are true *need* not be the case. It's easily conceivable that I *could* have chosen not to type this chapter right now, or even, not to come to this bar right now. What each of these situations describes is other ways things could have worked out.

That I am at a bar is a *contingent* truth—meaning that it is true, but it didn't have to be that way. A contingent truth can be contrasted with a *necessary* truth. Contingent truths are those where we can conceive that they might not have been true. There is no absurdity in supposing that something else might have happened instead. Necessary truths are those where we just can't conceive of them not being true.

That I am wearing a white shirt is a contingent truth. It's true that I'm wearing a white shirt—take my word for it—but it's easy to imagine me wearing a black shirt. However, that every triangle is three-sided is a necessary truth: it could not have been otherwise, we can't imagine a triangle with four sides—that four-sided thing you're thinking of isn't a triangle, it's a quadrilateral!

That I am typing this chapter is a contingent truth; it did not have to be that way. That I exist at all is a contingent truth, it did not have to be that way—I might possibly never have existed.

Each different potential outcome of how things are represents the many different possible worlds that could have existed. However, it seems to most of us, only one of those possible worlds is also real: the actual world. In fact, woven into the very fabric of the *Man in the High Castle* storyline is the continual tease of other possible worlds. Randall, the prisoner in the cell next to Frank Frink, describes the mysterious newsreel films being collected, showing the world not as it is, but as it could be—showing different possible worlds.

The Proximity of the *Man in the High Castle* World

What makes *The Man in the High Castle* especially interesting is not just thinking about a possible world where the Nazis celebrate VA Day. Instead, we're asked to explore how close this fictional dystopia is to our world. Trying to cash out how close a possible world is to the actual world is difficult. One way of seeing the idea is to think about the number of truths that would differ between the real world and the possible world.

For example, the person sitting next to me in this bar has a black shirt on. In one very close possible world, everything about the actual world is the same, except she's wearing a green shirt. So there could have been a world that's exactly the same as our world, except for this woman's different shirt choice this morning. That possible world seems very close to our actual world—the difference is very minor. In another possible world, we can imagine this woman's parents never meeting. So this woman wouldn't exist and couldn't be sitting next to me in the bar. The world where this woman's parents never met is further from the actual world (much more different) than the world where this woman merely chose a different color shirt this morning.

What makes *The Man in the High Castle* so exciting is trying to figure out just how close the fictional dystopian world really is to our actual world. The fictional world seems to be very much like the actual world. Both worlds revolve around human relationships on the planet Earth. Both worlds have the same physical laws and most of the same human history. In fact, as far as we can tell, both worlds are identical up until some point in the 1930s. We're left to wonder exactly how and when the two worlds became different.

There are some clues as to what's different. We know a nuclear bomb was dropped by the Nazis that fundamentally changed the course of the war. We know that America lost the war and the Nazis and Japanese won. We know this is why VA day is celebrated.

However, we also know there are a lot of similarities between the actual world and the fictional world. In the fictional world Frank still has a sister named Laura. In the fictional world there's still a San Francisco and a New York (of course, in the fictional world these have ceased to be cities in the United States!).

Brett Coppenger

Knowledge in the Real World

Traditionally, philosophers have thought that knowledge is "justified true belief." Just because someone believes something, does not mean they know it: some of our beliefs are false. But just because someone has a true belief does not mean they have knowledge: the person may have arrived at their true belief simply by chance. Think of someone who believes that the US president is in New York City simply because they consulted a magic eight-ball and it told them the president is in New York City. Such a person doesn't really *know* the president is in New York City, even though they believe it and it happens to be true. For them to know it, their belief has to be, not just true by chance, but true *and justified*. So, the argument goes, some kind of justification—such as good evidence or good reason to believe it—is needed for a true belief to qualify as knowledge.

Recently the theory that knowledge is justified true belief has fallen on hard times. A number of philosophers, beginning with Edmund Gettier ("Is Justified True Belief Knowledge?"), have pointed out that you can have a belief that is true and justified, and yet still not knowledge.

Here's an example of a Gettier-type problem (though this one was put forward not by Gettier but by Alvin Goldman). Consider the (imaginary) example of Barn Façade County. Barn Façade County is part of an extensive movie set. In Barn Façade County most of what appear to be real barns are simply barn façades. The producers of the movie wanted a landscape with a lot of barns, so they constructed a lot of barn façades, since it was a lot cheaper to construct a lot of barn façades than to build a lot of real barns. There are some real barns in the landscape, but only one in ten of what look like barns are real barns. The other nine out of ten are just barn façades.

Now imagine the following scenario:

> As Joe Blake drives from New York to the Neutral Zone he naturally forms lots of beliefs about the world around him. He believes the air smells clean and refreshing, he believes the road is open and

> smooth, he believes he will not be caught with the film, and he casually believes that the structure directly to his right is a very nice barn. However, as it turns out, unbeknownst to him, he is actually driving through Barn Façade County. But by an unlikely coincidence, the structure directly to his right really is a very nice barn, a real barn and not a barn façade.

In this case, it seems as if Joe's belief is justified: he's looking (in broad daylight) at the structure to his right. If any of our perceptual beliefs are ever justified, then surely this one is! In addition, the belief is also true. As it turned out the structure is a real barn! However, many philosophers tend to agree that in that kind of case Joe would not *know* that the thing to his right is a really nice barn. Mere chance played too crucial a role in this scenario.

Remember, the vast majority of the barns in question are not really barns, they are barn façades. If he had pointed in any other direction, we can imagine, the thing that he would have pointed at would have been a barn façade. Joe was rather lucky to have actually pointed at the one thing in the vicinity that was a real barn.

Robert Nozick's Account of Truth Tracking

According to Nozick (*Philosophical Explanations*) knowledge requires meeting a very specific set of conditions. According to Nozick, "To know that p is to be someone who would believe it if it were true, and who wouldn't believe it if it were false." Nozick's analysis of knowledge can be boiled down to the following four necessary conditions where p = some proposition, S = some subject:

Condition 1: p is true.

Condition 2: S believes that p.

Condition 3: not-p → not-(S believes that p).

Condition 4: p → S believes that p.

Conditions 1 and 2 are straightforward enough. My knowledge that today is Friday requires that it actually is Friday (the proposition is true), and that I believe it's Friday (the proposition is believed.) The remaining two conditions express subjunctive conditionals; if something *were* the case what *would* happen. Condition 3 requires that our beliefs be safe, If p weren't true, S wouldn't believe that p. Condition 4 requires sensitivity, If p were true, S would believe that p.

Nozick uses the idea of possible worlds in an effort to help explain safety and sensitivity. Thus, to understand condition 3 we need only consider the closest possible world where p is false. If, in that world S would not believe that p is true, then S's belief is safe. Additionally, to understand condition 4 we need only consider the closest possible worlds where p is true. If in that world, S would believe p, then S's belief is sensitive.

Nozick's Account in Action

Nozick's account is aimed at capturing the intuition that says this should not be an instance of knowledge. To see why Nozick's account delivers this result, one need only consider the closest possible world where it is not the case that the thing in front of me is a very nice barn. Clearly, in that world, the thing I would be pointing out would be a barn façade (remember, this is the closest possible world: we're trying to imagine the scenario most like the scenario in the example except for that one detail). However, if the thing in front of me was a barn façade, crucially, I would still believe that the thing in front of me was a very nice barn.

And so, since in the closest possible world where the thing I believe is false, it would still be the case that I would believe the same thing. As a result, my belief would be a violation of condition 3, and thus, would not qualify as knowledge. Put another way, in the closest possible worlds where p is false my beliefs do not change, so my belief is not safe. In Nozick's terms, whatever it is that is that's causing my belief in this world, that thing is not tracking truth in close possible worlds, and as a result the belief fails to be knowledge.

The Problem for Nozick: Abominable Conjunctions

Although Nozick's account of knowledge looks good at first glance, it does have problems. If Nozick's right, then it seems as if we can imagine some hypothetical situations that would result in some very awkward results. Consider the following couple of examples:

Example 1

Imagine that the Nazis have conspired to murder the Crown Prince of Japan. Now suppose that the statement that Jones murdered the Crown Prince is true and I believe it. I believe it on the basis of a newspaper I read. That would fit Nozick's theory: according to Nozick, I would know that Jones murdered the Crown Prince.

But now, consider the following circumstances. Jones was ordered to murder the Crown Prince by an SS officer who was very cautious. To ensure the Crown Prince's death, the SS officer ordered ten other hit-men to carry out the assignment. Each individual hit-man had instructions to kill the Crown Prince only if the hit-man in front of them failed.

Furthermore, this very cautious mastermind also hired someone to falsely report to the newspaper that Jones murdered the Crown Prince in case all the hit-men failed. As a result, it seems as if, according to Nozick's account, I know that Jones murdered the Crown Prince. This is because in the closest possible worlds where it was false that Jones murdered the Crown Prince I would not have believed it (I would have read in the paper that one of the other hit-men murdered the Crown Prince). However, even though I can know that Jones murdered the Crown Prince, it seems as if I do not know that someone murdered the Crown Prince. This is because, in the closest possible worlds where that statement would be false, I would still believe that it was true (even though the Crown Prince was not murdered, the newspaper would still report that he was). So, I'm left with the conclusion that I can know that Jones murdered the

Crown Prince, but at the same time not know that the Crown Prince was murdered. And this is weird!

Example 2

After making it to the Neutral Zone, Trudy is famished—and broke. Imagine that she finds herself at an all-you-can-eat pancake breakfast. Trudy allows herself to indulge; she will worry about how to pay later.

Consider the statement that Trudy ate less than a pound of pancakes. Suppose that this statement is true, and that she believes it. Perhaps she loves eating pancakes, does it often, and has become very good at judging how much pancakes she consumes. However, imagine the possibility that she eats more than fourteen pounds of pancakes. In such a case let's say it's true that such over-eating would result in hallucination: Trudy's accurate sense of how many pancakes she had eaten would completely desert her.

So, in the case where she eats more than fourteen pounds of pancakes she cannot know that she has eaten less than fourteen pounds of pancakes. But then we're left with the conclusion that Trudy can know that she ate less than a pound of pancakes, but at the same time not that she ate less than fourteen pounds of pancakes. And that is weird!

What each of these examples is illustrates is that our beliefs, even if tracking the truth, can fail to amount to knowledge.

Returning to the High Castle

Even if the implication of Abominable Conjunctions proves too bitter a pill to swallow for an account of knowledge, it might still be interesting to consider how safe and sensitive the beliefs of the characters in *The Man in the High Castle* are. Or, to put it another way, just how close is that world to our world?

Much of the commonsensical knowledge of the characters tracks the truth. I know that the Moon travels around the Earth. I know that Germany during the 1940s was a country. Each of these beliefs (and many, many more) would count as knowledge in the actual world and in the fictional dystopia of *The Man in the High Castle*. In the closest possible world where the Moon does not orbit the Earth, the Earth would have no Moon. But, in that world I would not believe the Moon orbits the Earth. In the closest possible world where Germany was not a country, I would never have learned about Germany being a country.

In addition to the knowledge that overlaps, there is also knowledge that is relative to each specific world. That the characters know that the Nazis won the war is safe. If the Nazis had not won, then none of them would have believed that the Nazis had won. Similarly, in the actual world, we know that the Nazis lost. In the closest possible worlds in which the Nazis had won, we would believe that they had won.

The Man in the High Castle consistently plays on the idea that this dystopian world is so close to our own world. We seem to have so many truths in common. The realization that our world could have been so easily this eerily different world is captured by the idea that so much of our knowledge in this world would still be knowledge in that world. In fact, it's suggested that it was just the actions of a select few that separate that world from our world.

In the closing scenes of the last episode of Season One, Adolf Hitler asserts that "Destiny lies in the hands of a few men." While there are many different possible worlds, it's most interesting to consider those possible worlds that, while being mostly like ours, are just a few big events from being very different.

17
When Worlds Diverge

ANANYA CHATTORAJ

"If the Allies had lost World War II, then North America would have been ruled by Germany and Japan."

That's a pretty common thought going through the heads of many students learning about world history for the first time. When trying to figure out whether that statement would be true or not, I'm betting that you'll imagine a new world that's exactly like our world up to the point of World War II. You'll probably try to figure out whether this world you're imagining is plausible, given what you know about our world.

In our world, you exist, I exist, and this volume of *The Man in the High Castle and Philosophy* exists. We also know that in our world, Nazi Germany lost World War II to the Allies, which led to the events of Nazi Germany not taking over North America. Our world is basically the world whose events and objects feel the most familiar to us. In Philip K. Dick's new world, instead of the Allies winning the war, the Allies end up losing the war. Dick provides us with the details of this new world in *The Man in the High Castle*.

Philosophers talk about counterfactuals (if-then statements), like the one above, through the use of possible worlds. A possible world is exactly what it sounds like—a world that resembles our own but is different in some meaningful way. It's just a way our world could have turned out if things had been slightly different. Nazi Germany winning World War II is definitely one of the possible ways in which our history could have been different.

In *The Man in the High Castle*, the Allies did lose the war, and now, much of North America belongs to the Nazis, and the West Coast of North America belongs to the Japanese with something like a demilitarized zone of the Rocky Mountain States separating the two regimes. When reading or watching *The Man in the High Castle*, we realize that though this fictional world is definitely different from ours, it's not *that* different. It's not like pigs fly around in *The Man in the High Castle*, or it's not like gravity flipped the other way, or it's not like aliens are controlling everyone's minds (well, they might be, but much like if we were being controlled in our world, *The Man in the High Castle*'s characters wouldn't know about it, just as we don't).

Let's assume that in the fictional *Man in the High Castle* world, all pre-1933 events were the same as in our world. The people who existed in our world before 1933 also existed in the pre-1933 *Man in the High Castle* world. The difference only starts in 1933 with the assasination of Franklin Delano Roosevelt. So what's the deal with Tagomi travelling between the two worlds? Is that even possible if the two worlds are actually distinct possible worlds? And if it is possible to travel between worlds in the way that Tagomi does, are they really separate worlds or just parts of some larger world that seems to revolve around Tagomi?

What in the World Is a Possible World?

The main philosophers' definition of possible world comes from David Lewis. Lewis (while he was alive) argued that possible worlds are quite real in the same sense that our actual world is real. We really have no reason to think that possible worlds aren't real—after all, we use them when thinking of the if-then statements for events that didn't occur like the one I mentioned at the start of this essay. Lewis outlines four doctrines of possible worlds in his book *Counterfactuals* (pp. 85–87):

1. **Possible worlds exist**
2. **Possible worlds are the same sorts of things as our world**
3. **Possible worlds cannot be reduced to something more basic**
4. **When we distinguish our world from others by claiming that it alone is actual, we only mean that we live here. "Actual" has no meaning other than referring to the world we live in.**

Lewis also goes on to describe more about possible worlds in his book *On the Plurality of Worlds* (pp. 69–81) which leads us to two more criteria for possible worlds:

5. **Possible worlds are spatiotemporally isolated from each other (worlds cannot be related to each other either in space or time)**
6. **Possible worlds are causally isolated from each other (the events of one world can't affect the events of another world if both are separate possible worlds).**

Given these six criteria a possible world must fulfill, we can start assessing the world portrayed in *The Man in the High Castle* to see whether or not it really is a possible world. Points #2, #3, and #4 may be the easiest to show, so I'll start with those ones.

The Same Sort of Thing as Our World

When Lewis says that possible worlds are the same sorts of things as our world, he asks the reader to explain what sort of world our world is. Whatever sort of world that is, he claims, is the same kind of thing as a possible world (*Counterfactuals*, p. 85). When thinking of possible worlds in this way, we can merge points two and three. Our current world is just the type of world with some sort of a structure filled with a bunch of stuff. For instance, our world is the type of world that has objects (whatever these objects may be), but it is not reducible to these objects. Regardless of whether these are your favourite pencils, toasters, and people, you wouldn't say that the world is reducible to a pencil, toaster, or even a person that exists in our world. The world simply is something which has objects in existence.

Our world is also generally accepted to be the type of world that has some form of causality, so there's a predictable order of events; if I place a piece of paper over a campfire, it will burn. The fire causes the paper to burn. Again, the world is not reducible to any one set of chain of events or even any physical laws. If we were to try to describe our world to the aliens that may or may not be controlling us, we wouldn't just say that the world is defined as someplace where fire causes paper to burn. This obviously wouldn't be an exhaustive description of our world, but it's enough for us to begin to understand what type of world our world and a possible world must be. A possible world must be the same type as our world, one with objects and events maybe some other stuff.

With this description, it certainly seems pretty clear that the world represented in *The Man in the High Castle* meets points #2 and #3 as well. It seems like there are objects in this world—Mr. Childan makes sure of that with his shop of "antiques," Tagomi has his Zen garden, and *The Grasshopper Lies Heavy* is certainly a thing of great interest for our main characters.

There are even people in the *Man in the High Castle* world similar to how our world has people. These people do the same sorts of things as our people—they fall in love, they go on adventures, and they work in cubicle-esque government jobs hoping to someday fall in love and go on adventures. There's also some sort of structure in the way objects are that is similar to the structure in our world—gravity certainly still exists in *The Man in the High Castle*. The world is also not reducible to either its objects or its structure alone. *The Man in the High Castle*'s world is as rich in its history, people, and culture as our world.

What if Our World Wasn't the Actual World?

Point #4 refers to how the term "actual" relates to us. This means that our world isn't the actual world for people like Tagomi, Mr. Childan, Frank, or Juliana. Our world is only the actual world for us because it's our frame of reference when talking about other worlds. Mr. Childan, Frank, or Julia think that their world, the *Man in the High Castle* world, is the actual world and the videos from the High Castle represent the "possible world" where the Allies won the war.

Tagomi, on the other hand, might be more confused about which world is the *actual* world, because he has had the opportunity to see both our actual world and his own actual world. What he identifies as the actual world is still presumably the *Man in the High Castle* world, because he supposedly has more ties to that world and he knows how to navigate the *Man in the High Castle* world (after all, he was confused by seeing the freeway construction in the TV show and by not being respected at the coffee shop in the book).

The key point to take away is that a possible world will be the actual world to the inhabitant of the possible world. This doesn't conflict with anything we've learned about the *Man in the High Castle* world either through the TV show or through the book. Going back to point #2, since the inhabitants of our world are the types of objects to assume that the world we live in is the actual world, it only makes sense to assume that the inhabitants of the *The Man in the High Castle* world are the type of people to assume that the world they live in is the actual world.

What if Tagomi Got to Visit Our World?

Point #5 is where things start to get complicated, thanks to Tagomi being able to "visit" our actual world (his possible world). Remember that Lewis's fifth point in the list above states that possible worlds are not connected to each other through space or time. This means that if any two parts of a world are related in space or time, then they are part of the same world. If Tagomi is related to our world in some way, then it must mean that the *Man in the High Castle* world is actually part of the world we live in. Now, I don't think this is necessarily the case, at least not in Season One of the TV show. Despite Tagomi's "visits" to our world as represented in the show, the *Man in the High Castle* world is still distinct from our actual world due to the nature of Tagomi's "visits." Mr. Tagomi's relation to our actual world in the book is slightly more complicated due to his interactions with the police officer and the people on the street.

In the show, we don't get to see very much about Tagomi's visit—we can't even be sure it is a visit. He doesn't interact with people by speaking to them, and nobody acknowledges him. He just stands up from the bench and looks around in awe at the vastly different world. To us, the viewers of the show, it could just be a vision he got from holding onto the new American jewelry. Going off of what we saw in the last episode of Season One, his first experience in our actual world had no interaction.

Going back to what point #5 actually means, Lewis writes that for any possible individual, if every part of them is related to another possible individual's parts, then the two individuals must inhabit the same world as "worldmates" (*Plurality of Worlds*, p. 71). Worldmates are simply beings who belong to the same world (not people who live in different possible worlds)—if I may be so bold, you're my worldmate and I'm yours.

Being spatially related to someone essentially means that you can measure a distance between them and yourself, and being temporally related to someone means that you can use phrases like "I bought a miniature pig ten minutes after I saw that eccentric couple have a fist fight under this streetlamp," or "I ate all the chocolate cake an hour after she told me not to touch it, since it was for our friend's birthday"—you can relate yourself to the other individual using time as a metric. TV-show Tagomi cannot boast any such relation to our actual world just from what was shown in the last episode alone. Since TV Tagomi did not interact with any person, nor did he have a two-way interaction with any object in our actual world, it's not clear that he really visited our actual world. It's quite possible that all he had was some sort of a vision, or an imaginative experience about what seems to him to be a possible world.

The book version of Tagomi, however, is a whole different story. In the book, Mr. Tagomi interacts with a police officer regarding his puzzle jewelry, a passerby regarding the upcoming Embarcadero Freeway, and a coffee shop patron regarding his lack of respect for Mr. Tagomi (*The Man in the High Castle,* pp. 220–26). Not only can Tagomi now say that "I spoke with a police officer before speaking to a passerby before speaking to a man in the coffee shop," but those individuals can say the same thing; the police officer can tell his child, "I spoke to a man who has the same puzzle as you earlier today"; the passerby can tell his friends, "I spoke to a man who had never even seen the freeway before!"; and the coffee shop patron can certainly make a remark about this odd Japanese fellow expecting to be revered. They all now have a story they can tell about Tagomi, some more interesting stories than others. Book Tagomi is related to these individuals, and the individuals are now related to Tagomi. This means that the *Man in the High Castle* world presented in the book fails criterion #5, and now it cannot be considered a possible world. Instead, it must be a part of our own world.

Lewis does briefly discuss island worlds in his talk of possible worlds (*Plurality of Worlds*, pp. 75–76). Island worlds are connected worlds that could form a possible world when taken as a whole. For instance, in the book, the world where Mr. Childan, Frank, and Juliana reside is one island world where the Allies lost World War II, and the world where Mr. Tagomi visits and interacts with the three people is another island world where the Allies won World War II. We can take the two worlds to be islands of the same, larger possible world. Tagomi is essentially the bridge between the two islands.

What if Tagomi Influenced Our World?

Now the question remains whether the TV show *Man in the High Castle* world holds up to the requirements of point #6, which says that a possible world must be causally isolated from other possible worlds (p. 78). This means that in any world, if an event A causes an event B, and in the closest possible worlds to that world, A does not occur, neither does B. For example, if reading this article causes you to read more philosophy, in the closest possible world that doesn't have your Doppelgänger reading my Doppelgänger's article, your Doppelgänger wouldn't read more philosophy.

Now, if an individual causes event B in world one, the closest possible worlds wouldn't have that same individual causing event B. By closest possible world, I simply mean possible worlds that resemble the actual world in as closely as possible and with the fewest changes. For example, if in the actual world, Abendsen wrote *The Grasshopper Lies Heavy* which incited political unrest, then this political unrest cannot spread to the possible world since the possible world must remain unaffected by the actual world.

Since Tagomi has had no two-way interaction in Season One of *The Man in the High Castle*, it's safe to assume that he hasn't been the cause of any events in our actual world. However, he holds a position of power in *The Man in the High Castle* world, and can presumably cause a great number of events. What happens, then, if he starts causing events using the knowledge he gains from the visit to our actual world? This may be similar to Abendsen in the books, since it is implied that he uses the *I Ching* to somehow glean information about the truth of how things ought to have been (the Allies winning the war) in order to write *The Grasshopper Lies Heavy*.

Mr. Tagomi, as the trade minister of the Pacific States of America, can influence the course of events when interacting with the Reich. What if it were the case that Tagomi used the things he saw in his vision to cause certain events in the *Man in the High Castle* world? Would this transgress criterion #6? It seems to me that this does not transgress point #6, if there is no two-way interaction between him and our actual world. His using this information to influence *The Man in the High Castle* events would be the same as anyone starting to influence events in their own world using spiritual revelations or even through information they learn about themselves through dreams.

The book version of Tagomi does have two-way interactions with members of the other world. By speaking to each of the members of our actual world, Tagomi seems to be the cause of these events. Here, I'm defining events as loosely as possible—the police officer, passerby, and man in the coffee shop simply speaking where they may not have spoken were Tagomi not present counts as an event in itself. These events would mean that both the *Man in the High Castle* world has Tagomi, event A, cause conversations with individuals, event B. The actual world referred to in *The Man in the High Castle*, then, is no longer causally isolated from *The Man in the High Castle*, leading us to believe that the two worlds in the book are actually part of the same world where *The Man in the High Castle* is one "island world" and the representation of our actual world is another "island world."

What if Tagomi Really Did Exist?

I left the discussion on point #1 until last, since the notion of asserting, as David Lewis does, that the *Man in the High Castle* world represented in the TV show is a really existing world may seem odd. It's hard to suspend belief on the fact that this is a TV show, and is so clearly fiction.

At the beginning of this chapter, I mentioned the if-then statement: "If the Allies had lost World War II, then North America would have been ruled by Germany and Japan." We can use possible worlds to assess the truth of this statement; if in the closest possible world to our actual world where the Allies had lost World War II, North America had been ruled by Germany and Japan, the statement would turn out to be true. To be close to our world, the other world should have the least amount of differences as possible, and the differences that do exist should be plausible. It certainly seems to me that if the Allies had lost World War II, it's possible that North America would have been taken over by Germany and Japan. The possible outcome of North America being ruled by Germany and Japan were the Allies to have lost World War II exists. It's this existence of the possible outcome that we can refer to when thinking about how exactly possible worlds exist. If we think that the if-then statement above is true, then we must think that the world where such a thing occurs exists.

There are some philosophers, called "strict modal realists," who would say that these possible outcomes in the form of worlds really exist in time and space in the same way that our world exists. Remember that we wouldn't be able to interact with this world (points #5 and #6), if it's truly a possible world. In this manner, the world and individuals represented in *The Man in the High Castle* may really exist in the same way as our actual world, assuming that watching the TV show that represents this world doesn't actually count as us interacting with the world, it could even be a possible world that makes the statement, "If the Allies had lost World War II, then North America would be ruled by Germany and Japan" true.

Mini Worlds

The Man in the High Castle gives us an excellent chance to think about the "What if . . ." scenario of the Allies losing World War II. David Lewis presents a few criteria for a world to be considered a possible world, and the TV representation of *The Man in the High Castle* can represent an actual possible world with Tagomi as a key individual in this world because it doesn't go against any of Lewis's criteria.

The book version of the *Man in the High Castle* world, however, fails Lewis's criteria of world isolation since Tagomi really does interact with members of the new American-led world he visits. This does leave the option for the book in its entirety to represent a new possible world—one with two mini worlds, the mini–*Man in the High Castle* world and the mini-representation of our actual world where Tagomi visits.

I have only been considering Season One. Tagomi's actions in the middle of Season Two certainly change the TV show's classification as a possible world, so it may no longer be the case that the world presented in *The Man in the High Castle* can make our opening if-then statement true, and the world we think of when we think about the alternate possibility of World War II wouldn't be *The Man in the High Castle*.

VI

A Video Darkly

18
How to Deal with Reality when We're not Built To

T.J. ZAWADZKI, STEPHANIE J. ZAWADZKI, AND MACIEJ A. CISOWSKI

> We do not have the ideal world, such as we would like, where morality is easy because cognition is easy. Where one can do right with no effort because he can detect the obvious.
>
> —Baynes in *The Man in the High Castle,* p. 236

Philip K. Dick's writing can be infuriatingly confusing. It feeds readers many ambiguous signals that convey no real sense of closure—and *The Man in the High Castle* is no exception. Perhaps bewildering the audience is the intent, not a side-effect.

We crave closure for many of the questions we find in Dick's books, and he consistently denies us any real sense of arriving at definite answers. Lingering confusion and the gnawing feeling that the true nature of reality is just out of our grasp have been the dominant themes of both Dick's narratives and philosophical and psychological studies for decades. Together, they all attest to how important understanding and embracing confusion can be in the business of dealing with reality.

~~Detecting~~ Disrupting the Obvious

Much of Dick's writing can be read as an internal dialogue, telling the story of a person who is venturing into the outermost limits of his ability to understand reality. Through his ventures, Dick shows us just how universally limited human cognition actually is, and how he just can't seem to shake the feeling that his brain may not have his best interest at heart.

Dick and his characters are unusual, statistically speaking. A person stuck in an uncomfortable state of indecision and confusion is considered psychologically anomalous. Philosophy begins in wonder, claimed Socrates, but most of us effectively avoid wondering too much about the overwhelming world around us. We are great at building simplified models of the world that fit neatly within the bounds of our comprehension.

There's a mountain of evidence that the vast majority of people are excellent at both ignoring and misrepresenting reality. In *The Man in the High Castle*, characters' lives are shaken when those simplified models come into question. As the characters' coping strategies break down, they react differently to the signs that another, parallel reality might exist. What ties these various reactions together are the characters' efforts to rebuild reality into a single, predictable, and sensible whole.

Cognition Is ~~Easy~~ Hard

The world we live in is far more complex than any one person can comprehend. In the mid-twentieth century, psychologists (and, apparently, Dick) were simultaneously inspired by the boom in technology and horrified by the crimes of the recent two world wars. And so, they sought the limits of human understanding and moral decision making. They didn't have to look nearly as far as they had hoped.

Psychologists quickly discovered just how much information our brains are tasked with processing and how poorly they cope with funneling that information into our consciousness. Over the decades, thousands of psychological experiments have demonstrated the surprisingly constrained limits of human understanding. Our brains have incredibly short attention spans and an extremely tight bottleneck through which they ingest the world's information. It turns out that our brains are fundamentally lazy to a point where research psychologists started calling the human mind a *cognitive miser*. Nearly every study seemed to uncover a new way that our brains prevent themselves from spending energy to, you know, *think*.

People are not sponges that passively absorb all the information they're exposed to. To be able to process and react to our highly complex world in a meaningful way, we need social and cognitive programs—a kind of brain software that helps us organize and filter information. The conditioning we experience as children (in addition to some basic programming that we receive right out of the box) teaches us how to perceive and understand (and distort) the world, allowing us to become functioning members of society.

Patting ourselves on the heads and stroking our bellies at the same time is already a tall order for our brains—not to mention keeping us upright citizens who salute the proper flag and reasonably respond to infinitely complex moral dilemmas. To deal with the incessant demands of life, our cognitive misers have developed endless arrays of coping strategies which fundamentally change the way we view and interpret the world.

Our brains are incredibly selfish and insincere, hiding from us just how many cognitive blind spots they really have. The research is in: our brains are lazy and they're lying to us, especially when we're under pressure. Left alone, few of us would rationally and peacefully come to terms with the existence of parallel realities, even if the evidence was clear as day on a screen right in front of our eyes.

Psychologists revel in such self-deprecating knowledge. They've spent decades cataloging and defining what they like to call *cognitive biases* that demonstrate just how stupid we are as proud members of our species. They've found hundreds of them. These biases affect every aspect of our thinking. You don't have to be Obergruppenführer Smith to be susceptible to the *just world bias*, which allows him to dismiss his war atrocities as "necessary evils" in the face of a people (his *own* people, by the way) whose "decadence" was adequate justification for their country's subsequent division and occupation. Because, in a just world, there are no unjust punishments.

These hundreds of cognitive biases suggest a fact which Dick was equally thrilled to revel in: *our perception of reality is a creative process*. Neither he nor psychologists were the first ones to toy with this idea. Philosophy's *radical skeptics* have a long-standing tradition of undercutting assumptions about what's considered obvious, real, and objective.

Why is this *skepticism* so *radical* (and possibly *far out*)? It questions the validity of our most fundamental experiences and thoughts. Here's a thought experiment: Bertrand Russell's "five-minute hypothesis" challenges readers to prove that the universe did not spring into existence five minutes ago and instill in them a complete set of false memories. Radical skeptics challenge the very foundations of reality with the same tools that other philosophers use to build apparently seamless rules of linear reasoning. Likewise, *The Man in the High Castle* skillfully builds a compelling and feasible alternate world, just so it can leave us confused about this new world's fundamental nature.

Philosophy's radical skepticism, mainstream psychology, and *The Man in the High Castle* share a common sentiment: our brains aren't able to handle much more than an unshakable sense that we are competent in dealing with reality. Instead of freezing our mental processes in an endless loop of trying to prove that the world exists, we move on. In order to function, we need closure and a feeling that the worldview we've created does not contain glaring holes and inconsistencies. So, our brains manufacture a view of the world that works around skeptical questions.

Creating ~~an Ideal~~ a Justified World

"But I thought my brain and I were close . . . Aren't we on the same side?"

Unfortunately, you're not. Your brain is limited, selfish, constantly under assault by your senses, and incessantly bothered for direction from your body. Your brain needs an easy way to protect itself from you and the world around you. It needs a blanket to hide under.

Consistency is a Snuggie for your brain. Consistency makes your brain feel good, like warm apple pie in your favorite Canon City diner. As soon as any new obstacle or decision crosses your path, your brain seeks its comfort zone in the familiar and the known. Feeling consistent lets your brain go into autopilot mode, content with its cognitive frugality. No extra thought wasted.

But, sadly for our little cerebral misers, we're sometimes forced to make choices in situations that are radically new, with no readymade answer, or to act in ways that we don't believe are morally right. These situations cause our brains to panic, creating what psychologist Leon Festinger called *cognitive dissonance*.

Presenting a brain with anything that challenges its usual functioning causes great discomfort to its owner. While Dick was writing *The Man in the High Castle*, Festinger was running experiments that showed just how easy it is to instill this deep psychological discomfort. Cognitive dissonance occurs every time we act inconsistently with our existing beliefs, feelings, or previous actions. It causes intense emotional and physical irritation, like needing to pee with no bathroom in sight. After having his worldview challenged in many ways and being forced to act against his fundamental values, Tagomi tries urgently and endlessly to restore his balance. No wonder! His brain was experiencing a dissonance overload.

A lengthy conversation with a radical skeptic might result in a similar response. The questions they have for us, not unlike the confusing events that *The Man in the High Castle*'s characters have to deal with, can burrow into our deepest sense of self and upset the unwavering certainty with which we assume the world to be a concrete, real, and stable object.

Usually when a new situation appears that requires we think or act inconsistently with our previous beliefs or behavior, our brains immediately want to know who's to blame. If there is something outside of us telling us how to act or think or feel, then there's no problem. We have an excuse, an *external justification,* for our inconsistency. Voilà! We were only following orders. Dissonance dissolved. Feeling consistent again brings the needed sense of a satisfying resolution.

In the show, Frank Frink, a previously upstanding citizen of the Pacific States of America, has an impressive battery of such external excuses for his newfound rebellious and dangerous behavior. Frank's cellmate talks him into opposing the Kempeitai and ultimately expediting his sister's death. The Kempeitai's murderous actions inspire his assassination plot of a peace-loving crown prince. Juliana Crain's recklessness leads Frank into absurd standoffs with the Yakuza, the Resistance, the Kempeitai, and the Nazis. And while his actions might be seriously inconsistent with his previously cautious character, he has plenty of external justifications.

Not everyone can be so fortunate. For Joe Blake and John Smith finding excuses will not be so easy. Joe, a Nazi double agent infatuated with a Resistance member, will have to figure out how to reconcile his allegiance to the Reich and his love for the woman he's been ordered to kill. John, on the other hand, will have to decide whether it will be easier to kill his own son or try to keep him alive in the Reich's America.

When there's no one else to blame, *internal justification* is the only cure for cognitive dissonance. We simply have to change our perception (of ourselves or the world) in order to stay consistent and eliminate any lingering confusion. Both Joe and John will have to either change their belief in the Nazi ideology, or change their beliefs about the people they hold dear. Only once they settle on an internal justification can their brains kick back and click the consistency autopilot back on.

In the book, Tagomi, an otherwise balanced and peaceful man, murders two Nazi assassins disguised as street hooligans. Baynes fears that Tagomi will never mentally recover from having committed the murders. The mental math is just too clear: two lives killed to save one cannot be justified. The evil Tagomi has committed does not fit with his understanding of a balanced, Taoist world.

Where One Can Do ~~Right~~ Wrong with No Effort

Situations like Tagomi's are where Dick's views on the discomfort of cognitive and moral confusion shine. Following the murders, a traumatized Tagomi swims in a muddled reality. He doesn't know what to do next. He doesn't know how or if he can ever go back to his old way of thinking. He wanders to a park bench. Uncomfortable and overwhelmed, he grips a small token of reality—a shapeless, formless piece of jewelry. He stares at it, seeking an answer, desperate to know why his life has led him to this point. What could possibly justify his actions? However, he does not seek any external justification, an outside excuse to explain away his shame and discomfort.

In the height of his confusion, drowning in dissonance, but refusing to be fooled to fall into a cognitively biased assessment of his actions, Tagomi becomes the only character in *The Man in the High Castle* to be transported to a parallel universe—one in which his murderous actions never occurred *because they never had to*. Pushing through this cognitive agony allows Tagomi to experience a side of reality only otherwise accessed by *The Man in the High Castle*'s characters indirectly through spiritual practice (via the Oracle known as the *I Ching*). His experience might be Dick's dramatic example of transcending the self to better understand our place in the world. This is the case even if that understanding means a farewell to his peace of mind and a warm welcome to cognitive and moral anguish.

While Tagomi is the character closest to experiencing a cognitive revolution and achieving any degree of true clarity, other characters tread through calamity into new modes of thinking as well. Juliana also goes through murderous and near-death experiences which propel her toward evidence revealing alternate realities.

Karl Jaspers, a German-Swiss philosopher and psychiatrist, called circumstances that elicit such illuminating responses *limit situations.* Like cognitive dissonance, *limit situations* are deeply confusing and bring extreme discomfort. These uncomfortable situations force us to go beyond our usual boundaries where we happily stew in cognitive limitations.

What happens when you see your sister gunned down by the Kempeitai or you fall in love with a woman you've pledged to kill? According to Jaspers, events like these are opportunities to mutiny against our cognitive misers and acquire a new mode of thinking—one that goes past simply changing our minds. Unfortunately, limit situations often push people beyond language, so their experiences can't easily be written down or relayed to someone else.

To show the unnamable is an artistic goal of many, including Philip K. Dick. He weaves elaborate narratives of confusion, ambiguity, and deprivation. Both his characters and readers are purposefully perplexed and overwhelmed by the worlds that Dick describes, to a point where they often succumb to radical skepticism themselves and question the very foundations of their realities.

Dick often provides only a single, relief-like product to his readers by guiding his characters through confusion to perceptual epiphany. In *The Man in the High Castle*, the Oracle guides some characters through crisis with no personal growth, while others are brought spiritual and cognitive revelations—and mortal danger. Radical skeptics likely wouldn't be surprised by the paradoxical nature of these outcomes. To them, it's only logical that paradoxical challenges are best explained by the absurd.

Morality Is ~~Easy~~ Hard

In Dick's *The Man in the High Castle*, challenging our perceptions is the role of spirituality and its scripture. The *I*

Ching is revered as a window to collective wisdom. But, it doesn't really give the characters the clarity they seek. At best, it offers a blurry glimpse of what might be happening behind the scenes.

Unlike in the TV show, readers of the novel, *The Man in the High Castle*, will find most major characters seeking the *I Ching's* guidance to help cope with their confusion. Dick's Tagomi, Juliana, and Frank all use it to justify their decisions. In the book, Juliana is so familiar with the *I Ching* that she alone is able to uncover the secret of the Man in the High Castle. After numerous consultations with the *I Ching*, Frank is able to create art that inspires Tagomi's cognitive revolution. Even the book's characters who don't directly appeal to the *I Ching* are influenced by its direction. Robert Childan is finally able to make a non-conformist, deeply moral decision against his own material interest because he is given a lecture on the spiritual importance of *Wu* (and Frank's *I Ching*-inspired jewelry is chock full of *Wu*).

The *I Ching* is supposedly able to offer insight far greater than any single brain could manage to produce. Like his characters, Dick sought direction out of the fog of his confusion in spirituality that relies on collective wisdom. It feels natural that his characters glimpse realities beyond their personal biases after they delve into ancient philosophies written millennia ago by countless people—it's what their author did. As he was writing the novel, Dick consulted the *I Ching* to resolve major plotlines and conflicts in the story, making it an integral creative part of the work. In turn, the book's Man in the High Castle writes his book (*The Grasshopper Lies Heavy*) by consulting the *I Ching*, making it an integral part of the characters' story. In contrast, the only person using the *I Ching* in the show is Tagomi.

Such as We Would Like

Did Amazon's *The Man in the High Castle* deprive the rest of its characters of the paradoxical revelations that the *I Ching* delivers in the book? Not necessarily. The subversive magic of the *I Ching* is brought to life through a battery of scattered newsreels, forming a videographic version of *The Grasshopper Lies Heavy*. Through these films, the power to confuse characters and audiences remains firmly intact. Both versions of *The Man in the High Castle* drown everyone involved in limit situations and dissonance-inducing moral dilemmas, making both versions of *The Man in the High Castle* gloriously confusing alternate histories of each other.

The Man in the High Castle is full of signs that elicit meaningfulness—but rarely any immediate clarity. It's a challenging stream of consciousness that by design can't be bothered to be a standard cohesive whole with a satisfying conclusion. So the next time you sit down to read or watch *The Man in the High Castle*, let yourself confront your own perception of reality. And do what many of Dick's characters do.

When confronted with confusion, force your brain out from its warm blanket of consistency and into the turbulent limits of cognitive dissonance and radical skepticism. Turn on *Radio Free Albemuth*. Tune in to the frequencies of the *Vast Active Living Intelligence System*. And drop out of the rut of your own reality with some *Chew-Z*.

19
What if Evil Had Won?

VERENA EHRNBERGER

What if things had played out differently during World War II? What if some crucial battles had been lost? What if evil had won? This question lies at the heart of *The Man in the High Castle*. The alternate universe Joe and Juliana live in, shows us a world where evil is such a common phenomenon that the people living with it on a daily basis tend not to question it anymore.

Juliana's long-time boyfriend Frank says that he's happy in their basement apartment; as Americans that's the best housing he and Juliana can get, and he doesn't know any different. Discrimination against people because of their race or religious beliefs is such a common thing for them that it is deeply ingrained in the culture they live in. And, although nobody talks about the concentration camps and killings, everybody knows that those killings take place.

When Joe is on his way through the country, he wonders about the weather and about something that looks like falling snow, until a policeman tells him that the "snow" is coming from the hospital: "Tuesdays they burn cripples, the terminally ill—drag on the state." In this alternate universe, taking the lives of innocent people is just another order that people execute to a large extent without questioning it. Doing evil is a simple job that needs to get done.

This is what philosopher and political theorist Hannah Arendt calls the "the banality of evil" that she observed during the Eichmann trial (Arendt, *Eichmann in Jerusalem*) that followed World War II. Arendt was one of the most influential and most controversial political philosophers of her time. Like many others, she tried to make sense out of the horrible experiences of World War II. Her reporting of the trial of Adolf Eichmann for *The New Yorker* won her fame and contempt (from some) at the same time.

In a world where everybody is doing the wrong thing, doing the right thing suddenly seems wrong. And, as Arendt realized, the problem doesn't lie in the fact that those people are evil beings, but rather in the fact that they choose to look the other way.

No One Has the Right to Obey

Wickedness may be caused by absence of thought.

—Hannah Arendt

SS-Obersturmbannführer Adolf Eichmann gained notorious fame after World War II for having organized the Holocaust. It was Eichmann's task to execute SS-Obergruppenführer Reinhard Heydrich's plan to solve "the Jewish question." He was responsible for the mass deportations into concentration camps. During his trial in 1961 Eichmann stated again and again that he had just obeyed the orders of his superiors and that everything that he did was in accordance with the law of that time.

The universe of *The Man in the High Castle* shows a similar point of view. Asked about the concentration camps, Obergruppenführer Smith states: "It was necessary work. We did it." Smith uses the same justifications for his deeds as Eichmann did. In a system, where everybody gets assigned his small part nobody really feels responsible for those big decisions about life and death anymore—especially not when those grave decisions are totally within the realms of the current legal order.

The society and the legal system of the Third Reich were organized in such a way that "the Führer's words had the force of law" (as Eichmann explained, during his trial). It is a common legal principle that orders, to be disobeyed, must be evidently unlawful. Shockingly, this was really not the case with the orders Eichmann obeyed. The orders he received, the orders to take part in the system which killed millions of innocent people, were in total harmony with the laws of his time, and with the philosophy of the society he lived in. So, why should he have ever considered disobedience?

Obedience is also the concept the society in *The Man in the High Castle* is based on. "Those weren't your orders," Obergruppenführer Smith has to remind Joe, time and time again. "The law is the law," says Chief Inspector Kido to Frank, when he captures him. "We are all subject to rules, and if we fail to live by them, the consequences are severe," says Chief Inspector Kido to Juliana during her questioning.

Obedience has its advantages, at least at first sight. Living by strict rules that don't allow any individual thinking can give a certain level of security. Life's a lot easier if you don't have to think for yourself. If you don't have to decide according to your own moral judgement, you don't have to bear the responsibility for the difficult decisions life demands of us, because all those decisions already have been made. It appears to make the world a much simpler and more predictable place. It makes the world more secure. And we all love security.

Obedience is the easy way out of the human dilemmas we all have to face. It's easy because we don't have to think (which requires intelligence), we don't have to make judgments (which requires a moral code), we don't have to make decisions (which requires self-confidence), we don't have to stand by those decisions (which requires a strong will), we don't have to defend our opinions against the will of a group (which requires courage) and we don't have to bear the responsibility for our doings (which requires strength). Obedience is easy.

And, obedience is also convenient. It spares us all of the hard work we, as humans, have to do. Being human is complicated. And obedience conveniently scratches some difficult tasks from our lives' to-do lists. This is what Arendt means when she says: "No one has the right to obey." She calls it a "right" because obedience has lots of advantages for people who don't want to put in the hard work to become an intellectually and emotionally fully developed human being. And it has just one big disadvantage that those people don't really care about (especially when they are the ones profiting from the rules): the surrendering of personal freedom.

Obedience can give a lot of security. It just takes away our freedom. So, the concept of obedience is at the very core of the human condition. Because isn't that what all our human struggles are ultimately about? In the end, our existence within any system we are born into—be it family, a social caste, or a whole society—takes place between those two poles, security and freedom. And every system comes with its own set of rules. Each and every one of us has to decide which rules to follow and which rules to break.

The Man in the High Castle depicts a system in which we can perfectly see those human needs for security and freedom play out. Although it is, of course, easier to trade security for freedom, if you belong to the ruling class of a society (like Kido and Smith), this trade is not always merely based on the merits of privilege alone; it is rather a trade that is based on the individual person's need for security. After all, there are people who trade security for freedom in the inferior classes too (like Frank and Mr. Childan). The characters in *The Man in the High Castle* can't, as we soon realize, be divided into categories like "ruling class" or "inferior class." Rather they can be divided into people who value security more than freedom, and people who don't.

There are people who dare to think on their own—irrespective of their social status: Trade Minister Tagomi, Nazi Rudolph Wegener and Juliana Crain. For those people freedom is a good worth losing their life over. And then there are people like Frank and Mr. Childan. They don't mind living a limited life, as long as the oppressors leave them alone for the most part. That's not because they believe in their oppressors' ideologies, but because they prefer the security of obedience to the insecurity of freedom. For people who are so prone to want security, it takes a lot of injustice to drive them to the point where they finally react. For Frank, it takes the murder of his sister, nephew, and niece.

Freedom is definitely a good worth fighting for. But there are also those characters where we can't really figure out what they are fighting for. Some might not so much be fighting for freedom, but rather against their status as an inferior class. And some might not be fighting for security, but rather for their privileged position. Mr. Childan, who needs security just as much as Frank, makes no secret of his fight against his inferior status. And Oberst-Gruppenführer Heydrich, who is risking a war, might be rather fighting for his privileged position (in contrast to Chief Inspector Kido who is risking his life to prevent one); neither freedom nor security seems to matter to Heydrich. Chief Inspector Kido seems to be fighting for security and is even willing to kill himself to prevent a war. Obergruppenführer Smith strongly believes in the Nazi ideology, and he values the security the system provides for him and his family, but is he fighting for his personal and professional security or is he rather fighting to stay a member of the ruling class?

Even if obedience might sometimes seem the easiest way out of trouble, there's always a cost to obedience: We might just not notice it at first. "Don't let them take your soul!" Frank's cell mate shouts while being taken away. The soul, in this context, is a metaphor for our humanity. As humans we think and we feel. If we stop thinking and feeling in order to obey, we lose everything which makes us human. As Frank finds out when his family (who always obeyed) gets murdered, the security obedience provides, is only an illusion. And the cost of obedience might even be higher than the cost of fighting for freedom.

Is the world of *The Man in the High Castle* so much different from our own? We too have to follow the rules (go to work, spend money on consumer goods), or we have to live with the insecurities that the absence of a regular job and luxurious consumer goods lead to. In the much smaller context of family life we oftentimes find this conflict between security and freedom (if we're unlucky enough to be born into a family that doesn't respect personal freedom to a certain degree). In this case, we either live by our family's rules, and are not able to decide our fate on our own, and thus risk a certain degree of obedience (that we're more or less comfortable with, depending on the level of security we need); or we're free but without the security of the system with whose rules we refuse to conform. The idea of obedience is deeply ingrained into our societies, too. Every system has its rules. The rules may vary. But the existence of certain rules is a given. And humankind is too varied, in its ways of being and thinking, to ever find rules all of us can agree upon.

What *The Man in the High Castle* is showing us mercilessly is that obeying the rules no matter what without ever thinking for ourselves is the one fatal error we as human beings can make. Because obedience takes away what makes us human: our ability to think, and our ability to feel—our rational and emotional intelligence—and, last but not least, our freedom. We, as humans, are thinking and feeling beings. If we let somebody take away our right to think and if we learn to dismiss our feelings in favour of a ruling system—how much humanity is there left in us, then?

The Banality of Evil

> The sad truth is that most evil is done by people who never make up their minds to be good or evil.
>
> —HANNAH ARENDT

When Eichmann referred to his orders during his trial, the judges first believed that he was trying to talk himself out of his culpability, that he was trying to hide his true motives by using empty words and phrases to fool the judges, that he (like so many criminals before him) was pointing fingers to avoid responsibility. Hannah Arendt noticed that that was not the case. "Except for an extraordinary diligence in looking out for his personal advancement, he had no motives at all." Her following realization forever changed the way we think about evil: "He merely, to put the matter colloquially, never realized what he was doing."

One of the most unsettling moments in *The Man in the High Castle* is when we get to know the family Smith on a deeper level. As a Nazi family, we expect them to be evil. But what we see is a loving mother, well-behaved children struggling with ordinary problems, and a genuinely caring husband and father—Obergruppenführer Smith; whom we took for an utterly heartless and cruel being, right up to that moment.

When Obergruppenführer Smith and his son Thomas talk about one of Thomas's classmates, a boy who is a "proud non-conformist" who dares to challenge teachers in class, we learn a lot about the paradigms on which the Smith family's life is based. Conformity, for them, is a greater good than freedom. Thomas has been taught to conform to society's rules, to bring honor to his family and to his school, and to serve his country by being a high-performance citizen. For Obergruppenführer Smith individuality is synonymous with egoism, which is "the path to moral decay," as he explains to his son Thomas. For him, the success of the group is more important than the fate of the individual. And who's to say his take on society is worse than the next one?

If we take a closer look at the ideology the family Smith believes in, we can see that it is not all bad. They just value other goods than we might value. Being useful to society matters more to them than their individual life. The will of the group is more important than personal emotions. Their life is based on family, achievement and community. When we look at these priorities, we might even understand them. It is not their priorities that are evil. Just one crucial thing is: the idea of blind obedience.

What's so disturbing about Obergruppenführer Smith's family is the co-existence of normality and cruelty. It's hard for us to believe that a man so evil could be capable of love. This normal and almost likeable side of a cruel Nazi disrupts our ordinary conception of evil. Evil like that, our moral instinct tells us, is done by cruel psychopaths. But it is not psychopaths we're dealing with, it is ordinary people profiting from a system that privileges them and who are not asking questions, just like Smith. That doesn't mean that Obergruppenführer Smith is not cruel. He certainly is. (We've seen him mercilessly torture human beings, after all.) But Smith does not enjoy cruelty as much as, for example, Heydrich does. Smith simply sees it as a necessity; a job that needs to be done. And he doesn't focus on his feelings of repulsion, if he has any.

To examine "the strange interdependence of brainlessness and evil," as Arendt put it, became a task that occupied her mind for the rest of her life. Arendt realized that evil doesn't lie in the malicious character of bad people. It lies in the unreflecting character of ordinary people; people who choose to forfeit their right to think. "Might the problem of good and evil, our faculty for telling right from wrong, be connected with our faculty of thought?" she asked.

What Arendt observed during the Eichmann trial was that the accused didn't feel guilty for his bad deeds, because he was not the one who gave the orders. According to Nazi ideology, personal opinions and feelings do not matter. In a society, where the individual does not matter, there is no one left to blame. These questions—the question of how his deeds might be judged, or perhaps even how he himself might judged—never even occurred to Eichmann. He did not question his deeds because that was simply not part of his orders. Challenging the existing order and making judgments was simply not a part of his upbringing. (Just like it is not a part of Thomas's.) Evil lies in this failure to think. And therein also lies its banality: when we try to understand this kind of evil, we realize that there's nothing there. No deeper ground on which it is based upon. Eichmann, and many other Nazis, did evil without deeper motives; they did it just out of sheer blind obedience.

Arendt had set out to understand the human mind but all she found was brainlessness.

This blind obedience was the mindset of Eichmann's times. In *The Man in the High Castle*, it still is. That is as true for the Nazi Empire as it is for the Resistance. The men who send Joe on his mission to the Neutral Zone expect him not to ask questions and to follow their orders, just like the Nazis or the Japanese do. Being obedient is a part of this time's upbringing. Therefore, what we observe in *The Man in the High Castle* is not so much a fight between the "good" resistance and the "evil" Nazi-Japanese Empire. It is rather a fight between the typical "brainlessness" of those times and people who dare to think for themselves.

See No Evil, Hear No Evil, Speak No Evil

> His guilt came from his obedience, and obedience is praised as a virtue.
>
> —HANNAH ARENDT

In *The Man in the High Castle* we see a society full of people who don't ask any questions anymore—because it's simply more convenient not to. Not speaking about evil, not questioning deeds that go against humanity, is a recurring theme throughout the show. This mindset is depicted in the show by the three monkeys, a Japanese proverb that Juliana stumbles upon when she is looking for "Sakura Iwazaru." The three monkeys, as a Japanese colleague explains to Juliana, are Mizaru, who sees no evil, Kikazaru, who hears no evil, and Iwazaru, who speaks no evil. Juliana realizes that Iwazaru ("Speak no evil") is the one the surveillance room at the Nippon Building is named after.

This old proverb originally refers to the art of kindness. It suggests that we can live a much happier life if we choose not to focus on the bad deeds of others, and not to badmouth others. In the world depicted in *The Man in the High Castle* this proverb gets another, more sinister, meaning: looking the other way and letting evil take its course.

In a world where "the practice of self-deception had become so common" that it was "almost a moral prerequisite for survival," as Arendt noted, not noticing reality has been turned into a virtue. If you don't notice it, you don't have to think about it. This way you are able to live a much more anxiety-free life. Looking the other way might be the thing that comes most naturally to us, when we have to face hard truths. This mindset is represented in the character of Juliana's stepfather, Arnold. He works in the surveillance room at the Nippon Building, and therefore knows a lot about the evil that is going on, and still refuses to acknowledge it.

But even people who have learned to look the other way, will experience moral dilemmas which will force them to take a good hard look at reality. These moral dilemmas will make obedience a more difficult task, and will open up a chance for them to experience freedom. "Brainlessness" is not a static character trait; even people who prefer to follow the rules to feel safe, like Frank and Joe, can begin to think again, when their world of rules doesn't feel safe anymore. The inability to "see no evil" is what happens to Juliana when her sister Trudy gets killed by the Japanese. It's what happens to Frank when his sister and her kids get murdered. It's what happens to Joe when he meets Juliana. And it even happens to Obergruppenführer Smith.

Obergruppenführer Smith has to face quite a few moral dilemmas because of the ideology he believes in. While he justifies his killings in the concentration camps by reference to his orders, he throws Captain Connolly from the roof when he was following Heydrich's order to kill Smith. Then, Smith has to make the decision to hand his old friend Rudolf Wegener over to the SS. "Emotions can't be allowed to interfere with what is right," he explains to Joe, and to himself.

In a system where evil is so common, doing good is nothing but a temptation you have to resist. Obedience, on the other hand, is praised as a virtue. When Obergruppenführer Smith is sitting in the office of the doctor who diagnoses his son with a congenital disease, he can't not hear the evil the doctor is suggesting: the euthanasia of his son. This might be the first time in Smith's life that he realizes how unfree he actually is.

Freedom can make life seem unbearably complicated. That's why some of us want to follow the simple rules obedience provides. The banality of evil lies in the fact that men lack the courage to be free, that they'd rather not think for themselves. But it just as much lies in the fact that men lack the emotional independence to stand on their own due to their upbringing. The banality of evil lies not only in those undeveloped minds that don't use their capacity for thinking, but also, or even more so, in those undeveloped hearts that don't dare to, and have never learned to, stand on their own.

20
The Spirit of Abstraction

CHRISTOPHER KETCHAM

We abstract every day. We look at the larger world and see something in it that attracts our attention and we focus on it. That's abstraction. Just imagine if we could not abstract the tiger hiding in the jungle.

In traffic we abstract the car that is on course to pass us by from one that looks as if it is heading right for us. If you have a peanut allergy you must abstract whether that brown paste is peanut butter or hummus. How does it happen? Something catches our eye as being important, not quite right, or different. It produces a question which requires our focus to better understand what this thing is my mind has abstracted. Sometimes we just say, okay, that's what it is and move on. Sometimes like the tiger we go, uh oh, and prepare to deal with the danger posed by the abstraction.

However, what if the abstraction is another person? Not just the big hulking brute that we see towering over the crowd in front, but a *particular kind* of person we have been told is fundamentally bad, inferior, or some other derogatory term. The Nazis abstracted the Jews from all other persons and tried their best to exterminate them. In other words, the world where Germany and Japan won World War II in *The Man in the High Castle* maintains the idea that whole categories of people can be abstracted as non-persons, especially Jews and black Africans.

Right away you say, this is not right. However, it's easily done. Your hated rival football team you abstract from the colors of their uniforms and their logo. Is that bad? What if you sent in your goons, your thugs, into their stadium to beat up everyone wearing their hated colors of orange and white? That's not good. Who gave you the idea that your team is better than their team? What criteria other than the colors that they wear are different? Good question. Abstracting the tiger can be productive; but like the Nazi treatment of the Jews, abstracting can be damaging, hurtful, or worse.

Gabriel Marcel said, "As soon as we accord to any category, isolated from all other categories, an arbitrary primacy, we are victims of the spirit of abstraction." The spirit of abstraction arises when someone plants the idea that this or that people, culture, color, religious belief, or some other aspect of being is less than you, and as a result you are superior to them. You work with Baynes who just happens to like your rival team. Do you abstract Baynes as a lesser person? Only on game day. Alright, but what if you are in Nazi Germany and Baynes is a Jew and you are what the government calls Aryan? If you don't abstract Baynes the Jew and assert that you the Aryan are superior to him, you will not only be shunned by fellow Aryans but may also face other consequences. You like Baynes, so why do you have to abstract him into this arbitrary category called hated Jew? It is the arbitrary nature of abstraction that Marcel called the spirit of abstraction.

Anti-Semite and Jew

Put the shoe on the other foot. Let's say you are *the* Baynes in *The Man in the High Castle*. You were born a Jew. What do you do? Why not try to do everything possible to disguise your Jewishness? Baynes tells others and gets others to believe he's Swedish. He has abstracted himself from his Jewishness.

Baynes the "Swede" and Mr. Loetze, a German, happen to sit together on a rocket transport. They engage in simple conversation until Loetze, who sees a new building below, says "It looks as if it was designed by a Jew." Loetze then says he wants a good Aryan companion to help him navigate San Francisco, so he tells Baynes that they are both racially kin, that is, Germans and Swedes. Baynes carries on a conversation with himself asking what is it about the Germans and their abstractions? Is it something they are born with? Do they understand the destruction that they are causing? They have abstracted themselves as God!

Baynes has had enough. To Mr. Loetze in *The Man in the High Castle* novel he says, "You would not have known . . . because I do not in any physical way appear Jewish; I have had my nose altered, my large greasy pores made smaller, my skin chemically lightened, the shape of my skull changed." Baynes isn't some aging Hollywood starlet trying to restore her vanity. He is trying to "pass" as someone he is not. We can say the same about the starlet, but she doesn't get her plastic surgery to save her life. Baynes changes his appearance; Frank Fink (was Frink) in the television series hides his Jewish heritage so as not to be murdered by the Nazis. How did we come to a place where a person's physical identity must be altered or heritage silenced to live?

How did abstraction of the Jews begin in Hitler's Germany? The population was angry. Hyperinflation and war reparations bankrupted Germany after World War I. Hitler made the Jews the scapegoat. He created a caricature of the Jew so that they could be easily recognized on the street. He made up stories about their cleanliness, their personalities, and their greed. He created an abstracted picture of them and backed it up with "evidence of their malfeasance." *They* are all murderers and rapists. *They* are all unwanted immigrants and are an inferior race to the real original Germans. *They* are taking jobs from the real Germans. *They* are all lazy and won't work and are mooching from the real German people. *They* have taken all of the wealth of Germany for themselves and we, the real Germans, need to take it back. Oh, by the way, *they* killed Jesus.

Wait, how can *they* be taking our jobs and mooching off of us at the same time? If *they* are all mooching, how did *they* get all the wealth of Germany . . . from mooching? How do *they* find time to work if *they* are all murderers and rapists? None of this needs to make logical sense. It only needs to be emotionally powerful to work to marginalize, criminalize, and segregate the *they*. For the Nazis, the *they* were the Jews. Nazis then whipped up German emotions and anger against the Jews.

Isn't this spirit of abstraction a combination of evidence poured upon more evidence that bends both logic and emotion into each other and confuses both? This spirit of abstraction makes *they* different from *us*. It then says that we (*us*) are superior to them (*they*). For this to stick we must be emotionally attached to the idea of our superiority as much as we do when we root for our team at the expense of the other team. This Baynes saw in Loetze and wondered how this could have come to be. Jean-Paul Sartre also saw the emotional context of the abstraction of the Jew, "Indeed, it is something quite other than an idea. It is first of all a passion."

This abstraction is only the beginning. Caricatures of the Jew are plastered all over the newspapers and public places in posters and other visual media. You know a Jew when you see one. Hence, Bayne's plastic surgery to erase his Jewishness and to make him disappear from those who may have known him as a Jew.

The efficiency of Hitler's bureaucracy was its passion to catalogue your ancestry to brand you this or *that*. If you have any of *that* anywhere in recorded history, you are not a this. You don't want to be a *that* because existence is not pleasant for a *that*. Baynes determined to erase his *thatness* so even his neighbors and even relatives wouldn't recognize him and call him out as a *that*. However, not only are the *that* victims but the this are also victims in that they have been duped by the lies those who claim primacy for thisness.

Victims of the Spirit of Abstraction

Wait, how can we, the superior Germans who won the Second World War in *The Man in the High Castle* be "victims of the spirit of abstraction"? We made those who lost the war

(Americans and Europeans) and Jews victims, not us, you say. Understand this, you the so-called Aryan have been duped, snookered, trolled, and your emotions have been brought to boil by lies compounded by more lies that started the war in the first place. Those who protest such lies disappear. They are silenced. You only hear the lies. Nazis told the German people: Just look at our poverty compared to their wealth. They are eating our lunch.

Philip K. Dick echoes another of Gabriel Marcel's notions that lying and war are somehow intertwined and that the lie is both to ourselves and to others. We're never sure which is truth and which is not in *The Man in the High Castle*. Fink, born a Jew, has changed his name to Frink and makes counterfeit collectible jewelry. In the novel, Childan, a collector of long lost things, believes he has a valuable Colt 44, but the knowledgeable representative of Admiral Harusha explains that Childan has been duped by counterfeiters. Though this is true, Childan later finds out that the Admiral's ship was sunk during the war—so who is this "knowledgeable representative"?

Baynes tells Mr. Loetze that he has completely disguised his Jewishness. However, who is Baynes now? He keeps molting like a serpent. Characters lie to themselves and others and Dick often "lies" to us.

Sartre asked why intelligent people don't see through the lies. He said it is more complex than truth, "The rational man groans as he gropes for the truth; he knows that his reasoning is no more than tentative, that other considerations may supervene to cast doubt upon it." Even the rational among us are unsure until we are, sort of . . . Sartre explained, "The anti-Semite has chosen to hate because hate is a faith; at the outset he has chosen to devaluate words and reasons. How entirely at ease he feels as a result." The faith of unending evidence is a powerful tool of the spirit of abstraction.

At first, the rational person doubts what he hears about the abstracted *they* but listens to others. It is the insertion of emotion into rhetoric that begins his journey to become born again and to believe the rhetoric as a new-found faith which is difficult to undermine with a return to reason—because reason has been exorcized from the faith. The abstracted have been given what W.E.B. Du Bois called a *dual consciousness*. Meaning, deep down they know that they are rational humans but the lies and propaganda around them call into question their rationality until they find themselves living in the quasi-world of uncertainty about even themselves. Those in power have the capacity to keep them thinking this way . . . that they are an abstraction, not part of the majority, perhaps not even human.

As Dick did in *The Man in the High Castle*, Marcel saw through the patina of power, of self-proclamation. Marcel said, "It is only through organized lying that we can hope to make war acceptable to those who must wage or suffer it." It appears that in Dick's tale the lies the Nazis told about the Jews and others during the war have metastasized to where society itself has become a lie and those within it have become adept at lying to maintain existence in a bureaucratized world where the truth may not be easily discovered.

Recall that Hitler did not change any laws to implement his 'final solution' that became the Holocaust. He wrote nothing down, never publicly announced his plans, and his orders to his highest henchmen were given orally in secret meetings which were not recorded. He told the German people lies about where the Jews were being relocated to and built walls around the extermination devices he deployed in the death camps so that nobody could see in.

The lie of Marcel's spirit of abstraction begins in resentment for which there is abundance in Dick's work. This resentment eventually becomes like the Nazi's final solution, first for the remaining Jews and then Africans.

How did Hitler and his henchmen do this? Marcel explained. In order for me to agree to war with other peoples or other counties I must "lose all awareness of the individual reality of the being whom I may be led to destroy." I make them non-persons and believe this even with evidence that contradicts this abstraction. Make their real and human faces disappear. You abstract yourself into the victor, the good person, the superior person first. Then you must convert the target *other* into an abstraction, something not personal, not human.

Okay, but not everyone in Germany bought into Nazism, the war, or demonizing the Jews. Yet, the message found its target in those who had been harmed by the depression and those for whom resentment could be elevated to a fever pitch by the pitch of brilliant salespersons and orators—the Nazis and their propaganda machine. "Boycott the Jews" on posters in 1933 began the process of dehumanizing the Jews by blaming them for everything.

How Could Victors Be Victims?

How were German people then and in Dick's story now *victims* of the spirt of abstraction? While hyperinflation in 1920s Germany was real, the cause had many sources such as war reparations, worldwide depression, and inept government. What the Nazis realized is that they could use the spirit of abstraction to produce a kind of disease of the intelligence. This disease of the intelligence eliminates logic for the emotional response of resentment to a target, any convenient target that the Nazis could get people to focus on.

Wyndam-Matson in the *Man in the High Castle* novel and the purveyor of a counterfeit Colt 44 and false provenance explains the process. He tells love interest Rita about how he makes the story more valuable than the merchandise: "Sure. And I know which it is. You see my point. It's all a big racket; they're playing it on themselves. I mean, a gun goes through a famous battle, like the Meuse-Argonne, and it's the same as if it hadn't, unless you know. It's in here." He tapped his head. "In the mind, not the gun." I can make you believe anything with the right story if you have a mind to want to believe. I manufacture the target for your resentment.

To foster the depths of resentment to the target other also requires the making the German race superior as the Nazis defined it. Jews and the Allies from World War I were perfect targets to get economically depressed Germans to begin to resent both and then to declare war on both.

Not in America

That was Germany before and during the war. Even if we lost the war, as the fictional *The Man in the High Castle* proposes, surely, we proud Americans would not succumb to the spirit of abstraction. Remember, our nation was founded in the new idea of freedom for all.

Ahem. Our spirit of abstraction began in slavery. We fought a Civil War to end that abstraction as did the Allies to end the Nazi abstraction of subjugation and Holocaust.

While Lincoln emancipated the slaves in 1863, we were not through with abstracting African Americans. Many southern states declared segregation to be law of the land at the end of Reconstruction in the 1870s, which was just another abstraction to retain whiteness's primacy over blackness.

In what came to be known as Booker T. Washington's 1895 *Atlanta Compromise Speech*, few remember how he called for the southern states to recognize how industrious African Americans are and how they could contribute to the economy if given the chance. All the southern whites heard was his line, "In all things that are purely social we can be as separate as the fingers, yet one as the hand in all things essential to mutual progress."

Southern whites knew they were superior. In the South, it was the dominant rhetoric. It is no wonder then that whites could only hear a great black leader declare that their own sprit of abstraction, segregation, was a good thing, the right thing. They also heard that this same abstraction was endorsed by all black men and women through their leader, Booker T. Washington. How could one person and one person alone, someone who never held any elected office, become the sworn and authoritative voice of an entire race? Even the later Dr. Martin Luther King did not claim such authority.

Just one year After the Atlanta compromise speech, in 1896, the US Supreme court decided *Plessy v. Ferguson*. Homer Plessy was one-eighth black and sat in a white railroad coach. He was removed and jailed. When he sued, he argued that his reputation had been damaged and that whiteness is a form of property giving him right of action or inheritance. He normally could pass for being white. He was like Baynes or Fink in *The Man in the High Castle*, a person who had to disguise his identity to gain the same rights as others who had the property of privilege, whiteness. Plessy had to acknowledge the lie to try to overcome segregation's deprecation of blackness before whiteness—in the spirit of abstraction.

US Supreme Court Chief Justice Brown took up Plessy's property argument and said:

> Conceding this to be so, for the purposes of this case, we are unable to see how this statute deprives him of, or in any way affects his right to, such property. If he be a white man, and assigned to a colored coach, he may have his action for damages against the company for being deprived of his so-called 'property'. Upon the other hand, if he be a colored man, and be so assigned, he has been deprived of no property, since he is not lawfully entitled to the reputation of being a white man.

This case cemented segregation into our system of justice for the next sixty years. It also gave credibility to the notion that whiteness *is* property and is something to value.

Abraham Lincoln reinvigorated the notion of the proud heritage of the people of the United States during the American civil war in his 1863 Gettysburg Address: "Fourscore and seven years ago our fathers brought forth on this continent a new nation, conceived in liberty and dedicated to the proposition that all men are created equal."

This does not sound like the birth of a nation mired in the spirit of abstraction. Yet, the Constitution did not outlaw slavery. A slave was declared to be three-fifths of a person to determine the number of congresspersons for each state. Plessy asked the Supreme Court how this could still be so, and rather than consider the now defunct value of the black person in terms of congressional representation, the court plumbed further into the depth of race itself to abstract primacy for the color white over the color black.

War in Peace

Abstraction, Marcel agreed, is a necessary mental operation to help us achieve our goals and purposes. When we isolate and give arbitrary primacy and the reverse, we become victims of the spirit of abstraction. Primacy isn't only the placing of Aryans before all other races, it is the arbitrary use of the *I Ching* (the book of changes) in *The Man in the High Castle* to determine future action without proper reflection. It is both the resentment and acceptance of the hegemony derived from war.

It is a peace derived from war said Marcel, "but which contains war in a latent condition." Dick leaves us fighting the war now called peace and we are never sure who won. However, as Marcel explained, if peace is derived from the idea of war then there is always war, and peace is only an aspect of war. Dick never assumes the war is over because its peace is never certain and it remains undecided who won, if anyone did. Peace and war become intertwined lies that bleed in and out of society and the characters who live the lie. As Hitler said the day before he invaded Poland on false pretenses, "The victor will not be asked whether he told the truth." Will you ask? Will you question the abstraction?

Dick introduces this mysterious novel called *The Grasshopper Lies Heavy*. It is an alternative history to Dick's own alternative history of *The Man in the High Castle*. Will you see through the alternate reality that the pundits and politicians are spinning to look for your own grasshopper lying heavy? At the end of the *Man in the High Castle* novel Juliana (Frink's wife) says that the purported author Hawthorne Abendsen has not written *The Grasshopper Lies Heavy*. The oracle has, and that oracle is the *I Ching*. The *I Ching* is the truth teller that Germany and Japan lost the war.

Hawthorne explains that yes, he lived in a high castle once, but in a drunken moment decided that his elevator was the vehicle to take him to heaven and Jesus. He moved out of the high castle. He feared the truth about death, the afterlife, and even what the *I Ching* had told him to write. Just who can we believe? Who owns the truth? Certainly it isn't the Nazis for they have created a mythical world that cannot be sustained. Their clinging to power in the face of an alternate truth is not the answer. They have abstracted so much from reality that reality has been bent to where it is unrecognizable.

Dick didn't ask us to believe in the alternate reality but to question it in our daily lives. Race, religion, gender, uniforms are all abstractions that do not define the person. If we can reverse the abstraction and ask about the person inside, we will see that the lie has been perpetrated—not only the abstracted other, but the target of that abstraction.

The believer in the spirit of abstraction's disease of the intelligence has become the victim, the victim of manipulation. To whose benefit is the abstraction? Not you who have been duped by the spirit of abstraction; it benefits only those in power to help them get and keep that power.

21
After Death It Can Get Worse

SAM DIRECTOR

Imagine you're an author who wrote many famous science-fiction books. Unfortunately, you recently died. Sorry about that.

After you died, a producer decided to make a TV adaptation of one of your books. Your writing is almost impossible to adapt literally to the screen, so this producer instructed the screenwriters to make big changes to your original work. The show's a big hit, but it looks significantly different from your book.

In changing your work without your permission, did this TV producer harm you? And, did he harm you even though you're dead? Well, I guess it's pretty hard for you to answer those questions . . . because you're dead.

This fake story about you (unless you really are a famous science-fiction author who went through this experience) is a true story about Philip K. Dick. *The Man in the High Castle* is one in a long series of screen adaptations based on Dick's work. In fact, Dick is the second most adapted fiction writer for the screen (after Stephen King).

Dick died before *any* of these adaptions were released, and many of them, including *The Man in the High Castle*, make big changes to Dick's original works. Were Dick alive and his consent obtained before these changes were made, we would not view these alterations as morally suspect, because the author himself would have consented to them. But the alterations to *The Man in the High Castle* and many other adaptions were made after Dick's death and without his consent.

By altering his work without his permission, have the creators of *The Man in the High Castle* TV adaptation harmed Philip K. Dick? This seems like a strange question to ask; surely, people can't be harmed after they die! If someone were to spit on my grave, that wouldn't be very nice, but it couldn't harm me, because I wouldn't exist anymore. Right?

Well, some philosophers disagree and have defended the idea of posthumous harm.

What Is Harm?

What does it mean to harm someone? Most philosophers agree that the correct theory of harm is the *counter-factual* theory of harm. This theory holds that actions harm people if those actions make people worse uff than they otherwise would have been.

In the original book version of *The Man in the High Castle*, Mr. Tagomi kills two German agents in order to defend General Tedeki and Mr. Baynes. Because he's a Buddhist and believes that no life should be taken, Tagomi is deeply distressed by this experience, and his entire sense of purpose appears to be uprooted. According to the counter-factual theory of harm, Tagomi has been harmed, because, if he had not killed these agents, he would not have experienced this psychological trauma. He would be better off if he had not killed these men. Killing these men harmed him.

Harmed After I Die? How Does That Work?

A posthumous harm is a harm done to a person after that person's death. This sounds pretty strange. If an act harms me by making me worse off than I would have been otherwise, and if death means that I don't exist anymore, how can I be made any worse off than just not existing? The Ancient

Greek philosopher Epicurus put the point pretty well in his *Letter to Menoeceus*:

> When death comes, then we do not exist. It does not then concern either the living or the dead, since for the former it is not, and the latter are no more. (pp. 30–31)

The Man in the High Castle supposes that Franklin D. Roosevelt was assassinated before World War II began. If FDR were alive to see the Allies lose the war, this would have been a great harm to him, because his deepest efforts for victory would have failed. But, in the world of *The Man in the High Castle*, FDR is dead when the Allies lose the war. So, it would be pretty strange to say that FDR could be harmed by the Allies losing. Because he's dead, he doesn't exist anymore, and it's hard to see how he could be harmed while not existing.

Why We Might Believe in Harm After Death

Some philosophers have appealed to intuition to support the idea that you can be harmed after you're dead. For philosophers, an intuition is much more than a gut feeling or a hunch.

When Juliana has a feeling that Joe is hiding something important from her, this is a hunch and not an intuition. An intuition is something stronger; although there are different definitions of "intuition," most philosophers agree that an intuition is a judgment which we don't need evidence in order to believe and which just seems to be true when we think about it. When I think about the claim, "Pleasure is better than pain," it just seems to be true, and I don't need evidence in order to believe it.

The case for the possibility of posthumous harm is based on the intuition that a person can be harmed by an event in her lifetime that thwarts her interests, even if she never discovers that this thwarting has occurred, and even if her subjective experience of her life is unaffected by it. While I'm still alive, I can be harmed by something even if I never find out that it has happened and even if it doesn't actually affect my experience of my life.

Not convinced? Well, take the case of slander. As the philosopher Douglas Portmore says, "it seems that the slandering of your reputation can be harmful to you even if you never become aware of it, even if you never experience any change in how others act around you, even if you never feel any less respected as a result of the defamation." If it turned out that all of your friends were very nice to you in person but were saying terrible things about you behind your back, it seems like you would be better off if they weren't gossiping about you. Because this gossip makes you worse off, it harms you, even though you don't know about it.

Consider the character Robert Childan. In the book version of *The Man in the High Castle*, it's suggested that some of Childan's merchandise in his Americana antiques stores is counterfeit. In this alternate San Francisco there is a booming industry producing counterfeit American antiques, many of which have likely been sold to Childan. For a person whose entire career is based on the authenticity of his goods, the fact that he has counterfeits in his inventory is deeply threatening to Childan. Childan, for much of the book, knows nothing of this. It seems true that, even when he didn't know about any of this, Childan was still harmed by the counterfeits in his inventory.

Joe (Cinnadella in the book, Blake in the show) lies to Juliana (Frink in the book, Crain in the show). In both the book and the show, Joe is a Nazi operative who lies to Juliana about who he is, even engaging in a sort of romance with her. It seems clear that Juliana has been harmed by this deception, even before she finds out about it. She has sex with a man who lied about his identity and with whom she would not have had sex had she known his real identity! Also, she was used without her consent as a part of an assassination plot. All of this is clearly harmful to Juliana, even while she doesn't know that these things are happening to her.

Why do we think that the examples just mentioned involve harm being done to people without their knowledge? We generally think that the thwarting of our desires is harmful to us. If you thwart my desire to do something, this means that you have prevented me, against my will, from fulfilling this desire. It's safe to say that, if my desires are fulfilled, this is good for me, and if my desires are thwarted, this is bad for me.

Admittedly, you may have desires which it is not good for you to fulfill, like a desire to eat a thousand hot dogs or to kill a million people. In the TV version of *The Man in the High Castle*, Joe Smith desires to kill members of the Resistance. It would not be good if Joe fulfilled this desire.

But, assuming that desires are within the bounds of morality and not physically harmful, it seems true that the fulfillment of my desires is good for me and that, if I am prevented from fulfilling my desires, this is bad for me. If something's bad for me, then it makes me worse off than I otherwise would be, which means that it harms me. If my desires are thwarted, then this harms me. And, it doesn't seem to make any difference whether or not I know that this has happened. Either way, I am harmed.

In Childan's case, he doesn't just want to *believe* that his merchandise is authentic; he desires that his merchandise *in fact* be authentic. The fact that some of his inventory is counterfeit means that his desire for authentic merchandise has been thwarted. And, since the thwarting of his desires is harmful to him, even if he doesn't know that it has happened, then he has been harmed by the fact that his merchandise is counterfeit.

And, in Juliana's case, she obviously, like all normal people, desires not to be lied to, not to have sex with people who are manipulating her, and not to be involved without her knowledge in an assassination plot. Given this, Joe thwarts Juliana's desires without her knowing and harms her in the process.

Wait, So I Can Be Harmed After I Die? That Sucks

If we can be harmed while we're alive without ever knowing that this harm has occurred, posthumous harm seems possible. If we can be harmed without ever knowing that this has occurred, then why does it matter if we're alive or dead? Either way, we won't know that the harm has taken place but we have been harmed all the same.

The philosopher Douglas Portmore asks, "If it is not necessary that you learn of the slander, or experience any ill effects as a result of it, for it to be harmful to you, then why would you need to be alive at the time of the slander for it to harm you?" This is made even clearer by the fact that we can have desires that extend beyond our lifetimes. As Portmore says in the case of slander, "Since you can desire to be respected not only while alive but also after your death, the slandering of your reputation, even after your death, can harm you." If the thwarting of my desires can harm me without me knowing it, and if I can have desires that go beyond my lifetime, then I can be harmed after my death.

Consider this thought experiment based on Mr. Baynes:

> Mr. Baynes wants to inform the Japanese government about Operation Dandelion, which is a Nazi plan to obliterate the Japanese Empire in a deadly surprise attack. Baynes painstakingly arranges a meeting with General Tedeki in order to tell him about Operation Dandelion. After much difficulty, he succeeds in telling General Tedeki about the plan. Although this deviates from the book, suppose that Baynes is fatally shot by the Nazi soldiers who infiltrate the *Nippon Times* Building. Then, suppose that, General Tedeki escapes and boards a ship back to Japan to inform the Emperor about Operation Dandelion. Due to the importance of this information, he tells nobody about it, waiting to tell only the Emperor. However, Tedeki suffers a heart attack halfway through the voyage and dies. Nobody ever finds out about Operation Dandelion.

In this case, we intuitively want to say that Baynes has been harmed. His desire was not just to give the information to Tedeki; rather, his desire was that the Japanese Emperor would learn of this information in time to act upon it. That desire was thwarted, and Baynes was harmed as a result, even though he was dead when this occurred.

Has Amazon Harmed Philip K. Dick in His Grave?

The question now facing us is whether or not the changes made in the TV adaptation of *The Man in the High Castle* thwarted some of Dick's desires, thus harming him.

The Man in the High Castle is a difficult book to adapt to a video format. As executive producer, and former adapter of another Dick book, Ridley Scott, said in an *Entertainment Weekly* interview, "it's a hell of a book to break down. There are about nineteen stories in the first twenty pages. How do you make that work? How do you get it down to the bottom line?"

Well, the answer is that, in order to adapt Dick's writing to the screen, many changes are inevitable. The creators of the TV show were well aware of this, but they tried to make changes in ways that preserved Dick's vision. As the creator of the show, Frank Spotnitz put it, "we departed from the novel, but we only did it to try to be more faithful to the ideas, and find ways to dramatize them more clearly."

As Caitlin Gallagher has observed, the three major plots in the TV show (Mr. Baynes in San Francisco, Frank Frink in San Francisco, and Juliana with Joe in Colorado) are also in the book. In other ways, the TV show deviates from the book. The TV show alters the timeline of events that comes from the book. In the book, the very first line begins with the story of Robert Childan, but in the TV show, Childan first appears in episode 4. The TV show changes certain facts about the characters, as well as introducing new characters. In the book Juliana and Frank are already divorced, and Juliana already lives in Colorado. In the TV show, they are engaged, and she begins her story in San Francisco. In the book, Joe's last name is Cinnadella, whereas his last name in the show is Blake. The TV show creates the characters of Chief Inspector Kido, Juliana's half-sister Trudy, and John Smith, none of whom appears in the book. In the book, *The Grasshopper Lies Heavy* is a book, whereas it's a newsreel in the TV show.

Have These Changes Harmed Dick?

Remember, the thwarting of my desires makes me worse off than I would be otherwise, which harms me. And, not only do I not need to know that this has happened in order for me to be harmed, I also can have desires that go past my lifetime; if these desires are thwarted, I can be harmed after my death. If the alterations to *The Man in the High Castle* have posthumously harmed Dick, they must thwart or hinder some desire that he possessed while he was alive and which can extend beyond his death. Which of Dick's desires might have been thwarted by the TV adaptation?

Dick might have desired for movie adaptations of his work not to be made. If this were true, then the TV adaptation would have harmed Dick, because it would have thwarted a deeply held desire. But, the evidence suggests that Dick did not possess this desire. Although he died before he could watch the theatrical cut of *Blade Runner*, Alex Santoso reports that Dick saw "a special effect test reel of the movie" before he died. Upon seeing this version of the movie, he was overjoyed, saying "it was my own interior world. They caught it perfectly." If Dick were against adaptations of his work, he surely would not have had this reaction to *Blade Runner*. So, the TV adaptation of *The Man in the High Castle* can't have thwarted Dick's desire for his works to not be adapted, because he had no such desire!

Second, perhaps Dick was fine with his work being adapted, but desired that no substantial changes be made in the adaptation. If this were true, then Dick would be harmed by the TV adaptation of *The Man in the High Castle*, because it contains fairly significant changes to his book. But, again, Dick's reaction to *Blade Runner* suggests that he did not possess this desire. *Blade Runner* contains substantial alterations to *Do Androids Dream of Electric Sheep?* Dick declared himself happy with *Blade Runner*. If he had desired that no noticeable changes be made to his works in their adaptations, he would not have had this reaction.

Third, maybe Dick, like most authors, desired for his work not to be altered to the point of losing its original purpose. Thus, if the TV show changed his book so much that it lost its original purpose, then the adaption would have harmed Dick. But it seems pretty clear to me that the TV version of *The Man in the High Castle*, despite its changes, is faithful to the overall purpose and trajectory of Dick's book. So, this desire has not been thwarted.

Fourth, Dick cared deeply about the success of science-fiction as a genre. In a letter that Philip K. Dick wrote before his death, he discusses his excitement that *Blade Runner* would help revitalize Sci-Fi as a genre:

> The impact of *Blade Runne*r is simply going to be overwhelming, both on the public and on creative people, and I believe, on science fiction as a field. Since I have been writing and selling science fiction works for thirty years, this is a matter of some importance to me. In all candor I must say that our field has gradually and steadily been deteriorating for the last few years. Nothing that we have done, individually or collectively, matches *Blade Runner* . . . Let me sum it up this way. Science fiction has slowly . . . settled into a monotonous death: it has become inbred, derivative, stale. Suddenly you people have come in . . . and now we have a new life, a new start.

Here Dick signals how deeply he cared about science fiction and how much he desired for it to thrive and innovate. Furthermore, he thought that *Blade Runner* contributed in a major way to this goal. So, if *The Man in the High Castle* had reduced the success of science fiction as a genre, then this would have been harmful to Dick. But, quite to the contrary; the production of this TV show will very likely enhance the recognition of science fiction.

The very fact that you're reading *The Man in the High Castle and Philosophy* shows that *The Man in the High Castle*'s TV adaptation has created a demand for more writing and theorizing about science fiction! So, if anything, the TV adaptation has not thwarted, but rather has fulfilled, one of Dick's deeply held desires.

Parting Thoughts from the Man in a Medium-Sized Chair

If posthumous harm is real, then we should be careful with how we treat the legacy of the dead. When we adapt the work of a deceased author, we ought to have in mind this author's desires. If we don't, we may posthumously harm the author.

However, in the case of *The Man in the High Castle*, Philip K. Dick has not been posthumously harmed by the changes made to his work, because the TV show has not violated any of Dick's desires. Sadly, Dick is dead, but he's no worse off, and maybe even somewhat better off, because of the TV show *The Man in the High Castle*.

Bibliography

Anthony, Karl K. 1988. *A Guide to the I Ching*. Anthony.

Arendt, Hannah. 2006 [1963]. *Eichmann in Jerusalem: A Report on the Banality of Evil*. Penguin.

Arnold, Kyle. 2016. *The Divine Madness of Philip K. Dick*. Oxford University Press.

Augustine. 1964. *On Free Choice of the Will*. Pearson.

Aurelius, Marcus. 1983. *The Meditations*. Hackett.

Balaguer, Mark. 2010. *Free Will as an Open Scientific Problem*. MIT Press.

Baynes, C.F., trans. 1994. *The Classic of Changes: A New Translation of the I Ching as Interpreted by Wang Bi*. Columbia University Press.

Benjamin, Walter. 1968. Theses on the Philosophy of History. In Benjamin, *Illuminations: Essays and Reflections*. Schocken.

———. 2005. The Work of Art in the Age of Mechanical Reproduction. In Lawrence Rainey, ed., *Modernism: An Anthology*. Blackwell.

Berlant, Lauren. 2011. *Cruel Optimism*. Duke University Press.

Bertschinger, Richard, trans. 2011. *Yijing, Shamanic Oracle of China: A New Book of Change*. Singing Dragon.

Boonin, David. 2014. *The Non-Identity Problem and the Ethics of Future People*. Oxford University Press.

Bruner, Jerome. 1987. *Actual Minds, Possible Worlds*. Harvard University Press.

Constantine, Murray [Katharine Burdekin]. 1937. *Swastika Night*. Gollancz.
Coppenger, Brett, and Kristopher Phillips. 2011. Is Justified True *Bluth* Belief Knowledge? In Kristopher Phillips and J. Jeremy Wisnewski, eds., *Arrested Development and Philosophy: They've Made a Huge Mistake*. Wiley-Blackwell.
Cover, Byron. 1974. Interview with Philip K. Dick. *Vertex*.
Crary, Jonathan. 2014. *24/7*. Verso.
Cormack, Mike. 1992. *Ideology*. Michigan University Press.
Debord, Guy. 2000 [1967]. *Society of the Spectacle*. Black and Red.
Denton, Sally. 2012. *The Plots against the President*. Bloomsbury.
Derrida, Jacques, Giovanna Borradori , and Jürgen Habermas. 2003. *Philosophy in a Time of Terror: Dialogues with Jürgen Habermas and Jacques Derrida*. Chicago University Press.
D'Holbach, Baron Paul. 2011 [1770]. Of the System of Man's Free Agency. In d'Holbach, *System of Nature*. Theophania.
Dick, Philip K. 1962. *The Man in the High Castle*. Putnam.
———. 1977. *A Scanner Darkly*. Doubleday.
———. 1991. *The Selected Letters of Philip K. Dick 1974*. Underwood.
———. 1991. *In Pursuit of Valis: Selections from the Exegesis*. Underwood.
———. 1993. *The Selected Letters of Philip K. Dick 1975–1976*. Underwood.
———. 1993. *The Selected Letters of Philip K. Dick 1977–79: Book Five*. Underwood.
———. 1996 [1968]. *Do Androids Dream of Electric Sheep?* Del Rey.
———. 1997. *The Selected Letters of Philip K. Dick 1938–1971*. Underwood.
———. 2010. *The Selected Letters of Philip K. Dick 1980–82*. Underwood.
———. 2011 [1966]. *Now Wait for Last Year*. Mariner.
———. 2011 [1981]. *Valis*. Mariner.
———. 2011. *The Exegesis of Philip K. Dick*. Houghton Mifflin.
———. 2012 [1956]. *The World Jones Made*. Mariner.
———. 2012 [1969]. *Ubik*. Mariner.
———. 2013 [1970]. *A Maze of Death*. Mariner.

———. 2016 [1964]. A Game of Unchance. In *The Eye of the Sibyl and Other Classic Stories by Philip K. Dick*. Citadel.
Epictetus. 1983. *The Handbook (Encheiridion)*. Hackett.
Epicurus. 1994. *The Epicurus Reader*. Hackett.
Feinberg, Joel. 1987. *Harm to Others: Moral Limits of the Criminal Law*. Oxford University Press.
Fumerton, Richard. 1987. Nozick's Epistemology. In Steven Luper-Foy, ed., *The Possibility of Knowledge: Nozick and His Critics*. Rowman and Littlefield.
Gallagher, Caitlin. 2015. How Does "The Man in the High Castle" Compare to the Book? It May Be the Most Faithful Philip K. Dick Adaptation Yet. *Bustle* (November 21st).
Gallagher, Paul. 2012. Nothing Matches *Blade Runner*: Philip K. Dick Gets Excited about Ridley Scott's Film. *Dangerous Minds* (April 18th).
Garber, Megan. 2015. "Edelweiss": An American Song for Global Dystopia. *The Atlantic*. www.theatlantic.com.
Gettier, Edmund. 1963. Is Justified True Belief Knowledge? *Analysis*.
Goldman, Alvin. 1976. Discrimination of Perceptual Knowledge. *Journal of Philosophy*.
Hawthorne, John. 2004. *Knowledge and Lotteries*. Oxford University Press.
Hitler, Adolf. 1998. *Mein Kampf*. Houghton Mifflin.
Holiday, Ryan. 2014. *The Obstacle Is the Way: The Timeless Art of Turning Trials into Triumph*. Penguin.
Hume, David. 2000 [1738]. *A Treatise of Human Nature*. Oxford University Press.
Ihde, Don. 1993. *Postphenomenology*. Northwestern University Press.
Kang, Inkoo. 2015. "The Man in the High Castle" Creator Frank Spotnitz Dishes about Building a Nazi America. *The Village Voice*.
Kattago, Siobhan. 2001. *Ambiguous Memory: The Nazi Past and German National Identity*. Praeger.
———. 2012. *Memory and Representation in Contemporary Europe: The Persistence of the Past*. Routledge.
Lamont, Corliss. 1990. *Freedom of Choice Affirmed*. Continuum.
———. 1999. Freedom of the Will and Human Responsibility. In John Burr and Milton Goldinger, eds. *Philosophy and Contemporary Issues*. Prentice Hall.

Lampe, Evan. 2015. *Philip K. Dick and the World We Live In*. CreateSpace.
Laplace, Pierre-Simon. 1996. *A Philosophical Essay on Probabilities*. Dover.
Lefebvre, Henri. 2014. *The Critique of Everyday Life*. Verso Books.
Lewis, C.S. 1952. *Mere Christianity*. Harper Collins.
———. 2015 [1944]. *The Abolition of Man*. Harper.
Lewis, David K. 1973. *Counterfactuals*. Blackwell.
———. 1986. *On the Plurality of Worlds*. Blackwell.
Lewis, Sinclair. 1935. *It Can't Happen Here*. Doubleday Doran.
Li, Shirley. 2015. Man in the High Castle on Amazon: Ridley Scott, Frank Spotnitz Preview the Chilling Thriller Set in an Alternate History. *Entertainment Weekly* (November 18th).
Lynn, Richard John, trans. 1967. *The I Ching or Book of Changes*. Princeton University Press.
Minford, John, trans. 2015. *I Ching: The Essential Translation of the Ancient Chinese Oracle and Book of Wisdom*. Penguin.
Marcel, Gabriel. 2008. *A Path to Peace: Fresh Hope for the World. Dramatic Explorations*. Marquette University Press.
Mason, Timothy W. 1995 [1981]. Intention and Explanation: A Current Controversy about the Interpretation of National Socialism. In Mason, *Nazism, Fascism, and the Working Class: Essays by Tim Mason*, Cambridge University Press.
———. 1995. *Nazism, Fascism, and the Working Class*. Cambridge University Press.
Maass, Donald. 2012. *Writing 21st-Century Fiction: High-Impact Techniques for Exceptional Storytelling*. Writer's Digest.
McLuhan, Marshall, and Quentin Fiore. 1967. *The Medium Is the Massage*. Bantam.
Meyrowitz, Joshua. 1985. *No Sense of Place*. Oxford University Press.
Morris, Tom. 2004. *The Stoic Art of Living: Inner Resilience and Outer Results*. Open Court.
Musil, Robert. 2012. *Posthumous Paper of a Living Author*. Penguin.
Nabokov, Vladimir. 1955. *Lolita*. Olympia.

Niebuhr, Reinhold. 1987. *The Essential Reinhold Niebuhr: Selected Essays and Addresses*. Yale University Press.

Nozick, Robert. 1981. *Philosophical Explanations*. Harvard University Press.

Olander, Joseph B., and Martin Harry Greenberg, eds. 1983. *Philip K. Dick*. Writers of the 21st Century Series. Taplinger.

Panter, Nicole. 2003. The Second Coming of Philip K. Dick: The Inside-Out Story of How a Hyper-Paranoid, Pulp Fiction Hack Conquered the Movie World 20 Years After His Death. *Wired* (December 1st).

Paskin, Willa. 2015. "What does 'Peak TV' really mean?" in *Slate*. www.slate.com.

Plato. 1992. *Republic*. Hackett.

———. 1995. *The Statesman*. Cambridge University Press.

Platt, Charles. 1987 [1980]. *Dream Makers: Science Fiction and Fantasy Writers at Work*. Ungar.

Popper, Karl R. 1982. *The Open Universe*. Routledge.

Portmore, Douglas W. 2007. Desire Fulfillment and Posthumous Harm. *American Philosophical Quarterly* 44:1.

Rickman, Gregg. 1985. *Philip K. Dick: The Last Testament*. Valentine.

———. 1988. *Philip K. Dick: In His Own Words*. Valentine.

Roberts, David D. 2006. *The Totalitarian Experiment in Twentieth-Century Europe: Understanding the Poverty of Great Politics*. Routledge.

Russell, Bertrand. 1925. *What I Believe*. 1925. Routledge.

Santoso, Alex. 2014. Philip K. Dick Never Saw *Blade Runner* and Ridley Scott Never Finished Reading the Novel It Was Based On. *Neatorama* (January 30th).

Sartre, Jean-Paul. 1995 [1948]. *Anti-Semite and Jew: An Exploration of the Etiology of Hate*. Schocken.

Schaefer, F.C. 2014. *Beating Plowshares into Swords: An Alternate History of the Vietnam War*. F.C. Schaefer.

———. 2017. *All the Way with JFK: An Alternate History of 1964*. F.C. Schaefer.

Seneca. 1969. *Letters from a Stoic*. Penguin.

Shirer, William. 2011. *The Rise and Fall of the Third Reich: A History of Nazi Germany*. Simon and Schuster.

Sternhell, Zeev. 1986 [1983]. *Neither Right nor Left: Fascist Ideology in France*. Berkeley: University of California Press.

Sternhell, Zeev, Mario Sznajder, and Maia Asheri. 1994 [1989]. *The Birth of Fascist Ideology: From Cultural Rebellion to Political Revolution*. Princeton: Princeton University Press.

Suvin, Darko. "Dick's Opus" in Joseph B. Olander, and Martin Harry Greenberg *Philip K. Dick*. Taplinger.

Taylor, James Stacey. 2012. *Death, Posthumous Harm, and Bioethics*. Routledge.

Turtledove, Harry. 1992. *The Guns of the South*. Del Rey.

———. 1994. *In the Balance: An Alternate History of the Second World War*. Del Rey.

———. 1999. *Colonization: Second Contact*. Del Rey.

———. 2010. *Hitler's War*. Del Rey.

Van Inwagen, Peter. 1986. *An Essay on Free Will*. Oxford University Press.

———. 2017. *Thinking about Free Will*. Cambridge University Press.

Vaneigem, Raoul. 2012 [1967]. *The Revolution of Everyday Life*. PM Press.

Waite, Geoff. 1996. *Nietzsche's Corps / e: Aesthetics, Politics, Prophecy, or, the Spectacular Technoculture of Everyday Life*. Duke University Press.

Waldron, Jeremy. 2004. Terrorism and the Uses of Terror. *The Journal of Ethics*.

Warrick, Patricia. 1980. The Encounter of Taoism and Fascism in *The Man in the High Castle*. *Science-Fiction Studies*.

Washington, Booker T. 1995 [1895]. *Up from Slavery*. Dover.

Wilhelm, Richard and Cary F. Baynes, trans. 1967. *The I Ching, or Book of Changes*. Princeton University Press.

Williams, Paul. 1986. Only *Apparently Real: The World of Philip K. Dick*. Arbor House.

Wittkower, D.E. 2011. Time in Unfixed You Are. In Wittkower, ed., *Philip K. Dick and Philosophy: Do Androids Have Kindred Spirits?* Open Court.

Žižek, Slavoj. 1991. *Looking Awry: An Introduction to Jacques Lacan through Popular Culture*. MIT Press.

———. 2017. *Trouble in Paradise: From the End of History to the End of Capitalism*. Melville House.

Agents of Philosophical Propaganda

Emiliano Aguilar got his MA from the Universidad de Buenos Aires (UBA), Facultad de Filosofía y Letras (Argentina). He has published chapters in books such as *Orphan Black and Philosophy: Grand Theft DNA* (2016) and *Mr. Robot and Philosophy: Beyond Good and Evil Corp* (2017). He likes to watch little windows showing alternate realities slightly different from ours. People call them "movies in Blu-ray."

There is surely a possible world where **Ananya Chattoraj** fulfills her dream of being a professional knitter, binge TV watcher, and cat cuddler. In her actual world, she settles for studying philosophy of science in her PhD program.

Maciej Cisowski holds an MA in Philosophy, though he's not actually sure if it has *wu*. He spends his time writing ethically questionable code for the Tyrell Corporation. In an alternate timeline he would surely be less prone to discussing skeptical paradoxes and parallel universes. In an alternate timeline he would surely be more prone to discussing skeptical paradoxes and parallel universes.

Marc W. Cole is a PhD candidate at the University of Leeds, who works on Aristotle's metaphysics of mind. When not busy with this, Marc likes to think about the role of law in politics. In his free time, he does martial arts of all sorts. Armed with philosophical knowledge and sweet kicks, Marc resists the Nazis permanently.

BRETT COPPENGER fears the rise of the Nazi regime in all possible worlds. To assuage his fears, he keeps himself busy by teaching philosophy. He is an Assistant Professor of Philosophy at Tuskegee University. His research and teaching interests are in epistemology, philosophy of science, and philosophy of religion. He previously contributed to *Arrested Development and Philosophy*.

SAM DIRECTOR is a PhD student in the Philosophy Department at the University of Colorado—Boulder. His research focuses on issues in both applied ethics and political philosophy. Specifically, he is interested in investigating the nature of rights, consent, and autonomy, with the goal of applying them to issues in ethics and political philosophy. He is rarely not doing philosophy. But, when he takes a break from philosophy, he enjoys talking about movies and literature.

VERENA EHRNBERGER currently works as a legal expert in the corporate world, which sometimes reminds her a lot of *The Man in the High Castle* universe. Nonetheless she is convinced that in some parallel universe everything is just fine. Verena studies philosophy and psychotherapy at the University of Vienna and is determined to do something with these skills in the future, because humankind has too much potential to just accept the status quo. Just like Juliana, she always bets on the best in people. She also blogs for TEDxVienna on a regular basis.

BENJAMIN EVANS hails from the alternative reality called Canada. A not-so-secret member of the Resistance, Evans has earned four graduate degrees in philosophy, humanities, and fine arts, most recently a PhD from the New School for Social Research in New York City. When he's not plotting revolution or writing about aesthetic theory, he likes to track down strange movies of unknown origin.

JOSHUA HETER received his PhD in philosophy from Saint Louis University and has contributed to both *Orphan Black and Philosophy: Grand Theft DNA* and *The Princess Bride and Philosophy: Inconceivable!* When he's not teaching philosophy at Iowa Western Community College, he spends his time contemplating whether (given the technology and opportunity) he would be morally justified in traveling back in time to assassinate the young Adolf Hitler.

Corey Horn is finishing his undergraduate degree in Philosophy at Eastern Washington University. His main area of focus is within the realm of political theory and cosmopolitan idealism, but in his spare time you will find him with his friends at the bar, contemplating the ethics of Nazis, villains, and whether or not pineapples belong on pizza (the answer is they do).

Timothy Hsiao teaches philosophy at Florida Gulf Coast University and Florida South Western State College. His research focuses on applied ethics, where he plans to Make Natural Law Theory Great Again. His articles have appeared in journals such as *Public Affairs Quarterly*, *Philosophia*, and the *Journal of Agricultural and Environmental Ethics*. His website is timhsiao.org. He welcomes correspondence (and hate mail from vegans).

Tim Jones received his PhD from the School of Literature, Drama, and Creative Writing at the University of East Anglia. He has published several essays in the Popular Culture and Philosophy series, including "Mulder and Scully, You're Late!" in *The X-Files and Philosophy: The Truth Is In Here*.

John V. Karavitis was *compelled* to write his chapter for this book. There was no way out for him. And, as always, he was *compelled* to follow the dictates of his own personal oracle, his overworked and underappreciated Magic 8-Ball™. Did we say "dictates"? We meant "thoughtful suggestions and constructive criticism." Especially given that the oracle kept giving John the same reply to every one of his questions: "Concentrate and ask again." (Wait, what?)

Christopher Ketcham earned his doctorate at the University of Texas at Austin. He teaches business and ethics for the University of Houston Downtown. His research interests are risk management, applied ethics, social justice, and East-West comparative philosophy. He has done recent work in the philosophical ideas of forgiveness, Emmanuel Levinas's responsibility, and Gabriel Marcel's spirit of abstraction, after which, thank heaven he did not catch the disease of intelligence.

Bruce Krajewski is Professor and Chair of the Department of English at the University of Texas at Arlington. He has written about fascism in *The New York Times*, and published a few bits about philosophy and esotericism. He wonders whether Maurice Blanchot is correct in his famous essay on science fiction when Blanchot writes, "No one is interested in the existence of a completely different time of a completely different world."

Donald McCarthy is an adjunct professor at SUNY Old Westbury and a graduate of the City College of New York's MFA program. He's published both fiction and non-fiction at venues such as *Salon*, *Paste Magazine*, *Alternet*, *Plots with Guns*, and more. He has yet to visit an alternate universe, but his desire to do so grows with every passing day.

Lukasz Muniowski is a doctoral student at the Faculty of Neophilology at Warsaw University. He's working on a thesis entitled "Tools of the Weak: The Transgressive Art of Hubert Selby, Jr." In addition to a publication about *Last Exit to Brooklyn*, he also has a piece in *Acta Philologica* on Michael Jordan as a mythical figure.

Fernando Gabriel Pagnoni Berns (PhD student) works at Universidad de Buenos Aires (UBA) as Professor in "Literatura de las Artes Combinadas II." He teaches seminars on international horror film and has published chapters in books such as *Peanuts and Philosophy: You're a Wise Man Charlie Brown!* (2017) *and Horrors of War: The Undead on the Battlefield* (2015). He lives in an alternate universe where TV reality stars become presidents and people in the Oscars can't keep straight who's won the prize. How very self-indulgent of him.

Miguel Paley is a pataphysicist, head coach of The New School Men's Basketball team (The Narwhals), and a PhD candidate in philosophy at The New School for Social Research. When not screaming at his team to play defense, Miguel writes on Bergson's philosophy of mind and its influence on the work of Emmanuel Levinas, Alfred Whitehead, and Hans Jonas. He also deeply admires the names of Üexkull and Hundertwasser. Gabriel Garcia Marquez once made him gross lemonade.

Franklin Perkins is Professor of Philosophy at the University of Hawai'i at Mānoa, a position he came to through a number of factors, including a middle-school decision to study martial arts, an encounter with Leibniz's writings on China, and Allied victory in World War II. In *The Grasshopper Lies Heavy*, he is most likely a carpenter. In this reality, instead, he is editor of the journal *Philosophy East and West* and author of *Heaven and Earth Are not Humane: The Problem of Evil in Classical Chinese Philosophy*, *Leibniz: A Guide for the Perplexed*, and *Leibniz and China: A Commerce of Light*.

Elizabeth Rard is currently working on her PhD in philosophy at UC Davis in California. Neighbors describe her as perfectly pleasant, but with a rather distorted memory of history. She will regularly stare blankly while famous historical events are discussed, and will sometimes reference wars that no one else seems to remember, all while drinking her five-cent instant tea, admiring her marigolds dreamily, and enjoying a suspicious looking smoke from a packet marked "Land-o-Smiles."

Dennis Weiss is a fan of all-things televisual and when he's not watching television he is Professor of Philosophy at York College of Pennsylvania where he regularly teaches courses on the intersections of philosophy, technology, popular culture, and science fiction. He's authored articles exploring the philosophical implications of Buffy, Data, Dick, and Sarah (a certain clone) and is the editor of *Interpreting Man* (2003) and *Design, Mediation, and the Posthuman* (2014). He is currently at work on a project examining the rise of the posthuman in twenty-first century television.

M. Blake Wilson is Assistant Professor of Criminal Justice at California State University, Stanislaus. Before that, he was a graduate student working on political philosophy. Before that, he was a criminal defense lawyer. Before that, he was a law student tracking down Philip K. Dick books at a time when most of them were out of print. He contributed a chapter to *The Who and Philosophy* (2016) by pretending to understand Nietzsche, tragedy, and Pete Townshend.

As a PhD student in Environmental Psychology at the University of Gröningen, **Stephanie J. Zawadzki** spends most of her time in awe of humanity's ability to create problems (and how consistently it outshines our ability to solve them). She seeks spiritual clarity on her yoga mat and through soul-searching conversations with her cats. Together with the alphabetically inferior T.J. Zawadzki, Steph rails against the forces of space-time in their fight to occupy the same reality.

T.J. Zawadzki -(STOP)- TRIPLE ACADEMIC AGENT UNDERCOVER AS INTERDISCIPLINARY PHD STUDENT -(STOP)- TRAINED IN APPLIED AND SOCIAL PSYCHOLOGY BUT MAINTAINED STRONG TIES WITH GENDER AND SEXUALITY STUDIES -(STOP)- NOW DEFECTED TO DEPARTMENT OF ALTERNATE HISTORY AT UNIVERSITY OF EXETER -(STOP)- APPEALS TO ORACLE AKA ADVISORS TO HELP WRITE NEW HISTORY OF SEXOLOGY IN POLAND -(STOP)- TRUE ALLEGIANCE TO STEPHANIE J. ZAWADZKI AND HER CATS -(STOP)- ESCAPE TO HOLLAND VIA HOUSEBOAT IMMINENT

Index

POPULAR CULTURE AND PHILOSOPHY®

PHILIP
K. DICK
AND PHILOSOPHY
DO ANDROIDS HAVE KINDRED SPIRITS?
EDITED BY D. E. WITTKOWER

Milton Keynes UK
Ingram Content Group UK Ltd.
UKHW021258191023
430925UK00032B/369